Christine Merrill lives on a farm in Wisconsin, USA, with her husband, two sons and too many pets – all of whom would like her to get off the computer so they can check their e-mail. She has worked by turns in theatre costuming, where she was paid to play with period ballgowns, and as a librarian, where she spent the day surrounded by books. Writing historical romance combines her love of good stories and fancy dress with her ability to stare out of the window and make stuff up.

London, 1814

*A season of secrets, scandal and
seduction in high society!*

A darkly dangerous stranger is out for revenge, delivering a silken
rope as his calling card. Through him, a long-forgotten past is
stirred to life. The notorious events of 1794 which saw one man
murdered and another hanged for the crime are brought into
question. Was the culprit brought to justice or is there still
a treacherous murderer at large?

As the murky waters of the past are disturbed, so is the *Ton*!
Milliners and servants find love with rakish lords and proper
ladies fall for rebellious outcasts, until finally the true
murderer and spy is revealed.

REGENCY
Silk & Scandal

*From glittering ballrooms to a smuggler's cove in Cornwall,
from the wilds of Scotland to a Romany camp and from
the highest society to the lowest...*

Don't miss all eight books in this thrilling new series!

REGENCY
Silk & Scandal

Paying the Virgin's Price
by
Christine Merrill

All the characters in this book have no existence outside the imagination of the author, and have no relation whatsoever to anyone bearing the same name or names. They are not even distantly inspired by any individual known or unknown to the author, and all the incidents are pure invention.

First published in Great Britain in 2010
Harlequin Mills & Boon Limited, Eton House,
18-24 Paradise Road,
Richmond, Surrey TW9 1SR

© Christine Merrill 2010

ISBN: 978 0 263 87079 4

52-0710

Harlequin Mills & Boon policy is to use papers that are natural, renewable and recyclable products and made from wood grown in sustainable forests. The logging and manufacturing processes conform to the legal environmental regulations of the country of origin.

Printed in Great Britain
by Clays Ltd, St Ives plc

REGENCY
Silk & Scandal

COLLECT ALL EIGHT BOOKS IN THIS
WONDERFUL NEW SERIES

To Annie, Gayle, Julia, Louise and Margaret.
It's been amazing, working with you, and I love you all.

Chapter One

February, 1814. London

The air of the Fourth Circle gaming hell was thick with the usual miasma of tobacco smoke and whisky, blended with the tang of sweat that Nathan Wardale had come to associate with failure. *Another's* failure, fortunately for him. Nate stared over the cards in his hand at the nervous man on the other side of the green baize table. He was hardly more than a boy. And he was about to learn the first of manhood's lessons.

The manchild cleared his throat. 'If you could see your way clear…'

'I could not,' Nate responded without emotion, shuffling the cards. 'If your purse is empty, then you had best leave the table.'

His opponent bristled. 'Are you implying that my word is not good?'

'I am implying nothing of the kind. Experience has taught me never to accept an IOU. If you have nothing of value upon your person, then play is done.'

'It is most unfair of you to stop when I am losing.' Though he had just come of age, the young man was also a marquis. He was used to getting his own way, especially from one so obviously common as Nate.

Nate shrugged in response. 'On the contrary. It is most unfair of you to expect me to treat a promise of payment as a stake in the game. While I do not doubt that you would make good, I have found that gentlemen behave rashly when their backs are to the wall. Later, they regret what they have promised in the heat of play.'

The boy sneered as though what other men might do meant nothing to him. 'And what do you expect of me, then? Bet my signet against the next hand?'

'If you wish.'

'It is entailed.'

'Then you are finished playing.'

The other's chin jutted out in defiance. 'I will say when I am finished.' He pulled the ring from his finger and tossed it onto the table. 'This is easily worth all that you have in front of you. One more hand.'

'Very well.' Nate yawned and dealt the cards. And a short time later, when the play had gone the way he knew it would, he scooped the ring forward and into his purse, along with the rest of his winnings.

'But, you cannot,' the young noble stammered. 'It is not mine.'

'Then why did you bet it?' Nate looked at him, unblinking.

'I thought I could win.'

'And I have proven to you that you could not. It is a good thing for both of us that you were willing to trade such a small thing. It is only a symbol of your family's honour. Easily replaced, I am sure. I will add it to the collection of similar items that have come into my possession from people like you, who would not listen to reason.'

The boy watched the purse vanishing into Nate's pocket as though he were watching his future disappear. 'But what am I to tell my father?'

'That is none of my concern. If it were me, I'd tell him that he has a fool for a son.'

The boy slammed his fist against the table so

hard that Nate feared something must break, then he sprang to his feet, doing his feeble best to loom threateningly. Nate could see that his opponent was wavering on the edge of issuing a challenge, so he prepared to signal the toughs that the owner, Dante Jones, kept ready to eject angry losers. But as Nate stared up into the young man's eyes, he watched the other's expression change as he weighed the possibility that Nate might be as successful at duelling as he was at playing cards.

Then the boy stood down and walked away from the table without another word.

Nate let out his breath slowly, so as not to call attention to it. He could feel the weight of the signet in his pocket, but it would not do to examine the thing while here. It would appear that he was gloating over the fallen. And though the infamous gambler Nate Dale had many faults, he did not gloat.

He was quite sure that he had taken a similar ring from the boy's father, not two years ago. The current ring was not a true part of the entail, but a duplicate, made to hide the loss of the original. The real ring was in a box on Nate's bed chamber dresser. It was just one small part of a collection of grisly trophies to remind him what men might do when the gambling fever was upon them and they were convinced that their luck was about to turn.

He wondered what that feeling was like, for he had never had it. It had been years since there had been a doubt in his mind on the subject of *table luck*. There had been bad hands, of course. And even bad days. But things always came right again before he felt the sting of loss. He had but to remain calm and wait for the tide to turn. To all and sundry, he was known as the luckiest man in England.

So it was with cards or dice. And as for the rest of his life? He had learned to content himself with the fact that it was unlikely to get any worse.

He stared around the room at the typical night's crowd assembled there. Winners and losers, noise and bustle. A few widows who enjoyed games more intimate than faro. One of them gave him a come-hither look, and he responded with a distant smile and a shake of his head. What must that say of his state of mind if he had become too jaded to value her considerable charms over an evening spent at home alone? But the energy in the room seemed to sap his strength rather than restore it, and it was wearying beyond words to think that tomorrow night would be just the same as tonight.

At least tonight was over. Nate started to push away from the table, then felt a shadow fall across it. When he glanced up, another player was moving into the chair that had been vacated by the previous owner of Nate's new ring. The stranger was dark of hair, eye, skin and mood. Though he was smiling, the expression on his face was every bit as foreboding as a storm cloud on the horizon. Perhaps it was from the pain of a recent injury, for he bore his left arm in a sling.

Nate barely bothered to look at the man's face, turning all his attention to the shuffling of the deck in his hands. 'Fancy a game?'

The stranger nodded, and sat.

Damn. Nate kissed goodbye to his plan for a warm drink by his own fireplace, and a chance to sketch a bit with pen and ink, thinking of nothing at all. Whenever he tried to limit his play, the hours grew even longer. It was as though fate knew his intentions and laughed at them. Certainly it was not the location that drew the pigeons to him. Suffolk Street was a long way from the comfort of White's. The clientele at the Fourth Circle was a curious mix of true lowlifes, habitual gamblers, members of the aristocracy who were fallen from honour because of their gaming, and the curiosity seekers of the Ton.

And Nate. He was the curiosity they sought, known for his preternatural luck at games. They brought with them the idea that it was skill, and that his would prove inferior to theirs: the conviction that it was possible to beat the unbeatable. The naïve hope that their reputation would be made with their success. Others sought him out as a rite of passage. It seemed everyone in London had, at one time or other, lost his purse to the infamous Nathan Dale.

Nate wondered what category this man fell into, and decided either habitual gambler or local tough. Perhaps he was an actor. Although he carried himself with an air of nobility, his clothes were an odd mix of fashion and cast off, flamboyant enough to be laughable in a drawing room, though they suited him well. His blue velvet coat was well tailored, but unfashionably loose, and he wore a striped silk scarf in place of a cravat. There was a glint of silver peaking out from under the lace at his wrist. It was a bracelet or cuff of some kind: most unusual jewellery for a gentleman. He wore a thick gold hoop in his left ear.

Nate could feel the subtle shifting of attention in the room as the heads turned to follow him with interest. Depending on their natures, the men touched purses or weapons, as though to reassure themselves of their security. But from the females present, the man's striking good looks and exotic costume drew a murmur of approval. It was irritating to notice that the widow who, just moments before, had been overcome with disappointment from Nate's rejection, had more than recovered at the sight of the handsome stranger.

Nate looked across the table at him with the dispassionate eye of one who made his living by correctly judging his opponents. *Gypsy*, he decided. But a Gypsy with money, judging by the jewellery. And so the man was welcome at Nate's table. He dealt the cards.

His opponent took them in silence, speaking only when necessary, losing the contents of his fat purse quickly and without emotion over a few hands of *vingt et un*. Such disinterested play made the game even more boring than the continual whining of the last man. The Gypsy made no effort to remove his jewellery after the last hand. It was some comfort, for it proved that he was not too lost to know when to quit.

And it was with relief that Nate watched the man reach into his pocket, as though searching for one last bank note or perhaps a sovereign that had become lodged in the coat lining and left for emergencies. 'If you are without funds,' Nate drawled, 'then it is best we not continue. I should have warned you when we began that I will not accept a marker.'

'I have something better than that, I am sure.' The man's continual smile was most disquieting. In Nate's experience, losers were not supposed to be quite so jolly. 'One more hand. I have something you will accept from me, because you have no choice.' And then, the Gypsy reached into the pocket of his coat, and dropped the thing onto the table.

A scarlet silk rope lay there like a snake, coiled upon itself. The end was carefully tied in a hangman's noose.

For a moment, it looked no different from the one Nate had seen so many years ago—on the day they'd hanged his father.

Nate pushed away from the table so quickly that it tipped, sending the rope, drinks and stakes into a heap on the floor. The man across from him took no notice of the mess, but continued to stare at him with the same fixed expression and knowing smile, as though satisfied with the reaction he had received.

Nate stared back into the dark face, noting the

lines in it, the shape of the eyes, and even the cold quirk in the smile. *He knew that face*—although coldness had not been there when last they'd spoken, nor the sharpness of the features, nor the hard set of the man's shoulders.

But if he could imagine this man as the boy he'd once been? Nate said in a voice made hoarse by shock, 'Stephen?' He looked again into the cold face across the table. 'Stephen Hebden. It *is* you, isn't it?'

The man gave a nod and his smile disappeared, as though to remind Nate that any meeting between them would not be a happy one, no matter how close they had been as children. 'I am Stephano Beshaley, now. And you call yourself Nate Dale, even though we both know you are Nathan Wardale.'

'Nathan Wardale died in Boston, several years ago.'

'Just as Stephen Hebden died in a fire when he was a child.' The man across the table held out his hands in an expansive gesture. 'And yet, here we are.'

Dead in a fire? It shamed him that he had given so little thought to what had become of his best childhood friend, after their fathers both died. But circumstances between the families had made the break between them sudden and complete.

Nate pushed the past aside, as he had so many times before. 'Very well, then. Mr Beshaley. What brings you here, after all this time? It has been almost twenty years since we last saw each other.'

'At my father's funeral,' Stephen prompted. 'Do you remember Christopher Hebden, Lord Framlingham? He was the man your father murdered.'

Nate pretended to consider. 'The name is familiar. Of course, my family was so busy that year, what with the trial and the hanging. But I do remember the funeral. It is a pity you could not return the favour and come to my father's funeral as well.' He waited to see if there would be a response from the man opposite him. Perhaps a small acknowledgement that Nate had suffered a loss as well. But there was none.

So he continued. 'When the hanging was done, we had to wait until he was cut down, and pay to retrieve the body. With the title attainted, using the family plot was out of the question. He is in a small, unmarked grave in a country church where the vicar did not know of our disgrace. I rarely visit.' He locked eyes with the man across the table, willing him to show some sign of sympathy, or at least understanding. But still, there was nothing.

'That burial was an intimate gathering, for all our friends had abandoned us. Although there was crowd enough to see him kicking on the gibbet. I thought the whole town had turned out to see the peer swing. And then your mad Gypsy mother screamed curses out of the window and hanged herself in full view of everyone. It made for quite a show.'

And that had done it. For a moment, Stephen tensed as though ready to strike him, the rage blazing hot in his eyes. And Nate welcomed the chance to strike back at someone, anyone, and to finally release the child's fury he had felt that day.

But then, Stephen settled back in his seat and his face grew cold and hard again. Despite that brief flare of temper at the direct insult to his mother, there was nothing left in his dark face to prove that the words had any lasting effect. If they had still been playing cards, Nate might have found him a worthy opponent, for it was impossible to tell what he might do next.

At last, Nate mastered his own anger again and broke the silence. 'Why are you here, Stephen?'

'To remind you of the past.'

He let out a bitter laugh. 'Remind me?' He spread his arms wide. 'Look at my surroundings, old friend, as I do whenever I feel a need to remember. Are they not low enough? Was I born to this? The title is gone, the house, the lands. My family scattered to the four winds. At least you found a people again. Do you know how long it has been since I have seen my own mother? My sisters? Do you know what it is like to stand helpless as your father hangs?'

'No better than to have him murdered, I suppose. And to know that somewhere, the murderer's line continues.'

Nate laughed. 'After all this time, is that the problem? I am as good as dead, I assure you. I have nothing left, and yet you would take more.'

Stephen snorted. 'You have money.'

'And a nice house,' Nate added. 'Two houses, actually. And horses and carriages. Possessions enough for any man. I gained it all at the cost of my honour. We are not gaming at Boodle's, as our fathers did, Stephen. Because we are not welcome amongst gentlemen. A Gypsy bastard and a murderer's son. Society wants none of us. We are in the gutter, where we belong.'

His opponent tensed at the word—*bastard*—but it was no less than the truth.

'I am sorry that I am not suffering enough to satisfy you. If you wish, we can go out in the alley, and I will let you remedy the fact. If you mean to frighten me into losing with this?' He looked down at the rope at his feet, and kicked it until it lay in front of his former friend. 'I have the real rope that did the job. My family bought it to keep it out of the hands of the ghouls gathered round the gallows. There is nothing left for you to do that will frighten me. Since irony is not likely to prove fatal, I suggest that you cease playing games. We are no longer children. If you truly want me dead? Then be man enough to shoot me.'

For a moment, he thought that the taunting had finally hit home. For Stephano the Gypsy nodded and smiled, as though there were nothing he would like better than to kill Nate and put an end to the meeting. But then, he said, 'I am afraid it is not that easy, Nathan Wardale.'

Nate cringed for a moment, and felt the old fear that someone might hear the name, and know him for the child of a murdering traitor. He might be cast out as unworthy, even from the Fourth Circle. And *then* where would he go? He recovered his poise and demanded, 'What is it to be, then?'

'That is not for me to decide. I am but an avatar in this. I bring you the rope. And now, fate will decide the method of your punishment.'

'My punishment?' Nate almost laughed. 'For what? When the murder happened, I was ten years old. Hardly a criminal mastermind, I assure you.'

'You are the son of the murderer.'

'Then your coming here serves no purpose, Stephen. My word is no good for anything but wagering. But if it were, I would swear to you on it that my family is not to blame for what happened.'

'Your father...'

'Was hung for something he did not do. He swore on the stand that Kit Hebden was dying when he found him. He did not strike the blow that killed him. He said the same to me, my mother and my sisters. By the end, there was no reason for him to lie to us. It would have gained him nothing, nor given us any comfort. He was sentenced to die, and we were quite beyond comforting.'

For a moment, he thought he saw a flicker of emotion on the other man's face that might indicate understanding, belief or some scrap of mercy. And then it was gone. 'If it is true that you are blameless, then circumstances will prove that fact soon enough. And I will break the curse and set you free.'

He laughed. 'It is a bit late to talk of freedom, Stephen. I have wealth, but no one to share it with. I have no friends. No one trusts me. No decent woman would want me. In the course of gaming, I have ruined many and caused men to do unspeakable things, convinced that one more hand will be all it takes to break me.

'And now, you will set me free? Can you wipe out the memory of the things I have done? Will you go to the House of Lords and insist that they clear my family's name? Can you get me my title? And my father, as well? Can you raise the dead, Gypsy? For I would like to see you try.'

Stephano the Gypsy spat upon the floor, and passed his hand before him as though warding off the suggestion. 'Your father was a murderer who deserved what he got. And I mean to see that you accept your share of his punishment.'

Nate had learned to see his past as a single dark shadow that threw his empty life into sharper relief. But now that the shadow had become the foreground, the picture created was so ridiculous, he let out with the first honest laugh he'd had in ages. 'My share of the punishment?' He leaned forward and grinned into the face of the man who had once been Stephen Hebden, daring him to see the joke and laugh along. 'Well I have news for you. You enriched me by a hundred pounds before you brought out the damned rope and began speaking nonsense. If this *is* a curse, then many would welcome it. But if you wish to see me punished? Then take my luck with you, and we will call it even.'

He pointed a finger at the rope on the floor. 'But do not come here, pretending to make my life worse with vague threats and portents of doom. There is nothing coming that will make things worse than they already are.'

And then the Gypsy smiled with true satisfaction. 'You think so, do you? We shall see, old friend. We shall see.' And he rose from the chair and exited the room, leaving the silk noose on the floor behind him.

In his dreams, Nate was at Newgate, again, surrounded by angry giants. They laughed and the sound was hollow and cruel, seeming to echo off the stone walls around him. He pushed through the crowd. But it was difficult, for he was so small and they did not wish to part for him. They had arrived early, to get a good view.

And he had come late, for he'd had to sneak from

home. Mother had said it was no place for the family. That father had not wished it. But was Nathan not the man of the family, now? It was his responsibility to be there, at the end. So he had forced his way through the mob to the front, and had seen his father, head bowed, being led to the gallows.

He called out to him, and William Wardale raised his head, searching for the origin of the cry. His eyes were so bleak, and Nathan was sure he must be lonely. There was no friend left who would stand by him at the end. He looked down at Nathan with such love, and such relief, and reached out a hand to him, as though it could be possible to gather him close, one last time. And then, his hand dropped to his side, and a shudder went through him, for he knew what Nathan did not. While he was glad that his last sight on earth would be his son, he had known what it would mean to a child.

The hangman bound his father's hands, and the Ordinary led him through a farce of meaningless prayer. And all around Nathan, the people were shouting, jostling each other and swearing at those who would not remove their hats so that the men in the back could see. Vendors were hawking broadsides, but he did not have the penny to buy one. So he picked a wrinkled paper from the ground before him, to see the lurid cartoon of his father, and his supposed confession.

It was *lies*. Every word of it. Father would never have done the things he was accused of. And even if he had, he would not have told the rest of the world the truth on the final day, after lying to Nathan, over and over. But even if it was lies, there were tears of shame pricking behind his eyelids as he read.

The hangman was placing the hood now, and a woman began to scream. He hoped it was his mother, come to take him home before he saw any more. His coming had been a mistake: there was nothing he could do and he did not want to see what was about to happen.

But it was a strange, dark-skinned woman leaning out of a window above the gallows. She was screaming in triumph, not fear, and her face had the beauty of a vengeful goddess as she stared down at the bound man and the laughing crowd.

And at him. She had found Nathan in the crowd, and stared at him as though she knew him. And then, she had shouted, in a voice so clear that the rabble had hushed to catch her words.

*I call guilt to eat you alive and poison your hearts'
blood. The children will pay for the sins of their fathers,
till my justice destroys the wicked.*

She pointed at him as she spoke of children.
And smiled. The adult Nathan screamed to the
child to look away. The woman was mad. He
should not mind her. And he should run from
this place. If he did not, it would be too late.

And then, there was a thump, and his father's
body dropped as the floor under him disappeared. As he fell, so did the woman in the
window, dangling from the silk scarf that was
wrapped about her neck.

In his child's mind, Nathan thought that the
worst was over. But since then, the adult Nathan
had seen enough in the Navy to understand what
happened to a hanged man if there was no one
to pull on his legs and help him to an easier death.

The kicking had begun. His father, and the
garish puppet of a woman hanging from the
window above him.

It had seemed like hours before the bodies
stilled, the crowds had begun to part, and his
mother had come for him.

When Nate woke, the bedclothes were wet
with sweat and tears. And there was the Gypsy's

silk rope on the dresser beside him. Why had he bothered to pick the thing up and bring it home with him? The gesture was macabre, and meant to upset him. He had been foolish to play along. And Stephen Hebden had managed to raise the old nightmare to plague him.

But Stephen was not Stephen any more. His old friend was long gone. The man who had visited him was an enemy. A stranger. A Gypsy who was as angry and full of tricks as his mother had been. He must never forget that fact, or Stephano Beshaley and his curse would taint his present, just as the man's mother had marked his childhood.

He might not be able to prevent the dreams, but during the day he would keep his mind clear of emotion, just as he did when he was at the gaming tables. His waking life would be no different, because of the Gypsy's visit. At one time or another, Nate had endured public disgrace, loss, starvation and physical hardship. There was little left that could move him to fear, anger or joy. He'd held a hangman's noose when he was still a child. The colourful rope on the nightstand—and its accompanying nightmare—did not compare to the horror of that day.

But his mind wandered to the people Stephen

might search out when his plans for Nate failed. His sisters, perhaps?

Even a Gypsy could not stoop so low as to hurt innocent girls. Beshaley's mother had stared directly at Nate as she'd said her curse. And he'd felt marked by the words, as if touched by a brand. Surely he was meant to pay the whole debt. Helena and Rosalind would be safe.

They had to be. How would the Gypsy even find them? When last Nate had seen them, they were tending their failing mother, waiting for him to come home. But he had lost them in the throng of strangers that was working-class London and had searched for them without success. Mother must have died, never knowing what had become of him, for she had been very sick, even before he'd disappeared. Helena and Rosalind were as lost to him as if they had never been born. It made him ache to think on it. But he could take some consolation in the fact that it would leave them safe from harassment.

Then who else would the Gypsy turn to, once he had failed with the Wardales? Did Nate owe Lord Narborough and his family a word of warning?

His own sense of injustice argued that he owed them nothing at all. They had heard about the curse as well. But they viewed it as little more than a joke. It had not scarred their lives as it had his. There was no sign that Marcus Carlow had been touched by fear. Nate should think of him as the Viscount Stanegate now that he had grown into his title. From the occasional mention of him in *The Times*, he had become just the man his father had hoped. Upright, respectable and honest. The sort of man that all their fathers had expected their sons to be.

If there was fault to be found, it did not lie with Marc or his siblings. It was their father who should bear the blame. Lord Narborough had claimed to be a friend of his father, but shut his doors to the Wardale family when they had needed help.

And Narborough had been the one to pin the blame on Father, when the murder had occurred. He had wasted no time in seeing to his apprehension and imprisonment.

It had gone so quickly. Too quick, he suspected. It was almost as though Narborough had seen the need for a scapegoat, and chosen William Wardale. Nate was sure, with all his heart, that his father was not a murderer. But someone had done the crime. And if there was a man alive who knew the truth, then it was most likely to be

George Carlow. The murder had been committed just outside his study, after all. And he had been the one who called the loudest for a hurried trial and a timely hanging. Suppose his father had blundered on to the scene just after George Carlow had struck the fatal blow?

Nathan tried to muster some glee that the Gypsy would visit them next. The Carlow family was due for a fall. But he could find no pleasure in it. While he was sure that the senior Carlow was a miserable old sinner, the Gypsy had called for the punishment of the next generation. Would it be fair to see the curse fall upon Marc or his good-natured brother Hal? And what of their sisters, Honoria and Verity?

Nate thought again of his own two sisters, hiding their identities from the shame of association with the Wardale name. Even if George Carlow had been the true murderer, did the Carlow girls deserve to be treated as his sisters had? If Stephano Beshaley removed the protection of the older brothers, then brought about the downfall of the family, what would become of them?

Even if justice for Lord Narborough was deserved and forthcoming, could it not be delayed awhile? The girls were infants when he'd seen them last. They must be near old enough to make matches for themselves. If it was possible to stall the Gypsy, even for a month or two, then they would be safely out of the house and with families of their own, when retribution came.

It went against his grain, but Marc Carlow deserved some warning of what was coming, so that he could watch out for his sisters. They had all played together as children, and been good friends—until after the trial, when their prig of a father had forbidden further association.

Stephen had been there as well, of course. Once, they had been as alike as brothers. He forced the thoughts out of his head. With nostalgia would come sympathy and regret. And after that: weakness and fear. He could not afford to feel for the man who wished his destruction. Stephen Hebden had died in a foundling-home fire. And Stephano Beshaley was a bastard Gypsy changeling, who had turned on them the minute he had a chance.

And the man who had once been Nathan Wardale would not let himself be ruled by curses and grudges and superstitious nonsense any more than he had already. The Carlows would be no more happy to see him than he would be to go to them. But he did not wish them a visit from the Gypsy, now that Stephano had taken it into his head to resurrect the past and deliver vengeance where none was deserved.

Nate dressed carefully, as anyone might when visiting the heir to an earldom, and tucked the length of silk rope and its accusing knot into the pocket of his coat.

Chapter Two

Diana Price resisted the urge to place her head in her hands and weep in frustration. The Carlow daughters were pleasant, and she viewed them more as friends than a responsibility. But some days her job as their companion was not an easy one. 'You will have to choose someone, Verity. The whole point of the Season is to find an appropriate match. It makes no sense to reject the entire field of suitors, before the rush is truly underway.'

She would have called the look on Verity's face a pout, had the girl been prone to such. 'I know what the point of coming to London was, Diana. But I had hoped that if Honoria would take care of the obligation and find herself a husband, then you would all leave off bothering me. Do you think Marc will force me to marry this year, even when I can see already that none of the available suitors are likely to suit?'

'Your brother will do nothing of the kind, Verity. But if you claim that none of the gentlemen in London suit you, then you are far too selective.'

'Only yesterday, Diana, you were criticizing Honoria for not being selective enough.'

'Because she was not. It does not pay to encourage the advances of every man who shows an interest, Particularly not when you are as lovely as Honoria.'

Verity gave her an arch look. 'And since I am not, I will be forced to marry a man who I do not love, just because he has offered?'

Diana reached out to hug the girl, who was quite as lovely as her sister, even though she lacked the older girl's confidence. 'That is not what I mean at all, dear one. It is simply that I do not wish you to discount gentlemen without giving them a fair hearing. You are young, yet. Though you might think that infatuation is the most important thing, it is not.'

'And you, Diana, are not so old that you should confuse the words love and infatuation. They sound nothing alike.'

'In tone, perhaps not. But when they are felt

in a young heart, they can be easily confused. I am sure if you are given time, you will discover that there are much more important factors to consider when accepting an offer.'

Verity sighed. 'Like money, I suppose.'

'While it is nice, I doubt you will need to concern yourself with the wealth of your suitors.' Any fortune hunters would have a hard time getting close, as long as Diana watched carefully. 'I am thinking more of kindness, stability, common sense…'

Verity rolled her eyes. 'All characteristics that can be gained with advanced age, I am sure.'

'It is not necessary, or even advisable, for a husband to be quite so young as his wife. In some cases, it might be better for a wiser man to—'

'Ugh.' Verity put her hands over her ears. 'Do not talk to me further about the need to find a sensible old man to offset my youth and inexperience.'

'Not old certainly, but—'

And now, Verity was shaking her head. 'If that is the sort of man you wish for, then you had best find him for yourself. But as for me, I will choose in my own good time. Even if he is rash or foolish, if he loves me, I will accept him. We will learn moderation together.'

Diana sighed. The conversation was ending as it had several times before, with Verity stubbornly convinced that when it came for her, love would conquer all. In Diana's experience, love was rarely a successful combatant against an uneven temper or an irregular income. 'In any case, it is not something we need worry about today. If you find someone this Season who interests you—'

'Which I shall not.'

'—we will discuss his qualities before you make a decision. For now, it will please your father to hear that you are dancing and laughing, even if he is too ill to watch you.'

Verity sighed. 'And there you have me, Diana. You know I will not refuse, if it is so important to the family. As long as I do not have to tie myself to that odious Alexander Veryan, just to make you all content. I swear, he is the biggest bore alive. The last time we danced, he trod on my toes half the night, while making sheep's eyes.'

Diana smiled in sympathy, thinking of the rather awkward young man and his pitiful attempts to capture Verity's affection. 'Your father would welcome a connection to the Veryan family, but re-spectability is not the only quality to seek in a husband. I am sure, if we put our heads together, we will find you a more suitable beau than young Alex.'

There was a quiet knock upon the door of the dressing room, and a maid entered. 'Miss Verity, there is a gentleman here. He wishes to speak with your brothers. But neither is home, nor expected. And Miss Honoria is…' The servant paused respectfully.

'Indisposed.' Verity looked helplessly in Diana's direction. They both knew that Honoria, who had none of Verity's reticence on the subject of marriage, had been up most of the night at a rout, dancing until nearly dawn. It would be quite beyond her to greet a visitor until noon, if then. 'I am hardly dressed to entertain. But I will come as soon as I am able. In the meantime, Diana, could you?'

Stall, while the girl finished her morning chocolate? It was full on ten o'clock, and Diana Price had been up for hours. She could hardly blame the Carlow girls for sleeping late. But she still found it vaguely annoying when the girls' suitors chose to arrive before lunch. With the men from the house, it left Diana in the awkward position of disappointing them. Until the girls had shown an attachment to any of the young men they had met, it would do the gentlemen little good to appeal to their older brothers on the subject.

She straightened her rather severe dress and put on her best chaperone's frown. 'I will see what it is about, Verity. If it is urgent, I will call for you. But if I do not, you may come down in your own good time. It serves the man right for arriving at this hour.'

Her friend gave her a relieved smile. 'Thank you, Diana. I don't know what I would do without you.'

She turned and walked out of the room and down the stairs to the salon. But the man waiting there came as a surprise to her, for he was a stranger. Her first impression was that he was far too old to be the usual post-ball suitor. His hair had not a touch of youthful colour left; It was a striking silver-grey. But on closer inspection, she could see that his back was straight, his skin tanned but smooth, and his green eyes had the clarity, if not of youth, then of a reasonable adult-hood.

Physically, he was not much beyond her own twenty-seven years. But there was a quality in those eyes that spoke to her. They had seen much, and not all of it had been pleasant. But whatever hardship he had seen did not seem to have broken him. There was a solidness about him, as though he were made of stronger stuff than most men. With his striking appearance, it seemed to her as though an ordinarily handsome man had been cast as a statue, with burnished metal for hair and skin, and glittering gems for eyes.

Here was the sort of man she had wished for Verity: someone who could inspire confidence and trust as well as make the heart flutter. And apparently, even she was not immune from him, for she could not help smiling a trifle too warmly in greeting. 'I am sorry to disappoint you. Lord Stanegate is from home. As is his brother. May I enquire as to the reason for your visit, Mister…?' She left the sentence open, to remind him that he had not bothered to introduce himself.

He tilted his head and stared closely into her face, as though searching his memory, 'Verity? Or is it Honoria? I cannot tell. It has been so long…' He used the same puzzled tone that she had used, and there was a pause as he looked at her, a faint smile forming at his mouth. It was as though he had not expected her, any more than she had expected him. But the surprise had been a pleasant one. He was taking her in, just as she had him, forming opinions, searching for her past in her eyes.

Without thinking, she reached up to touch her hair, ready to push a loose curl out of the way, even though there was none. And then stilled her hands, and kept them demurely at her sides. 'No, sir. I am companion and chaperone to the Carlow daughters. My name is Diana Price.'

She must have misjudged his stability after all. Her introduction seemed to stagger him, and for a moment, he tottered as though he were a feeble old man. He reached for the arm of the nearest chair, and unable to control the rudeness of his behaviour, dropped unsteadily into it, taking a deep gasp of air.

'Sir?' She stepped closer, ready to offer assistance. 'Are you ill?'

'No. Really. It is nothing.'

'A glass of wine perhaps? Or a brandy?' It was far too early. But the man needed a restorative.

He gave her the strangest smile she had ever seen. 'Water, only. Please. The heat…'

'Water, then. I will fetch it,' she said, pretending to ignore his condition. It was barely past winter. There was no heat to speak of, nor was it particularly cold. But if the man wished to make excuses for an odd spell, it would do no harm to allow it.

She went to the carafe on a nearby table,

poured out a tumbler, and brought it to him. As he took the glass from her hand, she felt the faintest tremble in his, as though the touch of her fingers had shocked him. He drank eagerly. When he set the glass down on the table beside him, a little of the colour had returned to his tanned face.

She sat in a chair opposite him so as not to call attention to his breach of etiquette.

He looked over and gave a weak smile of gratitude. 'Thank you for your kindness. Forgive me…Miss Price.' He took a breath. 'My name is…Dale.' His voice steadied again. 'I am an old friend of the family, but it has been a long while since I have had reason to visit this house. When I was last here, Miss Verity was but an infant and Honoria not much older. And seeing you, knowing that they are out…I was overcome with how long it had been. Are the girls well?'

'Yes, sir. Both are well-mannered and accomplished young ladies.'

'And lovely, I am sure. Just as I am sure that their good behaviour is a testament to your steady influence.' He fidgeted in his seat as though the burden of polite conversation was one that he was unaccustomed to. Then he stilled, as though gathering himself to the task at hand. 'But my business today is with their brothers. You say they are from home. Will they be returning soon?'

'Lord Stanegate is travelling with his new bride in Northumberland.'

'Marc married, eh?' Mr Dale got a distant look and he muttered, 'Felicitations. And Hal?'

'Somewhere on the Peninsula, I believe. He is a lieutenant in the Dragoons.'

The man nodded. 'It would suit him, I am sure, the life and the uniform.' And then he muttered, more to himself than to her, 'Very well, then. They are both safely out of the way, and I will not worry about them.'

It was good to hear that he seemed concerned, although why he should feel the need to worry over Marc or Hal, or think that it was safer to face Napoleon than be in London, she was not sure.

And now, he was looking at her again, as though he had forgotten that she was in the room with him and could not think what to do next. Then he said, 'If you could provide me with paper and pen, I would write a message to Marcus.'

'If the matter is important, I can give you the address at which he can be reached,' she offered.

Mr Dale waved a dismissive hand. 'If he is

happy and away from town, I would not dream of bothering him.'

'Perhaps Honoria…'

'No,' he said a little too quickly. 'Do not trouble the girls with this. I doubt it will involve them. This is a matter to be settled amongst gentlemen. And I would hate to think I'd been a source of worry to them. A brief note to Marcus will suffice. If you could relay it when he returns, I would be most grateful.' He favoured her with another bright smile. And this time, she was sure that he was deliberately attempting to charm her. Most likely, he wished to make her forget his strange behaviour.

And it annoyed her that he had succeeded. He had a nice smile, friendly and unthreatening, yet a little knowing. There was something about the way that he sat in the chair, now he had recovered himself, that made her think he was usually an adventurous man. Wherever he belonged, it was somewhere much more exciting than a drawing room. As she got up and went to prepare the desk in the corner for writing, she could feel herself colouring at the thought that he was behind her and might be watching her move.

Had it been necessary of him to give flattering attention to a paid companion, just to get writing materials? She would have given him what he asked, even if he'd frowned at her, Diana thought. But his charming behaviour only stood to remind her how hopeless her fantasies might be. In a short time, he would be gone and she would be here, delivering the note like the servant she was. He would have forgotten all about her.

And she would be left with the memory of that smile.

Mr Dale came and sat at the place she prepared for him, at the tiny desk by the window. He thought for a moment, then scrawled a few words on the paper, blotted it, and stared at the sealing wax for a moment. Here he would show how little he trusted her with the contents.

Then he put the wax away, and looked directly into her eyes—the green light in his sparkled like emeralds—and his smile changed to a thoughtful frown. 'Miss Price. I do not wish to trouble the girls with the reason for my visit. My fears for the Carlow family might be for naught. But you are their companion, are you not? A watchdog for their honour and reputation?'

Diana nodded.

'Then should they receive the attention of a

dark gentleman who calls himself Stephano Beshaley, know that he is a danger to them. Watch him carefully. And watch the girls as well, for he is just the sort to try and turn their heads. Should he appear, you must find Marc or Hal immediately and tell them. Can you do that for me?'

She nodded again, more puzzled than she had been before.

'Very good.' He handed her the folded sheet of paper. 'You can give this note to either Stanegate or Lieutenant Carlow, when next they are home. Marcus preferably, since he is eldest and most responsible. But either will understand its meaning. Thank you for your time, Miss Price.' He gave a short bow, and turned to leave.

'Wait.' She held up a hand to stop him before realizing that she had no reason to call him back to her, other than an irrational desire not to let him go.

He turned back, an expectant look on his face.

'If they wish to reply, where shall I direct the message? Or will you be returning?'

He gave the barest shake of his head. 'Do not concern yourself. They will not wish to reply to me, any more than they wish a visit from

Beshaley. But now, my conscience is as clear as I can make it. On this subject, at least.' He gave her another strange look, as though he were apologizing for something, even though he had done her no wrong. 'Good day, Miss Price.' And he was gone.

She walked slowly back up the stairs to Verity, with the note in her hand, wondering what she was supposed to do with the thing. She could forward it on to Marc on his honeymoon, she supposed. But he and Nell were not due back from Northumberland for weeks, and she hated to bother them. The time before their marriage had been stressful enough. Surely they deserved a few weeks of peace.

The paper before her was not sealed. Mr Dale had left it to her discretion. And although she would never peruse Marc's mail under normal circumstances, perhaps this one time it would be better to read the message to see if the matter was urgent.

There was only one line, scrawled hurriedly in the centre of the paper.

Marc,
The Gypsy has returned.
Nathan.

Her breath caught a little in her throat. The words were ominous: black and spidery against the white of the paper. But it was nothing that she did not already know. Nor would Marc be surprised. He had explained to her what happened, before he left, the harrowing fight, the single shot, and the evil Gypsy who had been calling himself Salterton falling to his death in the icy water. Marc had cautioned her to be on her guard and watch the girls closely, in case he had been wrong. If the man lived, he might return to bother them.

She bit her lip. If only there were some way to draw Mr Dale back and ask him if this information was recent or some time in coming. It was possible that he'd met the Gypsy before his demise on the ice some weeks ago. Marc had warned her before he'd left to be on guard against all strangers, particularly one with dark hair and skin. She was to summon him immediately if anything or anyone unusual appeared.

This morning's visit had certainly been unusual. But Nathan Dale was not dark, nor was he threatening. He had been trying to help, and had brought a scrap of information that was already known to the family. If a specific threat had been imminent, surely he would have said more, or seemed more worried. And he had been smiling just now. How serious could the situation be?

She would adopt a wait-and-see attitude, doing just as Marc had asked. She would watch the girls more closely than usual. And if Mr Dale returned, she would try to find a way to draw him out and gain more information—without revealing that she had opened his note.

On thinking of it, she very much hoped Mr Dale would return. She suspected he was a most interesting gentleman and it intrigued her to know more about him. It was as though hard weather had rubbed away at a softer, less substantial person, until the core of vitality could shine through to the surface. There was an air of confidence about him, as though he had already seen and survived hardship and knew better than to be rattled by anything less than the gravest circumstances.

Perhaps he had already dealt with the Gypsy's threat and was only tying up the loose ends of the contact, making sure that the man could do no damage elsewhere. If she needed his help during Marc's absence, there might be some way…

Of course not. She reminded herself firmly of her first suspicions regarding the man: that he might be a suitor of Honoria or Verity. If he was a friend of Marc's and sought the company of any of the women in the house, there was no reason to think that he would seek the friendship of their companion nor that he wished to be bothered with her concerns over the girls.

It was just that she had found the sight of him to be rather dashing, and now she was spinning fancies that they would have more time to talk.

She glanced down at the note, and *Nathan* written at the bottom. And she shivered. It was good that she had conversed with the man before seeing it, for past experience had taught her to dread that name, and all who carried it. If she had known he was a *Nathan*, she might have let an unreasonable prejudice colour her opinions of him. And then she would have been deprived of that marvellous smile. She smiled back, even though he was not there to see it.

Verity looked up as she entered the dressing room. 'Who was it?'

Diana tucked the note into the pocket of her dress. 'It was the most extraordinary man.' Without meaning to, she gave a little sigh of pleasure. She had nothing to fear from *this* Nathan. He looked nothing like the man her father had warned her of, ten years ago. Mr Dale was not cold, or emotionless or the least bit cruel. Her spontaneous attraction to him came from the openness of his countenance, his easy nature and his selfless concern for others. He had a robust physique and the healthy colouring of a man who enjoyed nature, not the stooped frame, pinched face and anaemic pallor of a habitual gambler.

In short, he was the diametric opposite of Nathan Wardale.

Chapter Three

Nate hurried out of the Carlow town house and down the street, feeling the cold sweat beading on his brow. Of all the people, in all the places, why had he been greeted by Diana Price? He had been nervous enough, going to the house at all. But once he had arrived on Albemarle Street, the feelings of his youth returned. As a boy, he had run across the chequered floor of the front hall, chasing and being chased, laughing and playing. It had been as a second home to him. And to feel that moment of pleasure, as the young woman had entered the room. The Carlow daughters grown to beauty? But no. A stranger. A very attractive stranger. Delight, curiosity, an awakening of old feelings in him, long suppressed.

She was a lovely thing, with shining dark hair,

and a small pursed mouth, ready to be kissed. Her large brown eyes were intelligent, but full of an innocence he never saw in the female denizens of the Fourth Circle.

She had looked at him without judgment or expectation, and a hint of responding interest that proved she was not wife to Marcus or Hal. Nate had felt quite like the man he once hoped to be. For a few moments, he was an ordinary gentleman meeting a pretty girl in a nice parlour, with none of the stink of the gaming hell on his clothes or in his mind.

And then he had discovered her identity, and it had all come crashing down. Thank God he had not decided to use his true name, for if she'd realized…

He hailed a cab in Piccadilly to Covent Garden and Suffolk Street, to the low haunts inhabited by Nate Dale the gambler. If the man he sought was anywhere, he would be here, waiting in the spot that he'd last been seen.

Nate went from the dim street, into the dim tavern connected by a tunnel to the Fourth Circle. 'Mr Dale, returning so soon? And in daylight.' Dante Jones saw him less as a friend than as a way to bring more people to the tables. 'To what do we owe this honour?'

'Mr Jones,' he responded, with barely a nod, resenting the grimy way he felt when the man looked at him as though he was nothing more than a meal ticket. 'Where is the damned Gypsy?'

'The man who you beat last night? In the same spot as when you left him. And I am glad to have him, for his play draws quite a crowd. He is very nearly as lucky as you.'

'Not any more.' Nate stalked past Dante and into the gaming room to find Stephano Beshaley, or whoever he chose to be called today, seated in Nate's regular chair, as though he owned it. He seemed impervious to the action around him, nursing his drink, long slender legs outstretched, as though he had been waiting for Nate's return.

Nate pulled the silk rope from his pocket, and threw it down on the table in front of the Gypsy. 'Take it back.'

Stephano only smiled and sipped his drink. 'Once it is given, there is no returning it.'

'Take it back. You have had your fun.'

'Fun?' Nate's former friend greeted this with a bitter twist of his mouth and an arched eyebrow. 'Is *that* what you think this is for me?'

'I think you take pleasure in tormenting me. But you have done enough.'

And there was the ironic smile again. 'You have changed much, in a few short hours. Last night, you said that there was nothing left to hurt you.'

'And I was wrong. I freely admit it. You have found the one thing.'

Beshaley laughed. 'I? I found nothing. But apparently you have. And I wish you to get what you deserve from it.'

'You knew where I would go, when you returned. And you knew that Diana Price would be there, waiting for me.'

'Who?' The Gypsy seemed honestly puzzled.

Nate reached into his pocket, and removed the tattered piece of paper that he had carried with him for ten years, like Coleridge's albatross. He set it on the table before his old friend, who read aloud.

Should I lose the next hand, I pledge in payment my last thing of value. The maidenhead of my daughter, Diana.
Edgar Price
June 3rd 1804

Beshaley sneered back at him. 'Just for a moment yesterday, I almost believed you. If you are innocent of any crime, then to carry vengeance to the second generation is to damn myself. But a man who would take such a thing in trade for a gambling debt deserves to suffer all that fate wishes to bring him.'

Nate glanced around, afraid that the people nearby might hear what he had done in that moment of madness. 'I was young. And foolish. And in my cups. Edgar Price was my first big score, and I was too full of myself and my own success to think of what I might do to others. When I suggested this bet, it was intended as a cruel jest. I'd taken the man's money. And his house, as well. I live there still. He'd bankrupted himself at my table to the point where his only options were debtor's prison or a bullet. And yet, he would not stop playing. Like every gambler, he thought that his luck would change if he played just one more hand. I thought to shock him. To embarrass him. That if I pushed him far enough, he would slink from the table. Instead, he signed this to me.'

Nate took the paper back and stuffed it into his purse so he would not have to see it any more. It still pained him to read those words. 'He cried when he lost. He begged me for mercy. And I told him that if I ever saw him again, or heard of him frequenting the tables anywhere in

London, I would find him and the girl and collect what was owed me. And to his credit, I never saw or heard from him, after that day. I keep the paper to remind me what can happen when a man is pushed too far at the tables. And I have not taken a single marker, since.'

'How noble of you.' The Gypsy looked ready to spit in disgust. 'You are lower than I thought you, Nathan. And after seeing this, I feel considerably less guilty about delivering the rope.' He pushed it back across the table toward Nate.

Nate stared down at the symbol of disgrace, and in his heart, he agreed. He deserved punishment. But his mouth continued to try to justify the unjustifiable. 'I thought the girl long married, by now. It has been years. She must know that I am no threat to her. But I went to warn the Carlows of you. And she was there. She is chaperone to Honoria and little Verity. You knew, you bastard. You knew it all along.'

The Gypsy smiled in satisfaction. 'I knew nothing, other than that I would bring the rope to you, and see what resulted from it. Normally fate is not so swift. By your actions, you have made your own hell. Do not blame me, if today is the day that the devil has come to claim you.'

'Whether or not you have staged this meeting

with the girl, it will be the last one between us. I mean to leave Diana Price alone, just as I have always done. Now take this back.' He slapped the rope upon the table.

Stephen arched his eyebrows. 'And what will happen, if I do? Will she vanish in a cloud of smoke? You created the problem, Wardale. You must be the one to solve it.'

'I can hardly be held to blame for what happened to her father, Stephen. He came to me, and he would not leave. He wanted to gamble. I am a gambler. I never set out to be what I have become. It is all the fault of your mother and your people.'

'You won someone's daughter at faro, and it is all my mother's fault, is it?'

That sounded even more foolish than the rest of it. God knew how mad the rest of his defence would sound. 'Did you know me for a gamester, before the curse?'

The Gypsy snorted. 'You were ten years old.'

'Yet I'd ruined my first man before I could shave. And that is the way it has been, from the very first wager. I am lucky. And it is all because of the curse your mother placed upon me.'

The Gypsy laughed. 'You believe in luck?'

'What gambler does not? I cannot claim that

skill has brought me all that I have gained. I win far too often to think that it is always by my own abilities.' He waved a hand in the direction of the faro tables. 'These tables? All gaffed. Dante cheats. Only a fool would play here. But if you like, I will beat them for you. No matter how much Dante might cheat, he can never beat me.' He stared at the tables in remorse. 'No one has ever been this lucky. No one save me. It is not natural. And if I cannot lose? Then to play against others is little better than robbery.'

'Then stop playing. Or tell them to.'

'I cannot.' He gritted his teeth. 'Every night, I swear I am through. But the next night falls and I come back to the tables. I mean to play until I lose. Not just a hand or a single pass of the dice. When I lose all of it, every last thing I have won, then maybe I will understand how the others have felt. Only then can I stop.'

The Gypsy's snorts continued, combining into a gale of laughter. 'First you thought I conjured the Price girl. And now you wish to blame me for your excessive good luck. That is the maddest thing I have heard yet.'

'You do not believe in your own magic?'

'I do not have to. Not if you do. I come here with a reminder of your family's villainy. And you proceed to fill in the rest. In less than a day, you are near to prostrate with guilt. If you want freedom, Nathan, use this rope for the purpose it is intended.' He held the noose at eye level, until he was sure the meaning was clear, and then tossed it back on the table. 'Then my doings with your family will be over and you will no longer be able to concern yourself with the families of your victims.'

His self-control was a distant memory, as Nathan felt the long-buried rage burning in him again at the old accusation. 'My father was hanged for a crime he did not commit. My family has paid more than enough, with that. Take back the curse, Beshaley.'

'No.'

'You dirty Gypsy. Take back the curse.' In fury, he reached out and grabbed his former friend by his bad arm, squeezing the bicep.

He had found the injury. Stephano Beshaley went as white as his dark skin would allow, and the pain of the contact brought him out of his chair and to his knees.

Nate was overcome with a shameful glee to see his enemy humbled before him, and he remembered why it was so important to keep one's emotions out of the game. When one always had the upper hand, it was too easy to take pleasure from the suffering he inflicted. He pushed the anger from his mind, and squeezed again with clinical precision, watching the other's face contort with pain. 'Take back the rope. Let me go, and I will release your arm. You have my word.'

The Gypsy took a deep breath, as though he were trying to drive back the pain with the force of his will. Then he raised his shaking white face in defiance. 'Your father was a coward and a murderer. And you are the sort who would gamble for a girl's honour. Your word means nothing to me.'

Though the first statement angered him, the last was so true that his grip slackened on his old friend's arm, and he watched as the colour returned to the man's face. And in the place of the nothingness inside him, there was now a deep bone-aching remorse. 'Please. I am sorry. For all of it, Stephen. *Let me go.*'

And for a moment, the man on his knees before Nathan was plain Stephen Hebden, as hurt and bewildered as Nathan was. 'I cannot. I am as much a slave to the curse as you are, for I was the one left to administer it. If your father was innocent, then you are already free and what you think is a curse is all your own doing. But if not?' He shrugged with his one free arm. 'I can do nothing for you.'

Chapter Four

'Well, this was a most satisfying afternoon,' Honoria announced, as they neared the end of their shopping trip to Bond Street. 'And perhaps next time, we will persuade Diana to buy something for herself.'

'There is nothing I really need,' Diana said, as much to persuade herself as the girls. It was always tempting, on these forays, to make a purchase of some sort. But even a small one was an unnecessary indulgence.

'Then perhaps what you need is to sit down and have an ice. It would be very refreshing, after such a long walk.' Honoria was looking longingly in the direction of confectionary.

'The walk was not very long at all, Honoria, and should hardly exhaust you. Exercise, when taken in moderate amounts, is beneficial to health. And

I am sure that tea at home will be refreshing enough.'

'Sometimes, Diana, you are far too sensible.'

Diana smiled at the accusation. 'I need to be. Or you would indulge every whim, and grow too plump for your new gown.'

'Is that the gentleman who called yesterday, Diana?' Verity Carlow was staring in the opposite direction, and making an unladylike effort to point over the stack of parcels she was carrying, at a man on the end of the block. 'Oh, do say it is him. For he is every bit as striking as you described him.'

Diana prepared a reprimand, and then glanced in the direction her friend was looking, and saw the sun glinting off the silver hair of the man she had seen in the parlour. In the last twenty-four hours, she had spent so much time thinking of him that it felt almost as if she had conjured his image to appear on the street. It was hard to believe she was truly going to see him again after such a short time. But he must be real, for he looked very different than he had when she had seen him in the house. Today he seemed carefree. He was without a hat. And with the wind ruffling his hair, and his green eyes squinting into the sun, he looked almost as though he belonged on the deck of a ship, staring out at the sea.

She wondered if that was his true job. Sea captain. Or perhaps privateer. Surely something very romantic and commanding. He stood on the sidewalk as though he had conquered half of London. And here she was, spinning more romantic fancies around the poor man. But she had to admit, the effect that the sight of him had on her was sudden and difficult to control. It brought with it a faint breathlessness that increased as she realized that he was coming in their direction. 'Yes,' Diana said, trying to keep the excess of emotion from showing in her voice. 'That is Mr Dale. Whatever can he be doing here?'

'Shopping, I am sure,' Honoria said. 'Just as everyone else is doing. Perhaps he is visiting the tobacconist or the bank.' Apparently, the man's imposing nature was lost upon her. She was looking at Diana in a most searching way. 'While you made his behaviour yesterday sound very mysterious, you noticed nothing about him that would prevent him from mixing in society, did you?'

'Well, no.' It was just that she did not ever remember seeing him here before. And she was sure, had he shared the street with them in the past, she would have noticed.

Diana doubted Marc's apparent friendship with the man would require his sister's association with him. If it did, Marc would introduce them properly, in his own good time. For safety's sake, she prepared to steer Verity and Honoria to the other side of the street. 'You are probably right. He is shopping, or running errands of some sort. But I doubt he means to mix with us. He seemed most uncomfortable when visiting yesterday, and was in a hurry to leave.'

Verity gave her a round-eyed look. 'He did not seem to hold us any ill will, did he?'

'Of course not. But neither did I have any reason to think he might wish our company today.'

'Nonsense,' said Honoria. 'We do not mean him any harm. We are only being friendly. It is not as if Verity and I are angling after him, no matter how flattering your description might have been.'

Verity shaded her eyes with her hand for a better look. 'Flattering as well as accurate. He is most handsome, is he not?' She grinned at Diana. 'And it would show an amazing lack of Christian charity to appear to shun our brother's old friend, if we meet him on the street.'

Although she was sure that Verity's heart was

at least partly in the right place, Honoria must know that an act of Christian charity by a marriageable young lady towards an attractive, eligible man was liable to be misinterpreted. But it was too late to explain this, for Honoria was waving her handkerchief at the gentleman in question. 'Here, Mr Dale! Over here!' She set out at a quick pace towards the man, who was momentarily curious as to the identity of the person greeting him. But then he recognized Diana, trailing in Honoria's wake. And his eyes took on a distinctly hunted expression.

'Honoria!' she said sharply, hurrying after the girl. 'You have not been properly introduced to the man.'

Honoria ignored the tone of warning. 'Nonsense. He told you he had seen us as children, did he not? Then surely we need not be so formal. But if it bothers you, then you must remedy the fact immediately, and present us to him.

'Mr Dale? I understand that you are an old friend of our family. I was most disappointed to be indisposed when you visited yesterday.' She favoured Mr Dale with her most brilliant smile and then cast a significant glance in Diana's direction.

Diana gave up, and said, with a resigned tone,

'Mr Dale, may I present Lady Honoria and Lady Verity Carlow.'

He gave a somewhat stiff bow, and answered, 'You are correct, ladies. We are already acquainted. Although you were both much too small to remember me, and I was but a boy when I last saw you.'

Verity said, 'Miss Price and I were speculating on your appearance in Bond Street. I do not remember seeing you here before.'

Diana coloured and gave a small shake of her head to indicate that they had been doing nothing of the kind, for the last thing she wanted was to reveal the true nature of her speculations. She was sure that her head-shake looked nothing like the saucy toss Verity was giving her golden curls, to make them catch the sunlight.

Nathan Dale was wearing the same poleaxed expression that men often got when the Carlow sisters turned their considerable charms upon them. He muttered, 'Tailor,' as though he could barely remember what had brought him out to shop.

'So you frequent the area?' Verity gave Diana a triumphant look. 'I suppose we have seen you in the past. But the renewed acquaintance of our families puts a fresh face on the experience. Now that we know you again, we shall be running into each other all the time.'

Diana was sure that this was not the case. She was convinced that she would have been drawn to the man's striking appearance, had she seen it before.

For his part, Mr Dale looked positively horri-fied at the notion that he would be seeing them again and again.

But Verity ignored this as well, and said, 'Now that we have found you, may I ask you to be of assistance? We are overburdened by packages. If you could help us regain our carriage?'

No gentleman could refuse, although this one looked like he wished to. He glanced around for a moment, almost as if he was embarrassed to be seen with them. But then he bowed again and took the packages anyway, then turned to help them find their transport. Once that was achieved, it seemed Verity would not be satisfied with the aid of servants, but required Mr Dale to escort them all the way back to the house.

Diana could see him struggling to come up with a polite refusal, his eyes finding hers and holding them with a mute appeal for aid. But then, Honoria linked her arm through his, and all but dragged him into the carriage to sit beside her. 'There,' she said, giving a sigh of satisfaction. 'This is much better, is it not?'

Mr Dale gave a nod of polite agreement. Although since she was seated opposite him, Diana could see from his miserable expression that this was the last place on earth he wished to be. He remained in strained silence as the normally quiet Verity prattled on in a most annoying way about the price of ribbons and the challenge of finding a sufficiently fluffy *coq* feather in exactly the right shade of blue.

Diana had no idea what had gotten into the girl, although she suspected it had something to do with silver hair and green eyes. But she was well on the way to giving her a megrim. Mr Dale seemed of a similar mind, squirming in his seat as though he wished to fling open the door and dart from the coach, willing to risk a fall beneath the horse's hooves, over slow death by millinery.

Honoria was no better, clinging to Mr Dale's arm as though she sensed his desire and was trying to prevent the escape. If the girl truly wished to gain the man's attentions, she would need to choose another approach entirely. And much to Diana's dismay, she could find no desire to help either of them. If the man took a sudden and violent distaste to the Carlow sisters, it would forestall the risk that she might have to chaperone any of them, enduring painful evenings of lingering glances, staring intently into her needlework while ignoring their whispered endearments.

Was it only yesterday that she had been eagerly awaiting the appearance of Verity's first real suitor? She loved the girl, and wished her well as she struggled in the shadow of her older sister. If Verity finally made a choice, then Diana should be relieved, not annoyed. Unless it was this particular man.

And while she was sure of Honoria's ability to captivate any man, she could not warm to the idea that the object of her affection was the enigmatic Mr Dale. No matter that she thought he was exactly the sort of man she could put forward as a steadying influence on either of them. To be forced to sit in the corner and watch as Nathan Dale grew increasingly besotted over either of the Carlow daughters would be the most difficult thing in the world.

Perhaps Mr Dale thought the same, for he was squirming again. He stretched his long legs out before him, and they brushed against Diana's skirts.

She gave a surprised jump as his calf touched hers. He straightened suddenly, mumbling apologies.

Honoria nudged Verity with her toe from the opposite seat, and there were a few muffled giggles from the two girls until Diana gave a disapproving cough.

Mr Dale seemed to fold in upon himself, trying to take as little space as possible and cause no further incidents.

At last, the carriage arrived in front of the Carlow town house, and before it could come to a full stop, Nathan Dale had the door open and the step down. He offered a hand to Verity and then to Honoria. Once he had seen them both safely to the ground, he turned back for Diana. He wiped his palm upon his coat-tail and gave an embarrassed bob of his head, as though he did not wish to look into her eyes. But at the last moment, he looked up, his amazing green eyes catching hers and holding them. And then, his hand touched hers.

Her feet were on the ground, and he was turning away. But she had the strangest sensation that an important moment had passed, though she had no recollection of it. And it was a shame, for if the time had been spent with her hand in his, she thought that she would very much have liked to have a clear memory of it.

She came back to herself offering a silent prayer of relief that the trip was over, only to hear Verity insisting that Mr Dale simply must stay for tea, and her sister heartily agreeing. Honoria had reached out to catch the man by the arm again, before he could escape into the street. And now, she was reminding him that it was teatime, after all.

After dragging him so far out of his way, it was only logical that the girls offer him refreshment. Diana should commend them for their hospitality. But the events so far had left Diana's nerves frayed to the point where she was sure her cup would be rattling on the saucer loud enough to block out the sound of conversation.

And Mr Dale, damn him, could not seem to find voice enough to refuse the girls. If he did not wish to be with them, then why could he not say so—and end her torment? Instead, he allowed himself to be led as meek as a lamb into the sitting room for tea and cakes.

They were barely seated, before Verity sprang to her feet. 'I wonder what is taking so long? Cook is normally much more prompt than this. Perhaps someone should go and check.'

Diana was weighing in her mind the possibilities. It would not do to leave the girls alone
in the room with a stranger, while she went to
talk to the help. If that was what Verity was attempting to orchestrate, she underestimated her
chaperone. She would tell the girl to ring for
Wellow, the butler, and lecture them both later
about the need to sit patiently when one had
guests.

But before she could take action, Honoria announced, 'I will just go and see after things.' And
she was up, out of her chair and out the door. She
turned back. 'And Verity, you must come with
me.'

Her sister rose. 'Can you not find your own
way to the kitchen?'

'Of course. But I suspect I shall eat all the
sandwiches before they are even brought here,
for I am famished. If you do not come to watch
over me, I swear, I will not leave a thing for Mr
Dale.'

'Really, I…do not require anything,' he finished to the closed door.

And Diana found herself alone again, with
Nathan Dale.

There was a moment of very awkward silence.
And then, he spoke. 'Miss Verity did not talk

nearly so much when last I saw her. Of course, she was an infant at the time.'

'She did not talk so much when last I saw her either, and it has been barely an hour. I do not know what has got into her.' Diana hoped it did not sound like an indictment of her friend.

Apparently, he feared the same. For he said, 'I mean no disrespect. For all her chatter, she is a pleasant girl, as is her sister. Have you known them long?'

'I came into the household when Verity was almost fifteen. She is still nineteen and barely out.'

'And Honoria twenty. The family must be very proud of them.' For a moment, his gaze grew distant, as if remembering the past. And then he focused on her again. 'And before coming here, did you have another position?'

'As companion to an elderly lady in Kent.'

He leaned forward as though he found her rather uninteresting life to be riveting. 'And did you prefer that job to this one?'

She smiled, surprised at his questions. 'One position is much like another, I expect. But on the whole, I find it more enjoyable to watch the young. It was difficult to see the person in one's care wither and die, knowing there was nothing to be done. Much more pleasant to see them blossom, as young Verity has.' She gave a small sigh. 'Soon, they will have no need of a chaperone here. The girls shall be fine married ladies, with husbands and houses of their own.'

'And you will be out on the street.' He looked as though the prospect alarmed him.

She gave a little laugh of reassurance to soften the blunt way he had described her pending unemployment. 'Hardly, I am sure. Lord and Lady Narborough have been most kind to me. They will see to it that I am properly placed somewhere. I trust them to help me, when I am no longer needed here.'

'You might be surprised.' He muttered the words under his breath, and for a moment, she suspected that his fondness for the family was not as great as it had at first appeared.

'Well, in any case, I am not too worried,' she lied. 'When this job is finished, I will find another family who needs me. There are always openings for sensible women of a certain age.' Although they might not be as enjoyable as her current place.

'*A sensible woman of a certain age.* I see.' Perhaps he found her good sense to be a disappointment. Or perhaps it was her age that bothered him. He was frowning at her. 'But should you not find a place to your liking, do you have family to return to?' He was on the edge of his chair now, as though her answer were deeply important to him.

She shook her head. 'It has been just me for almost five years. But my situation is hardly unique. And in some ways it was easier for me than it has been for others. My mother died when I was young. And I was well-settled in employment before my father died. There was no period of sudden turmoil, as I found myself homeless and alone with no plan for the future.' In fact, the turmoil was several years past, and her anger with her father had cooled by the time she'd lost him for good.

'But you have no one else? I mean: no prospects, other than employment?'

She looked at him sharply. Was he enquiring if there was a gentleman in her life? 'Certainly not.'

And now he'd realized how that question had sounded, for he fell into pensive silence, before beginning again. 'I am sorry if my curiosity was inappropriate. But if you should find yourself in constrained circumstances and there is anything I can do to help…'

And now it sounded as though he were about to offer a *carte blanche*. 'No, Mr Dale,' she said firmly, so there could be no question of her meaning. 'I can assure you, that whatever my circumstances might be, I will not be needing help with them.'

A short time later, Verity and Honoria returned followed by a footman with tea things. Apparently, the time away had calmed Verity's nerves, although Honoria had the same enigmatic smile on her face as before. They set about arranging the table for Mr Dale, like consummate hostesses. They were solicitous of his needs without clinging, and they conversed without the annoying chatter that had bothered her in the carriage.

It gave Diana the chance to retreat to a corner with her cup and stay well out of the flow of talk, allowing the girls to get to know the gentleman better. If he could be called a gentleman, for his behaviour to her had been most forward and more than a little strange. She wondered if she had given him too much credit the first time they had met, swayed by his charm and his physical appearance.

And if her silence now permitted time to observe the fine features of Mr Dale? Then she doubted he would notice, and she could hardly be blamed for it. She did find him to be a very handsome man. And she sincerely hoped she had misunderstood his intent toward her. He spoke easily enough with the girls, now that she was out of the way. There was nothing improper about his speech or manner. And he'd lost that curious sense of agitation he had brought to even the most mundane of his questions to her. When he rose to go, he thanked Verity and Honoria in turn, then paused as he looked in her direction, seeming to swallow his nerves before giving her the same polite words of thanks and a short stiff bow. And then, he was gone.

There was a moment of silence, as though Verity wished to be sure that the man was totally out of earshot, before she spoke, as though he could hear their opinions of him through the brick walls and on the street. Then she turned and smiled at Honoria. 'Well?'

Honoria smiled and nodded. 'Oh, yes. I think most definitely.'

And then she turned to Diana. 'And what do you think of the gentleman, Miss Price?'

Apparently, she was to render the final verdict, and she did not wish to, for her own opinion was most decidedly mixed. She took care to discount her own strong reactions, and did her best to view him as she would any other prospective suitor. 'I am glad that you are both so definite on the subject of Mr Dale. He seems a fine person, and was most courteous in his behaviour. Your inviting him into the house was not inappropriate, although it was somewhat unplanned. If there is a past history between your families it cannot be too terribly improper. But despite what you might think, we do not know him very well at all. I doubt your father or brothers would approve, should things progress to the point where he might make either of you an offer before they can be consulted.'

'Us?' Verity sat down, laughing heartily. 'Oh, Diana. If you do not see the truth of what has been happening, you must be blind. However are we to trust you with advising us on our futures, if you cannot manage your own?'

'What has my future to do with it?'

Honoria grinned. 'We heard the way you spoke of him, after his visit here yesterday. The vividness of your physical description was enough for Verity to pick him out of the crowd on Bond Street. And apparently, you did not see the way he looked at you when we met him.

His eyes followed you as though you were the only woman present. So we waylaid the poor fellow and made ourselves as tiresome as possible. Then we left you alone together, as soon as we were able. You did not expect us to play chaperone, did you? For that would be more than a little ironic.'

'Me?' Her voice cracked on the word.

'Yes, you, you goose,' said Verity. 'I wondered what would become of you, once I was wed. It would be so much better for me, were you to be a proper married lady as well, and not a companion to another. For then we could all remain friends and see each other as often as we liked.'

'Me? Married?'

'To Mr Dale,' Honoria completed the thought. 'You are right, Verity. It is the most perfect idea in the world.'

'Me.' And now that they had placed it there, the thought was stuck in her head and would not be dislodged. 'Married.' It had been so long since she had even thought of the word as it pertained to herself, that she could not manage to form a sentence around it. 'To Mr Dale.' If it had been one of the girls displaying an interest in the man, she would have given a lecture at this point about the importance of knowing a gentleman better before using such a word in connection with him. Horses should be put before carts. There should be frequent meetings between the interested parties. Affection and love were things that should be nurtured before a more permanent arrangement could be considered.

But suddenly, she felt as foolish as either young girl. Her head was flooded with visions of a home of her own, a husband of her own, and her own children, all with the sparkling green eyes of Nathan Dale.

If she were thinking clearly, then she would have told the girls that, if a gentlemen were as rushed into making an offer as they wished for Mr Dale to be, the offer he might make would be one that no proper woman could accept. What must he think of her? He must suspect that she had arranged their private conversation by manipulating the girls, all in an attempt to court him for herself. How would she be able to speak to the man, when next they met, if her head was full of romantic nonsense and his ideas were much more worldly?

She forced her fears into the background and looked at the girls with her most prim and sensible gaze. 'No. I am sorry. The idea does not appeal to me in the least. If this visit with him

was arranged for my benefit, then while I thank
you for the concern, I can assure you that no
further such plans are necessary.' She swallowed
hard, and lied. 'I am quite content to remain as
I am.'

Chapter Five

Nate went back to his house in Hans Place, with the Carlows' tea sitting uneasily in his stomach. The feelings of disquiet grew with each step towards his home. By the time he had stepped through the front door, it felt as though ants crawled upon his skin.

That was a near one. It had been a misfortune to meet the girl once. But to find her again so soon, after years of avoidance? It was another part of the Gypsy's damn curse, he was sure. As little Verity had been quick to point out to him, now that he had found Diana Price, he was unlikely to get free of her.

The thought flitted across his mind that he had no desire to be free of her. Under better circumstances, he'd have been enjoying the association immensely. And she seemed to enjoy it as well, if there was any meaning to the pretty blush upon her cheek when they'd been left alone.

But then, he had proceeded to make an ass of himself by prying into her personal life and asking questions that no stranger should care about. He had left her with the impression that he was the sort who would make advances towards a vulnerable woman within moments of being alone with her. Damn it to hell, he had only wanted to make up for what he had already done to her. Instead it had sounded like he wished to set her up in an apartment as his ladybird.

Although, once the idea had entered his head, he had to admit that there were advantages to it. If she were so inclined, it would be pure pleasure to watch those eyes widen in pretended shock at his suggestions, only to be lulled into catlike satisfaction when he acted on them. She must realize that the way she pursed those full lips in disapproval at him only made them more tempting. He suspected that, should she fold her arms beneath her high breasts, or place her hands upon those softly rounded hips in a gesture of disapproval, she could easily bring a strong man to his knees.

It was all quite hopeless. Even if she was less

than the proper lady he suspected, she was Edgar Price's daughter and therefore the last woman in London he should be wishing to bed. He might pretend to be Nate Dale for a while with her, he supposed. But knowing his luck when away from the gaming tables, it was only a matter of time before Hal or Marc arrived and recognized the man who was courting their sisters' chaperone. Or perhaps he would be the one to let some word slip that would make it clear to Diana Price his true identity.

Until a few days ago, it had been easy enough to think of himself as well and truly Nate Dale, and to think of Nathan Wardale as a distant memory. But now, he could not help but see his current life as a thinly drawn fraud. When the truth came out, he doubted that there were enough words in his vocabulary to talk himself out of the situation.

He looked around, at the entry hall to his house. Although the place had been home to him for almost four years, and he had long ago come to think of it as truly his, suddenly, he felt like an interloper in the home of Diana Price. As he glanced around, he was qualifying everything in his life into two enormous piles: things that he had bought and things that had been in the house when he had won it. Even the servants were Price's, although it had been many years since he had felt any disloyalty. Those who had not wished him as master had quit on the day he'd accepted the deed. But most were content enough, when they realized that the new master could easily meet the back payments on their salaries and manage a raise as well.

He had followed his sudden arrival with an unexpected six-year absence. And in that time, the servants might as well have been sole possessors of the house. The man of business he had retained to pay the bills knew better than to meddle in the mundane details of running it. They had relaxed in the knowledge that the chaos the house had undergone from the previous owner's gambling was at an end. If the new master was also a gambler? Then at least he was a winner. Their positions were secure.

And if any one of them had ever wondered what had become of Diana Price or her father, then they had never spoken the words aloud in his presence.

But now, everywhere he looked, he saw reminders that he had taken this house right out from under the woman who sat so patiently at the side of the Carlow sisters. He walked up the stairs and hurried down the hall to his room. It was the only place in the house guaranteed not to remind him of the previous owner, for he had bought everything in it, brand new, even stripping the silk from the walls and taking up the rugs to prevent the ghost of Edgar Price from intruding on his dreams. Once he was shut inside, he would have peace.

But to arrive there, he needed to pass the locked door at the head of the stairs. He almost made it by without looking. In truth, he had trained himself never to look in that direction. To not see the door. To imagine it as a blank square of wall. But once remembered, he could not seem to put it from his mind.

When he reached his room, he rang for the butler.

'Sir?'

'Benton, do you have a key for the room at the head of the stairs?'

'Miss Diana's room, sir?' The man had been butler of this house since long before Nate had come to it. And although he appeared loyal, now that he was pressed on the subject, he made no effort to hide the fact that there was still one area of the house that did not belong to the new owner. When Nate had returned from America, the single room had been left untouched, as though no one could bring themselves to store the contents. And now, Benton's tone was worried, as if the idea disturbed him that it might finally be time to pack the contents away.

Nathan nodded. 'Miss Diana's room.'

The butler did not say another word, but removed a single key from the ring in his pocket, handing it to Nathan as though he wanted no part in what was to happen nor in whatever cosmic repercussions might fall on his master's head as a result of his actions.

Nate sighed. 'Thank you, Benton. That is all.'

The man removed himself, and Nate made his way back down the hall to the locked door. He turned the key quickly and jerked open the door before stepping inside, leaving it open behind him, so that he could see by the light from the hall. The room was dustier than he'd remembered, but other than that, unchanged. The wardrobe doors were thrown open, as though the occupant had been forced to pack and leave in a hurry. She must have taken her day dresses; a large section of the wardrobe stood empty.

But the ball gowns had been pushed to the side, and left behind. She'd known, even then, that her days as a debutante were over. If one was about to seek a position, then one did not need finery. He glanced around the room, taking note of the things missing and the things left behind. The hair brushes were gone but the ornaments remained. The jewellery box was open, and the contents scattered, as though she'd thought to take it all, then come to the conclusion that it had been lost to her along with everything else and settled on taking a few small pieces as remembrance of her old life.

There was a book on the table by the bed, the reader's place still marked by a scrap of ribbon. Did she ever finish it, he wondered, or had the little book been forgotten in her rush to go?

He thought back to his own departure from Leybourne House. The way his mother had told him to pack only what was needed. He had just turned ten, and still thought toy soldiers and wooden swords to be among life's necessities. After seeing the enormous pile of his possessions, she had sat down with him, and explained that, from now on, life would be different.

It was the first time, in all the harrowing weeks, that he had seen his mother cry.

He looked again at the contents of the room around him. He remembered how it had felt to be so totally displaced. And yet, he had done it to others. To the sweet-faced girl who had absented herself from his conversation with the Carlow sisters with the talent of one whose sole job was to fade into the background. She should be dancing at balls beside Verity and Honoria, not sitting in the corner with her book.

He had done that to her. He had ruined her chances, and her life. She should be married by now, with children of her own and servants to care for her needs.

He could feel the marker, heavy in his purse, as though it sought to burn through the leather and scar his skin. He had been telling himself for years that he had done the best he could by Diana Price. That it was enough: not following through on the damn thing. As bad as he had been to take it in the first place, he could have been worse. He had never demanded payment. He held himself forever in check, trying to prove his good character by the one thing he did not take.

Small comfort to Diana Price. He had not made her his whore for a night. He had left her with her virtue while denying her a lifetime's comforts.

He sat on the edge of the bed and looked around the room. She had been happy here, he was sure. It was smaller than his room, of course, but well-appointed and cheerful. It suited her. Without thinking too much about it, he stretched out on the bed and he picked up the book.

He woke nearly an hour later. He could remember reading. It was a volume of Shakespeare's sonnets. He had read and enjoyed them many times before. But the surprising warmth of the room and the peace of it had overcome him. Was it the quality of the light through the windows? Perhaps, when he had chosen his own room, he should have taken this, rather than the master suite. He had rested better during the little nap than he had in his own bed. And now, he was shaking off the vision of a pretty young girl with wide dark eyes, sitting in the window seat of this very room, legs tucked under her skirts, a half smile on her sunlit face and the book in her lap.

In his dream, she had looked up at him, where he lay on the bed, and put down the book to come towards him. The glint in her eyes was as welcoming as he might wish, and she had smiled. And then, thank God, he had awakened. If the dream had gone as he expected—with her lying in his arms—he was sure that it would have ended in a nightmare, once he'd realized who she was.

He got up quickly, trying to clear the fog from his brain, then left the room, locking the door behind him and dropping the key into his pocket. Then he bypassed his own room and went down the stairs to his study. Or was it Edgar Price's study? He was no longer sure. He had been so proud, when he'd first won this house, although much less so of the rest of that evening. There would have been room for Helena and Rosalind, and Mother as well. They would have lived happily enough, he was sure, once he had found some way to persuade them that he had come by it properly.

He had meant to break the news to them gently, making sure that everything was legal and the way prepared. His mother had never approved of his gambling to make the rent. She had wanted him to find an honest trade to help contribute to the family. And if she had realized how high the stakes had risen, and how quickly? If it upset her that he was winning coins off navvies or a few quid off of drunken clarks to help pay the bills, then she would have been appalled to see what he had won from Price.

It would not do to drop his family into a house full of unwilling servants, with the previous owners' possessions strewn about and Price's pipe still burning on the mantle. So he had toured the premises, released any servants that did not feel they could make peace with a change of masters and arranged things so that his mother need never again be troubled with the butcher's bill. He topped up the household accounts with several more fine scores at the tables. When he was through, the place would run like clock-work. His mother need never think about the time he'd spent gaming for the money she lived on, or waste her fading energy in sympathy for the source of their wealth.

But it seemed that fate was working against him, yet again. For no sooner had he finished his plans, than he was set upon by a press gang. He did not wake from their tender ministrations until he was onboard ship and well on the way to France as a member of His Majesty's Navy.

When he had managed to make his way home, he found the house little different than it had been when he'd left it. He had returned to a life that was quite comfortable, and further gambling had made it even more so. But it meant nothing if there was no one to share it with.

And now he could not shake the feeling that it was not his life that he was living, but one that rightly belonged to another. He gathered paper and pen, and addressed a hurried letter to Miss Price, care of the Carlow family.

And what did he mean to say to her? 'I am sorry,' hardly seemed enough, nor would it do any good to explain himself. It might appear that he thought he had suffered more than she, and he doubted it was possible to compare burdens. At last, he decided to leave the contents blank. Then he turned out his purse and piled the folded bank notes neatly inside the paper, reaching for the wax to seal it all up tight before sending. He almost marked it, but thought better of it. She did not need to know the sender, nor the reason. After this afternoon, she would not wish to take a penny from Mr Dale for fear of encouraging his attentions. And if she should discover the real reason he had done it, he dreaded her response.

But if he could reimburse her, in some small part, for the damage he had done.

It was not enough. It could never be enough. But perhaps he could find other ways to help her, without giving the wrong impression, when her position with the Carlows was at an end. It was better than nothing.

But *nothing* was what he had done in the past, and he found it would no longer content him.

Chapter Six

As she sat enjoying morning tea in the small dining room with Verity, Diana tried not to think of the day before. So the girls were convinced that Mr Dale was considering marriage. The idea was as ridiculous as it was appealing. His interest could not be too strong, for she was sure he would not have returned to the Carlow home had Verity and Honoria not forced the issue.

But once there, he had been more than willing to speak to her. And it was more than that. It was far more telling that he listened. Anyone might speak when trapped alone in a room with a stranger, just to fill the embarrassing silence. He had said very little about himself, but made every effort to draw her out.

And he had made the curious offer of aid. Perhaps she had misunderstood him, putting too ominous a spin on the words. After years of watching out for the virtue of others, even the most innocent of unguarded comments might be seen as an improper advance. She replayed the exchange endlessly in her mind, trying to see it from all sides. But it became even more confusing with repetition.

And now, whether she saw him again or not, Verity and Honoria would tease her endlessly on the subject of Mr Dale, just to see her turn pink at the mention of the man's name.

But if she did see him?

It was all she could do not to moan aloud at the thought. Her curiosity about him had grown to fascination, and then obsession. If she saw him, she would make a complete cake of herself. Any interest he might have felt would turn immediately to distaste, once he saw her behaviour.

It was disaster.

She gave Verity a weak smile over her cup of tea, and wished Honoria a good morning as the girl appeared in the doorway, yawning and sorting through the morning's mail. 'Here, Diana. A letter addressed to you.' Honoria held it out to her, and then snatched it back, holding it to her temple, as though trying to divine the contents. 'Too thick for a *billet doux*. I wonder what it might be?' She passed the letter to her friend.

'What utter nonsense, Honoria. You really are being most unfair to me. If you are not careful, I shall remember this behaviour. And when you receive a letter, I shall return the torment.' She tried not to appear as excited as she was, but she rarely received mail. It was even more rare to receive it unexpectedly, and she had no idea what this might be. She ran a finger along the edge of the folded paper to pop the sealing wax.

Bank notes fluttered to the table in front of her. It was as startling as if she had opened the letter to a flight of moths. She leaned back in her chair, as though afraid to let the things touch her dress.

'Ohhh my.' Verity had no such fear and came to her side to scoop the notes off the floor and into an organized pile on the table, counting as she went. 'There is all of thirty-four pounds here. Who sent it?'

Diana's mind was too numb to scold her charge for the impudence of the question. In truth, she was curious to know the answer. She picked up the letter, searching both sides for information. 'I do not know. There is my address, right enough. But there is no return.' She turned the paper. 'And no message, either.'

'Why would anyone send such an odd number?' Honoria asked. Was there a debt that needed paying?'

Diana stared at the money on the desk. 'None owed to me.' There might have been, to her father. But it was far more likely a debt was owed by her, than to her. And why would the money have come to her now, so many years after it might have helped?

'Well it is nowhere near your birthday. Or Christmas, for that matter,' Verity said.

Honoria riffled through the stack. 'And it does not look as if the person went to the bank for the money. The bills are all odd. Creased. Old.'

'But legal tender, all the same,' she told them. The Carlow girls were used to their money, clean and neatly folded, going straight from their brother's hand into their reticules. They had never been forced to search their father's pockets after a night of gambling, hoping that there would be a little left to pay the grocer.

The memory shocked Diana, for it had been so long, she'd thought it forgotten. But at the sight of the somewhat ragged bills before her, the past came flooding back and brought bitterness with it. Pound notes hurriedly gathered and stuffed into a pocket or purse. Not stacked neatly, but front to back, and upside down. This was enough to be very near a year's salary to a paid companion. But someone had thrust it into an envelope as though it were nothing, and addressed it to her. She stared at the writing on the letter, trying to divine masculine from feminine. The letters were roughly formed, as though the writer had wished to conceal his or her identity.

'Well, whoever it was seemed to think it most important that you receive this,' Verity said. 'You are sure that you have no idea?'

'None.'

'No belated gifts from estranged godparents?'

'I have none, estranged or otherwise.'

'No family that has gone to the continent or the colonies to make their fortune?' suggested Honoria with a smile.

Diana held it up to her. 'It is a London postmark, Honoria. There is nothing exotic about it.'

'No pending bequests from rich uncles?'

Diana laughed. 'Of course not. You know I have no family. And even if I did, they would not be so secretive.'

Verity smiled in triumph. 'Then it must be from an admirer. Someone is pained to see you forced into the shadows, toiling to maintain our good name. That someone wishes you a chance to better yourself. And I know just such a one. It is from Mr Dale.'

'Verity!' Diana was sure that her cheeks could not get any more pink at the thought of the man, for she could feel them burning already. 'It can be no such thing, and I forbid you to say that again. Mr Dale would have no reason to send me a large sum of money, on a whim. And even if he did, the gesture would not be kindly in the least. It would…' She struggled to think of a way to explain, one that did not confirm her worst fears about the man. 'It would be most improper. Only one sort of gentleman would offer money to a female. And only one sort of female would accept it.'

'Do you think that he means to make you his mistress?' Honoria's eyes grew wide with curiosity.

'Honoria! It is most unladylike of you to entertain that idea. But if a gentleman well outside of his dotage gave me a substantial amount like this, I would not think that it was out of concern for my future or well-being. I would return it immediately, for I would assume that he expected something in exchange for it that I did not wish to give him.'

Honoria stared at the pile of bills on the table.

'Then he would be the most cold-blooded and foolish paramour imaginable. Surely he must know that jewellery would be a better temptation, when persuading a woman to part with her honour. And to not enclose an address?' She waved her hand over the money. 'It is very difficult to demand thanks for the gift if one does not identify oneself when sending. Is he likely to make an appearance, regretfully inform you that he forgot to enclose his card when offering a *carte blanche*, and then expect you to fall at his feet? I seriously doubt it, Diana. More likely, he was moved by your situation and feared you were in need of help. But the natural shyness and reservation he displayed towards you, when talking with us, left him awkward and unsure of how best to aid you. So he posted you the contents of his purse. But he feared that you would take it just as you have suggested, and throw the money back in his face. So he gave no return address to prevent you.'

Diana dearly wished that this was the case. For it would allay her suspicions about their last meeting. But if he had truly meant to offer help, why could he not have forgone the money and renewed the offer with a note of apology and explanation?

Unless he did not wish to see her again, or lead

her to believe that there was anything at all romantic about his interest in her. Her heart fell a little at the most probable truth. And then she looked back to the money and sighed. 'Well, whoever sent it, I certainly cannot keep it. They are mistaken if they think I need financial help. I am secure in my position here.'

'Until we are both married,' Verity pointed out. 'And I suppose that will happen soon. Honoria, you must make a choice from amongst your many admirers, for it is cruel to make them wait. And for me?' She sighed as well, as though the idea were a burden to her. 'There is the matter of finding an appropriate gentleman. But once I apply myself to the task…'

Diana cut short the girl's fears, for sometimes it did not sound as if Verity wished to marry at all. '*When* you settle is beside the point. You will do it when the time is right. You need not give a thought to what will happen to me after. But when you no longer need me, I have set aside a small savings that will keep me until another position can be found.'

Verity looked at the money again. 'We will not worry, for we know that you have at least thirty-four pounds. Enough for a year's worth of rainy days, right there on the table.'

It nearly doubled what she had set aside for herself. 'But I cannot keep it,' Diana said again, firmly so as to assure herself. 'It is far too much to be proper. Perhaps a deserving charity—'

'How utterly ridiculous.' Honoria's autocratic nature was showing again. 'You are worthy enough for this, Diana. And we will not allow you to get up on your high horse and give this away. Is there nothing you want? No unfulfilled dreams that might be achieved with the help of this money?'

'Dreams?' Diana resisted the urge to flinch at the word. She had worked very hard in the last ten years to rid herself of dreams. But now that the money was before her… 'No,' she said firmly. 'There is nothing.'

'There is,' Honoria said in triumph. 'I saw it in your eyes, just now.'

'It is not enough money. It hardly matters, really.'

Verity tugged her arm. 'Speak, Diana. Tell us. You know you want to.'

'A house.' Diana blurted the word. 'Just a cottage. It needn't be much. But all my own. And enough money to live in it, and know that it would be mine forever.' With a door to lock, should her father's biggest mistake ever catch up with her.

Honoria was looking at her with the eyes of one who had never known loss. 'Well. That is certainly not what I expected you to say. Not very exciting at all.'

Diana thought back to the day when they had been forced to leave her home, just minutes ahead of the arrival of the new owner, fleeing in terror of a man that she had never met. 'Excitement is not always what we expect, Honoria. It might not be pleasurable at all.'

Verity was blinking at her in confusion, with the blank look of one that had been coddled and protected her entire life. But good-hearted soul that she was, her expression quickly changed to one of sympathy and encouragement. 'How foolish of us. It is quite possible for your dreams and ours to be very different, and yet very important, is it not?' She held out her hands to her friend. 'Forgive us. If it is a cottage of your own that you wish, then there would be no harm in keeping the money, would there? Perhaps it is not enough. But surely, it could be a nest egg. You will have it on that day that you have no more silly young girls to care for.'

She looked down at the money again, letting Verity's words tempt her. Perhaps it would not be such a bad thing to hold the money for a while. At least until she could figure out who sent it. There might be a perfectly logical explanation that she had not thought of. And she would feel most foolish if she gave away a windfall that she was truly entitled to. 'You are right, I think. It does no harm to keep the money, as long as I do not mean to fritter it away on nonsense.'

'Like another trip to Bond Street?' Honoria suggested.

Which was tempting, Diana had to admit. It would be too easy to convert some of the money in front of her into a new bonnet, which was a thing she wanted, but certainly did not need. She shook her head. 'That is exactly the sort of foolishness I mean to avoid. It will be far better for us to go to the park for a time, and take some fresh air.'

Chapter Seven

Nate lifted his face to the sky, looking at the light dappling through the leaves in the trees of Hyde Park. The sun was shining bright today, and it was good to be out in it. After all the long months onboard the *Endeavor*, being burned and blinded, Nate had thought he'd had enough of the damned sunlight, and that the windowless gloom of a gaming hell was most preferable. But this morning had been different. When he'd sent the money off to Diana yesterday, he had felt the change. Even after gambling until almost dawn, he'd felt an unaccustomed lightness of spirit that had been buoyed as he'd tossed a portion of his winnings to the children begging on the street. He could not make all things right for the girl by putting a few pounds in an envelope, but at least he had done something.

Perhaps, with time, he could come up with a better solution.

On the cab ride back to Hans Place, he'd signalled the driver to let him out before the park so that he might walk the rest of the way. He needed a fresh breeze and spring sunlight on his face. He needed a change. He took a deep breath and smiled. This was what he needed: to walk in daylight like a normal man, instead of creeping home with the dawn and sleeping through the day. Even if it was just for the morning, he needed some proof that his life could be changeable, like the weather. A sign that he was on the cusp of a new season.

'Mr Dale!' The voice of Verity Carlow cut through him like a sugar-coated knife and reality came crashing back. It had been foolhardiness itself to attempt a walk through Hyde Park at this hour, when anyone might be taking the morning air. And if Miss Carlow was present, then that must mean…

He turned towards the voice with a pained smile. 'Lady Verity. And Lady Honoria. And Miss Price as well. How good to see you all.'

The ladies made their curtseys, and Verity addressed him again. 'And you as well, Mr Dale. It is just as I suspected. We are destined to meet.'

'Yes. I suspect it is our fate.' Damn that Gypsy. 'You are all well, I trust?'

'Very much so, sir.'

He glanced over at Diana Price, who seemed to be going pink in the early morning sun. 'And you, Miss Price, are better, I trust?'

'Better?' She looked at him curiously, with a slight smile. 'I do not recall being ill.'

Damn again. He had been thinking of the money, and the difference it would make to her future. He should know nothing of it, or what was the point of anonymity? 'Well, I mean. Well, as well. As well, as Lady Verity. That is to say. Also well.' And now the words were hopelessly tangled. He allowed them to trail into silence.

The younger of the sisters gave a small giggle and Lady Honoria said, 'We are going, after our walk, to Bond Street so that Miss Price might buy a new gown.'

'Or perhaps not.' Miss Price seemed to be of two minds on the subject, no matter how Honoria felt about it. And then, she turned back to him. 'And in answer to your question: Yes, thank you. I am most well. And you, sir?'

He was in hell. Suffering the torment of giggling debutantes and their dark-eyed companions. 'Fine also, thank you.'

And that should have been all that was required of him. But Lady Verity chose that moment to spy someone over her shoulder. 'Penelope and Charlotte Veryan are just down the path. I have been meaning to speak with them for ages. And Honoria, you have as well.'

'I have?' Lady Honoria seemed surprised by the fact.

Her sister seized her by the sleeve. 'Of course you have. Now come along immediately, or we will miss them. You do not mind walking a ways with Miss Price, do you sir?'

Nate's head ducked beneath his collar, and without thinking, he turned away, to make sure that the Veryan sisters did not spot him, even in profile. He could not remember if they'd even existed at the time of the scandal, but it seemed unwise to give them a reason to take a description of him back to their father, Lord Keddinton of the Home Office.

The man was the number one spy catcher in the country, and had made a good part of his reputation on the disgrace and hanging of the Earl of Leybourne. God knew what he would do if he realized that Nathan Wardale had resurfaced and was sniffing about the Carlow family. He smiled at Verity and then at Diana, and lied through his teeth. 'Do I mind the company of Miss Price? Not at all.' In truth, it was almost as awkward as a meeting with the Veryans.

Almost, but not quite. And since the Carlow girls were gone as soon as the words were out of his mouth, he could not very well run off like a rabbit and leave Diana alone. He turned to look at her.

She must have seen the helpless confusion on his face, for she gave a short laugh. 'Really, Mr Dale. It cannot be as bad as all that to be forced into my company. You are free to go, if you wish.'

He hung his head, embarrassed to have been caught in the thought. 'Forgive me, Miss Price. It is not your company that concerns me. Well, not precisely. It is just that—' He broke off, before he told her any more of the truth and ruined everything. 'I must apologize for yesterday's conversation. I am sure that my excessive curiosity was most inappropriate. But I meant nothing by it.'

'Then I shall take nothing from it.' She smiled at him with obvious charity. But was there a touch of disappointment in her eyes? Why would that be? Unless she had enjoyed his interest in her and wished it to be more than polite small talk.

Then he realized that he had allowed a gap in

the conversation, as he'd stood dumbstruck, trying to fathom what she might be thinking. So he cleared his throat, and said with a smile, 'And now, I am behaving strangely again, I think.'

She nodded. 'That is the way, sometimes. If one is by nature reticent, or unaccustomed to speaking with those of the opposite gender, then conversation can be difficult.'

She thought him shy did she? And awkward around women? The idea was so ludicrous that he almost laughed in response. It would not do for one so pretty as Diana Price to think him unable to talk to women. There were any number of ladies who could assure her that he was most charming. He was certain he had heard the word irresistible used on several occasions. 'That is not the...' And then he realized that the sort of women he normally conversed with could hardly be called ladies. And that there was a perfectly obvious reason that he found it so difficult to talk to Diana Price. But that he could not very well explain it to her. And so he allowed the untruth to stand, gave a shrug and added, 'It is far too difficult to explain.'

She smiled in encouragement. 'If you wish to attempt it, you will find me a most receptive listener.'

And there it was again. A sparkle in her eye and a hint that she would welcome his interest. He cast her a sidelong glance. 'I imagine you are skilled in that as well, since you are a professional companion.'

She nodded, making no effort to speak. Even in her silence, she was teasing him, and he relaxed enough to smile back. Without thinking about it, he turned and gestured to the path, away from Verity and Honoria. They began to walk, falling easily into step with each other. 'Perhaps I could persuade you to speak. It would be much easier for me to ask about you than to explain myself. Tell me more about yourself, Miss Price.'

She seemed just as surprised as he had been to have the conversation turned back to her. 'There is not much to tell that you have not already heard. I have been tending to the needs of others since I was seventeen. I believe we discussed it, when last we met.'

'And before that?' he asked gently.

She paused, and he wondered if it might stir some rancour or sadness in her. But her pace stayed as placid as it had been. 'I had an unremarkable childhood. My mother died when I was seven. There were no other children.' She gave a small frown. 'My father was very loving, but not particularly wise. He lost his fortune and our home, and I was forced to seek employment.' She glanced at him, quickly. 'That is not to say I did not love him very much. Or that he was not good to me, except in that one thing.'

'Of course.' He rushed to say it. 'But sometimes, when a man is a gambler, he does not realize what he has done until after.'

She looked up sharply. 'I did not say he was a gambler.'

'You did not?' Of course she hadn't. And how was he to explain that bit of knowledge? 'I am so sorry if I assumed incorrectly. But that is frequently the cause of sudden reversals of fortune amongst gentlemen.'

She sighed. 'You guessed correctly, Mr Dale. But the problem was long ago, and hardly concerns me, truly. It has not been a bad life, not really. After the night he lost the house…my father ceased gambling.'

There was an odd pause in the middle of the sentence that made Nate wonder how much she knew about what had truly happened.

'After he saw me safely employed, he went North for a time. But he visited me frequently. Our lives were harder than they had been, of course.' She smiled at him, the lines on her face smoothing to tranquillity. 'But better. Everything was so much better, once he put down the cards for the last time.'

Did she know the reason for her father's sudden abstinence? If she did not know the full truth, then perhaps she felt Nathan Wardale had done her a service by ruining her father. But he knew exactly what had happened, and would never feel right on the matter. 'So it ended well, then. That is good to know.'

She turned her head and smiled fondly back at Verity and Honoria. 'I have been quite happy with the Carlows. And I shall be most glad to see them make matches. Their brother, Lord Stanegate, has recently found a wife. Perhaps it will inspire them.'

He smiled. 'Marc is the first of us to marry, then. But he is at that time in life when a man must consider his future.'

'You knew him as a child, you said?'

'Yes. He was a bit younger than me. Still is, younger of course.'

'And already married.'

And it was obvious the direction the conversation had taken. Without meaning to, he was half way to offering for the girl. Which could have been a fine thing, since she was delightful. She would have been perfect for him, if she had been any other woman in the world. And if perhaps, he was a different man.

He reached into his pocket for a handkerchief to mop at the sweat he could feel springing out on his forehead, and heard a small thump as something fell from his coat and onto the ground at their feet.

And there, before them, was the little volume of poetry from Diana Price's bedroom, her ribbon still marking the place. Without thinking, he must have put it in his pocket on leaving the room.

Being the helpful sort of person that she was, Diana looked down at the thing, then stooped to pick it up. 'You seem to have dropped something, Mr Dale.' And then, she saw the title. 'Shakespeare?' she exclaimed. 'Is he a favourite of yours?'

'Yes. I like him very much.'

'I do as well. I used to have my own copy of the sonnets, and read it many times. But it has been so long.'

Of course she had. And here was her own hair ribbon in the same place she had left it, waiting to be recognized. He held his breath, expecting the moment of revelation. But it passed. For she opened the book, paging through it and re-moving the ribbon, tucking it to the back. It was a plain thing of blue satin, much like many others, he assumed. She was examining the book as though the marker held no special meaning. 'This is even the same edition I remember.'

'You must take it then.'

'That is not necessary,' she rushed to assure him. 'If I wished, the library…'

'It is hardly anything.' To give back something that had given her pleasure? That was less than nothing, for it only brought them closer to being even. But when he searched his heart, he knew that it was right, for it made him feel better to do it, even knowing that she might recognize the thing. 'Please. I insist. It is not new. But I would be honoured to part with it, if you enjoy it.' He reached out without thinking, and clasped Diana's hands to press the book into them. They were well shaped, tiny in his, smooth and warm in their kid leather gloves. He looked into her eyes which were shining bright with happiness.

And her gaze dropped demurely to the open book in front of her and the place where their hands were joined. 'The age of the book is not important. The words in it are just as true as they ever were. Thank you.'

So much joy from something so small. And the smile on her face made him feel like a Galahad. As long as the moment was taken out of context. Because otherwise…He looked up, desperate for a distraction. 'Ahh. I see the ladies are returning from their visit.' And not a moment too soon. He stepped hurriedly away from Diana and raised a hand to hail them.

The girls came back to them, in an obvious state of excitement. 'Diana,' Verity said breathlessly, 'the most wonderful news.'

Honoria continued, 'We have been invited to a party at Lord Davering's. Everyone of consequence will be there, I am sure. And we are to accompany Lord Keddinton and his daughters.'

And Nate watched as, without thinking, Diana forgot the book in her hand and the man in front of her, and dropped easily back into her role as chaperone. 'Would this by any chance be a card party?' She must know very well that it was, for the Davering parties were well on their way to being notorious.

'Small stakes only,' Verity insisted. 'A few hands of casino in the lady's room would do us no harm, surely.'

'A few hands?' Diana raised an eyebrow. 'It seldom stops at that.'

'It is nothing,' Honoria argued. 'Lord Keddinton is Verity's godfather. He does not think it improper, or he would not allow his daughters to go. And all the other girls—'

'Can do just as they please,' said Diana, closing the book in her hand with a snap. 'But they will do it without your help. You are not going to a card party, and that is my final word on the subject.'

And now, the girls turned to Nate, who took an involuntary step back as the combined weight of their charm was turned upon him. 'Mr Dale?' Honoria all but batted her lashes. 'Surely you can help us persuade Miss Price that it is nothing to be afraid of. She is tremendously silly on the subject of cards. She will not even let us play for buttons, when we are at home.'

'And if you accompanied us, as well?' Verity smiled. 'Then I am sure no harm would come to us.'

'No!' His denial shocked everyone with its suddenness, himself included. But the old swine, Davering, had learned of his reputation, and kept inviting him to those damned parties, hoping he would be the centrepiece of a night's play. What kind of a man would find amusement in watching his friends lose at cards? He gave the girls a stern look. 'Under no circumstances would you see me at such an event.'

The girls' faces crumpled in disappointment.

He took a breath, collected himself and said, 'I am sorry for the sharpness of my tone. But I am afraid I must agree with Miss Price on this matter. I do not attend such parties because I abhor gambling, and I would never encourage the activity for young ladies that I value as friends. You would do well to listen to your companion on the subject and shun anyone that encourages you to do otherwise.' He glanced up at the sky to read the time by the sun. It was late, and he had grown tired to the point of speaking nonsense. 'And now, if you will excuse me, I fear I must be going. Good day to you.' And he turned and walked away.

'How unspeakably odd,' Verity said, watching his sudden retreat.

'That you should try to coerce the man into escorting you to a party, instead of waiting for an offer? Your behaviour was shameful, both of you.' And utterly mortifying. Had their forwardness shocked him? Or worse yet, suppose he had seen through the obvious ruse of getting round the chaperone by tempting her with the diversion of his company? Either possibility was quite embarrassing. And it had all been going so well.

'But it does nothing to convince me that he doesn't fancy our Diana,' Verity added. 'See how quickly he came to her defence against us.'

'And more proof of how well they might suit,' Honoria agreed. 'His reaction towards a little card game was every bit as adamant as yours, Diana.'

And he had been so vehement that Diana wondered if there was more to it than just an interest in her approval. Was his past as scarred as hers, that he was so violently opposed to cards? A father, or perhaps a brother, lost to the game?

She felt a little fluttering in her heart at the thought. For although she did not wish him ill, if there was a greater proof that they would suit, she did not know what it could be. Today's visit had shown both a shared dislike and a shared pleasure. She held tightly to the book in her hands, and could not help smiling.

'And see how it has affected her.' Verity was positively grinning. 'It appears we shall not be able to orchestrate a meeting over the card table. But surely there will be another opportunity for us to make this match, Honoria.'

And should the opportunity occur, Diana doubted that she would resist their efforts.

'Well if she means to be courted, then she had best have a new gown,' Honoria said. 'Now that we have had our exercise, Diana, may we please go to Bond Street?'

Diana stared off in the direction that Mr Dale had disappeared, giving the book in her hands an affectionate squeeze. 'And perhaps after, we shall go to Gunter's for ices. Just this once.'

Nathan hurried down the path, out of sight of the ladies, the sweat on his brow turning cold with the early March air. And as he walked, there was the sound of masculine laughter, just behind him.

He turned to see the Gypsy leaning against a nearby tree. 'So you abhor gambling, do you?' Beshaley's grin was positively evil. 'It amazes me that you were able to say that aloud and with a straight face.'

The same thought had occurred to him, even as the words had left his mouth. He could not very well have let them go to Davering's. A misstep in such company would be the ruin of those poor girls. But neither would he offer explanation where none was deserved, lest it give the Gypsy something to use later against the Carlow girls.

Instead, he kept the focus upon himself. 'I did not choose my profession out of any great love for cards. I am sure you must know that many terrible things become palatable, once one's need is great enough.'

There was the slightest twitch at the corner of Stephano's mouth, as though he might know the truth of that even better than Nate. Nate filed the information away, hoping it could be ammunition of his own.

And then he smiled. 'If your object in troubling me was to see me make a fool of myself, then I hope you are satisfied. Not only did I tell a bold-faced lie, I gave her that damned book.'

And now the Gypsy grinned at him, and he cursed himself for saying too much. 'Do you think you can gain forgiveness for what you have done to her with such a paltry gift?'

'I think nothing of the kind. The book was an accident. I was reading it, and must have put it in my pocket. When she said that it was a personal favourite, what else could I do?'

He could have claimed it as his own and then put it away. Instead, he had stood there like a love-struck fool, and pressed the thing into her hands. But it would serve nothing to announce the fact to his opponent. So he gave Stephano a disinterested smile, as though what Diana Price might know or think meant very little to him. 'I doubt it shall be a problem. She was grateful, of course. But I do not plan to see her again to discuss the contents.'

The Gypsy gave him an enigmatic smile. 'I am glad you have such confidence in plans, Nathan. It is probably because yours have been so successful in the past.' And with that, he turned and walked away.

Chapter Eight

'Diana, another letter has arrived for you.' Honoria brought the morning's post into the small dining room, with even more glee than she had shown two days ago.

'Is this one full of bank notes?' Verity asked hopefully.

Honoria gave the letter a practiced squeeze. 'Too thin. I would guess that it is single sheet.'

'Too bad. Then we shan't persuade her to go shopping.'

'Much more likely, it is a love note from Mr Dale.'

'Give it here.' Diana said more sharply than she had intended, for she did not want to show unseemly interest.

'Not until you promise to tell us of the contents.' Honoria held the thing just out of reach.

'If I feel that the contents are likely to be of interest to you, then of course I will share them.'

This seemed to satisfy Honoria, for she handed the letter over, still crowding so close that Diana had to step back if she wished any privacy.

Miss Price,
Meet me again today at ten o'clock, in the place
where we last met. I have a matter of importance
I wish to discuss with you. Please come alone.

Another cryptic note. It was not signed. But she smiled, for she could easily imagine that the word Nathan had been omitted from the bottom of the page.

He wanted to meet her. Alone. This time there would be no pretence that he was interested in the Carlow sisters. It would be just the two of them, walking down the path in the park. She clutched the paper to her breast so that no one could see the words.

'Well?' Honoria still stood expectantly before her.

'It is nothing.' And that was an enormous lie. For in a few words, it was everything. 'Of no concern to you, anyway.' Much closer to the truth. For she did not want to share the message any more than she wished to share Nathan Dale. Even if it was just for one meeting, he would be hers alone, and so would the secret be.

Honoria smiled knowingly. 'I do not think you have to tell us, for the look in your eyes says enough. It is from Mr Dale, and the words are sweet. When you are ready, perhaps when we are all old and have children of our own, you must show us.' She reached out and enveloped Diana in a hug. 'But for now, all we need to know is that you are happy.'

Diana dressed carefully to prepare for the meeting and wished for a moment that she still had the fancy day dresses she had owned in her youth. It was a curse to be as sensible as she had become, for it showed in her wardrobe. And when she had finally allowed herself an extravagance on their last outing, what had she been thinking, to let Honoria persuade her to buy a dinner gown? It would have been far better to purchase one or two simple dresses, and some ribbons to refresh her tired bonnet. The green silk dress she had chosen instead would make it appear that she was trying to outshine the Carlows, should she wear it in public.

Although sometimes, it was nice to be noticed. She glanced in the mirror, smoothing her hair, and tying the sad bonnet ribbons into a creditable bow. Perhaps her plain appearance did not matter to him. He had taken the time to discover that today was her day free of duties, without bothering to ask her. He must be more than a little interested in the woman under the bonnet to take the trouble.

She walked to the park, doing her best to maintain an even pace, to arrive neither too early, nor late. It might not be that unusual for a young woman to walk alone in the park, but it would be too far outside normal decorum to appear to be loitering there.

But it was not necessary to be concerned. For at exactly ten o'clock, she saw him striding down the path in her direction in a purposeful way, as though he were no more interested in being caught lingering than she was.

'Mr Dale.'

She could tell he'd recognized her voice, for his head snapped up at the sound of it, looking for the source. But his face did not hold the welcoming smile. Instead he wore a look of alarm. His bright green eyes had a trapped quality, as though she were the last person he expected to be meeting.

And now, he was smiling as though he thought

it possible to disguise his initial reaction. 'Miss Price. What a coincidence to see you again, so soon.'

'Coincidence?' Something was very wrong. Perhaps she had misread the date on the note. But more likely, she had jumped to a conclusion as to the sender. She could feel the blush rising on her cheek and ducked her head hoping it was not too late to hide it from him. 'You are clearly in a hurry. Please, give me no mind, for I would not detain you. Good day.' And she made to pass, hoping that he would think she also had somewhere to go.

'Wait.' He reached out and caught her arm before she could get away, and the warmth of his fingers seemed to sink through the cloth of her gown. He was smiling sympathetically at her, as though he could sense her confusion and wished to put her at ease. 'This is not a chance encounter, is it? You do not seem at all surprised to see me.'

'I thought that you wished…But obviously not…' And now she was sure she must be crimson, gone past embarrassment and into mortification. 'I am sorry. I should go.' She turned from him again, looking desperately back up the path that would take her towards the Carlows' town house.

He renewed his grip on her arm. 'Please, wait. There is something wrong, isn't there? Explain it to me.'

She reached into her reticule for the note, and closed her eyes as she handed it to him. 'What must you think of me? I swear, I am not normally given to meeting alone with gentlemen. But I thought if it was you it would not be so wrong.'

'It is not signed.' He said it very reasonably, as though it surprised him that she could not see something so obvious.

'I know.' Without opening her eyes, she said, 'It was not from you, was it?'

'No, it was not,' he admitted.

She opened her eyes again, and gave a little shrug to hide her embarrassment. 'And now, I look a fool for jumping to such conclusions, based on an unsigned note that is obviously some sort of prank.'

He sighed, but then smiled back at her. 'I think it was a perfectly honest mistake. We had a lovely conversation when we were here before, did we not? And it was interrupted when I hurried off.'

'Yes.' She pursed her lips and tapped the letter with her fingers. 'But I am very angry with the girls, for I suspect that they are in some way involved with this.'

'You do?' He seemed a little surprised by the idea. But it was probably just that he did not wish to think ill of ladies. 'I suppose that is the most logical explanation.'

He was allowing her the benefit of the doubt, although he did not seem convinced. So she added, 'Of course, it does appear to be in a man's writing.'

He nodded. 'I do not blame you for your mistake, for it is rather like my hand. It appears Lady Honoria had an accomplice. A footman, perhaps?'

She thought for a moment to correct him on the likelihood of a footman having such a fine hand or for that matter, being able to write at all. 'Although it is just the sort of trick Honoria might play, if she meant to try to get around me. She must have got Peters or Richards to help her. Or maybe it was John the coachman.' She gave the paper a little rattle, hoping that rough handling of it now might make it less obvious that she had pored over the thing, reading and rereading, searching for a happy meaning to a few short words.

And then, his hand covered hers to still their movement. 'No matter. If I had a pen, I would solve it all by putting my name at the bottom of it and pretending that it came from me.'

And his smile was so warm and his touch so comforting that she felt her hand begin to relax. 'But you did not mean to see me.'

'That does not imply that I do not take pleasure at the meeting.'

'Thank you, sir.' And then, she added impulsively, 'And I enjoyed talking with you, as well.'

'Then it is settled. We are both glad to be out in the park on a lovely spring day. Especially after such a hard winter. Let us walk a ways together.'

When she looked up his eyes seemed very green, and staring down at her with an intensity that made her heart jump. And she remembered that their meeting was not really proper. She should have separated from him after the briefest of greetings. 'I am afraid it is not wise for us to be seen together. It might appear to some that we are having an assignation.'

He smiled, for he must have realized that that was exactly what she had been expecting. 'I have always thought it more a proof of the small minds around us, that they can be so eager to think ill of a lady of good character, such as yourself. But if it puts your mind at ease, we will keep to the less-travelled paths, away from prying eyes.'

And that was exactly what she should have

feared. A man who was less than a gentleman would take advantage of such privacy. But surely, Mr Dale was not such a one. So she said, 'Thank you for your understanding. Perhaps I am overly sensitive. Since it is my job to guard the reputations of others, I work very hard to set an example to them by my own behaviour.'

'Then I will take care to do nothing that is beneath reproach,' he said, offering her his arm.

She tucked the note back into her reticule, then reached out gingerly to put her hand upon the crook of his elbow. He turned and guided her off the main path. And then he said, 'What shall we talk of today? Poetry, perhaps? For if it is a shared interest…'

'No,' she said firmly. 'Today, I wish you to tell me something of yourself. For you have managed to ferret information from me that I would not usually tell a stranger. It is hardly fair. You must give me something in return.'

He thought on it for a moment, and a strange expression crossed his face. 'I suppose that is true. I must tell you about myself. Although, I am afraid that the story will not be pleasant.' And his arm tightened against hers, tucking her hand close to his side. 'I hardly know where to begin.'

She gave an encouraging squeeze to his arm.

'Begin with your family, then. Are they living? Or are you alone?' *Like me.* She had almost added the words, but did not wish it to seem that she was searching for more similarities.

'My father is…dead. He died when I was just a boy.' That seemed a difficult admission, and she wondered: had they been so close that it still grieved him?

'And what of your mother?'

'I have not seen her for many years, nor my sisters.'

'You are estranged from them?'

'Not by my doing, I assure you. I pray daily for their welfare.' It touched her heart that he looked so distressed that she might think him capable of abandoning them. It was just another example of his tender heart.

His eyes fell. 'After Father's death, there were difficulties. Our finances were strained. We children took employment, and each contributed to the family's welfare as best we could. But one night, when I was returning from…work. I was set upon by a press gang.'

'You were in the Navy, then?' It explained the commanding way he stood, as though the earth could move under him and he would not stagger.

He gave a sad smile. 'You make it sound very heroic. I was there against my will. Off the coast of France, and then the Americas. I spent the first months—sick as a dog from the motion of the water—trying desperately to contact my family, to explain why I could not come home to them. But I do not think the letters found them, for there was no response.'

'It must have been horrible, not knowing.'

His mouth made a bitter line. 'Six years of my life, wasted.' And then he looked at her, his eyes sombre. 'And this is where you will see me for the sort of man I truly am. For when I finally got the opportunity, I jumped ship.'

'You are a deserter?' She almost released his arm. For it was most shocking, and not at all in keeping with the man she was convinced that he was.

'Do you blame me? The law that took me was for trained seamen. It was never meant to drag in-experienced men to sea against their will so that they could lose the King's ration of bread and grog over the side whenever the ship crested a wave. I was a terrible sailor, from the day they took me to the day I ran.' He opened his hands, staring into the palms. 'Look here. See the scars? This is where I lost my grip on the sheets, and the rope near skinned my hands. I could show you the marks of the flogging I got for that, as well. And the places where the sun burned my skin to blisters. It was a hard life, and I was glad to be rid of it.'

'But to run away...' It was so different from what she expected from him that she hardly knew what to think.

'They had no right to take me, and their callous stupidity jeopardized the safety of my family. God only knows what happened to them, without my protection.' He frowned. 'I tell myself that my sisters are most likely married, with families of their own by now. But I know that is probably a lie. And it is a shame. For over the years my fortunes have changed much. If I could but find them, I could support them in luxury and quite make up for the hardship I left them in.'

And knowing the sort of things that might happen to a woman alone, or even through the carelessness of one such as her father, she had to agree. 'You were right to worry, and I can understand your actions in trying to get back to them. But to live under the stigma of desertion cannot be easy. Perhaps if you appealed to the Admiralty, they would give you a proper discharge.'

'Perhaps. My claim is legitimate. But I have,

shall we say, a certain lack of faith in the English courts. They have never been a friend to my family. And while the law clearly states that I am in the right, it would be scant comfort to have that as an epitaph, should they decide to execute me for desertion. Once I earned enough money in Boston to pay for a passage home, it seemed easier just to start anew. And mask my identity.'

The pause now was a long one, until he was sure that she understood. 'I am not at all the sort of man you might think me, Miss Price. Not in behaviour. Not even in name.'

Perhaps she did not know him as well as she thought. Yet, when she looked into his eyes, and felt his hand on hers, she was sure she did. 'It does not matter.' She reached out with her other hand, and laid it upon his sleeve, giving his arm a re-assuring squeeze that seemed to startle him.

He put his other hand on her shoulder. 'I did not wish for my story to sound like a morbid attempt to garner your sympathy.'

'I did not think you did. But it is a tragic story, all the same. It is all right. Your life has been difficult. You have done the best you could with it. I understand.'

He pulled free of her grasp and slipped his arm around her waist. 'You do not know how much your words mean to me, Miss Price. They are like a balm upon the old wounds. And I had never thought to hear them from your lips.' And with that, he pulled her close and kissed her.

The moment seemed to go on forever. But perhaps it was because she closed her eyes and held her breath, as if she could keep very still and hold time in place. She had spent much of the recent years interrupting such attempts by Honoria's suitors and thwarting their few successes. But at some point, years ago, she had quite given up the dream that a moment like this would ever come to her. And now that it had, she felt quite remorseful for depriving Honoria of the joy of it. For to feel the rough of his cheek brushing against hers, and the firm warmth of his hand, his breath upon her face, the softness of his mouth and the barest touch of his tongue against her lips was pure heaven.

And then he pulled his head away from hers, and looked hurriedly around to make sure that they were alone on the path and that none had seen what they had done. He took his hand from her waist, laid a finger under her chin, and said, with a nervous smile, 'I am sorry. I did not intend to take that liberty. But your absolution moved me more than I could resist. Thank you.' He squeezed her hand again, and then released it and stepped back.

She was quite at a loss. For what was she to say in a moment like this? Pretending outrage was quite impossible, but asking him to repeat the action was very wrong as well. And she was sure that her cheeks must be flaming scarlet.

He smiled down at her. 'Miss Price?'

'Mr Dale.' She touched her hand to her bosom, as though she were trying to catch her breath after strenuous exercise.

He tipped his head, waiting for her to clarify her feelings. 'Are you all right, then? Can you forgive me that as well?'

And she struggled again, taking in a huge breath and letting it out in a sigh. Then she smiled at him. 'That was the most miraculous thing, was it not?'

He grinned back at her. 'For you as well?'

'Perhaps it was only because I have no knowledge of such things. I did not know what to expect. It was my first kiss, you see.'

He was still smiling quite broadly at her. 'I would be lying if I said any such thing about myself. But if it gives you comfort to know, that was quite different from an ordinary kiss. I wonder, have I gained skill since the last time, or do you have undeveloped talents? Or was that an unusual occurrence?' He looked around again, making absolutely sure they were alone. 'Let us try an experiment.' And without further warning, he pulled her off the path, behind a nearby oak. Then he leaned in and kissed her again.

This time, his lips were still as gentle but he placed his hands on her shoulders in such a businesslike way that it felt rather like a scientific study of the kiss. He took the time to adjust his position to an angle that was most pleasurable. Then he pulled away, looked speculatively at her, as though he meant to catalogue her response, and held the pose until it made her laugh.

Then he laughed as well, and kissed her again, more quickly and less expertly, and she sighed and wrapped her arms about his neck, hugging him to herself.

When they parted this time, his piercing green eyes were less focused, and the smile on his lips was of a man well satisfied. He gave a sensible straightening of his coat and smoothed a few loose hairs from around her face, making sure that her bonnet sat squarely upon her head and showed no signs of disturbance. Then he tucked her arm tightly into the crook of his, peeked around the corner of the tree to make sure that they were still unobserved, and led her back out onto the path, so that they might walk together, side by side, as though nothing had happened.

He looked out over the park, as though making small talk, and said, 'This has been a most interesting morning, Miss Price. And most unexpected. I think that further experimentation will be necessary.'

'And I think, with things as they are between us, Nathan, that you should call me Diana.'

He stopped dead in the path, and pulled his arm from hers, the smug smile disappearing from his face. 'How did you know my name?'

'Your name?'

'My given name. Because I am sure that I never used it in your presence.'

She took a step back, even more confused by this than she had been from the kisses. If his behaviour toward her this morning did not render them close enough for first names, then she truly did not know him as well as she ought. 'It was written upon the note you left for Lord Stanegate. You did not seal it. I suppose it is horrible of me to admit the fact, but I read the contents. I was only trying to assure myself that the matter was not serious.' She coloured in embarrassment. For she had all but forgotten the note and her indiscretion in reading it.

Instead of aggravated, he looked strangely relieved. 'That is all, then? But of course. It makes perfect sense.'

'Then you forgive me for prying?' For his anger was gone as quickly as it had come. 'If it is any assurance to you, Marc already knows the fact you wished to relay.'

'Marc, is it? You call him by his first name as well?'

She had expected him to question her further about the note. But she could see by the blazing look in his eyes that he was much more concerned with the reason for such familiarity with another man.

Who had ever noticed or cared about such a thing in regards to her? She could not think of a time when she had been the sole focus of a man's attention, and the thought sent a small thrill through her. 'I call him by name because I have known him for years. He is deeply concerned for the welfare of his sisters. And since his father is unwell, he has taken it upon himself to act as their guardian.'

He seemed to relax a little. 'Then you two arc not—'

'Certainly not. He is my employer. And a happily married man. He would never…nor would I,' she added quickly, straightening her dress as though there were some way to retrace the last few minutes to prove to him that she was of better character.

'I am a jealous fool.' He said it softly as though it were some great personal revelation. Then he looked up at her again. 'Please forgive me. I am not usually prone to strange suspicions, baseless jealousy nor sudden rudeness.' He paused. 'Of course, until today, I was not prone to kissing young ladies in the park.'

'If you did not wish…'

He held up a hand. 'Let us start again. Or at least go back to the moment where you meant to call me Nathan and I was to call you Diana. Things were really going quite well, before that moment.' And then he smiled at her, full of mischief and shared secrets.

He held out his arm to her again, and they walked together, side by side down the path. And it occurred to her that their companionable silence was almost as good as the kissing had been, for it made her feel close to him, as though they were so much alike that words were no longer necessary. The little fillip of jealousy at the end of their encounter and his speedy apology for it stood as a proof that he was engaged deeply enough to want her all for himself. As did the lingering way he released her hand when they reached the end of the path and it was time for her to return to the Carlows—as though he had no wish to let her go.

And she realized that she had no idea what to say upon parting. Was it rude to seem eager for another meeting? And where could it be? She certainly could not go to his rooms, nor could she give him leave to call upon her, since she had no place of her own.

But he understood. For he said, 'I suppose I must leave you now, Miss Price. *Au revoir?'*

She gave him an embarrassed smile, and nodded.

'Perhaps we can meet again in the park. Next week at this time?'

'I would like that. Very much.'

'Very good. I shall write to you on the day, to remind you of our appointment.'

As if it would be possible for her to forget.

'And this time, I shall sign my name, so you shall know that it is really me.' His smile was teasing. He reached for her hand, bowed and brought the fingers to his lips, kissing the air above them in the most proper way imaginable.

As she turned to cross the street towards home, she could feel him behind her, watching her progress.

Chapter Nine

When Nate returned to his house, the rooms seemed brighter than he remembered. Perhaps it was because he usually slept so late that he did not often see them in full daylight. Or perhaps the sun was higher in the sky, now that winter was passing.

Or perhaps it was because he could not seem to stop smiling.

As he had watched Diana go back toward the Carlow house, he felt his lungs tighten. He had the most foolish desire that she should remove her bonnet as she walked, so that he might see the sunlight shine on her dark hair, or catch one more glimpse of her departing face as she went around the corner. Even the thought of that made him smile all the more. What a miracle she was. And what an impossible idea that she would walk bareheaded down the street, with her hair blowing in the wind.

Of course, all his thoughts involving Diana Price were impossible ones, and his position had just become more difficult than he could possibly imagine. He had avoided her for so long, thinking a meeting to be somewhere between ill advised and disastrous. And now?

He had discovered his soulmate. Her sympathy towards him, the gentle touch of her hands, was like nothing he'd known. And he'd never suspected that she would be so beautiful, so graceful and so easy to converse with. After his confession to her, he'd limited his talk to the most innocent of topics, and she had hung on every word, as though he were profoundly interesting. He had meant to tell her the rest and make a clean breast of it. But with such a woman at his side the past was easily forgotten. And soon, it would become impossible to imagine a future without her. There was only one small thing standing between them and happiness.

Nathan Wardale.

What good had that man ever done for either of them? Diana most assuredly would not want to see the fellow. And he'd been more trouble to Nate than he was worth. It was Wardale that had explaining to do, should the Navy ever come calling. And Wardale was the one living with the taint of his father's disgrace.

Wardale had lost his sisters and mother as well, damn him. If there was some way to find the women in his family, then it might be time to reclaim the name. If he thought that his sisters would see the news and come to him? Then it might be worth having Nathan Wardale risk arrest and appear in public.

But he was not even sure that they lived, or that they would wish a meeting with him, after the way he had abandoned them. When he'd returned, his inquiries after them had gotten no response. A louder, more obvious appearance, after all this time, was just as likely to upset the lives of his sisters than to benefit them.

And it would upset Diana as well. If she thought of him at all, she must wish Wardale were dead. If they lived, his sisters must think him dead as well. They had probably finished grieving for him long ago. It would hardly be a fresh loss to them, should Nate Dale put a permanent end to him.

There was the problem of his profession, of course. Diana had no tolerance for gambling, and he could hardly blame her. But he need not continue in it, if he did not wish. He had lived with the nagging feeling at the back of his mind that his gambling was somehow the fault of the Gypsy woman and that he could not stop. But he had never really tried, had he?

Beshaley had said the success of the curse was a result of his faith in it, and nothing more. So from this moment on, Nate would choose not to believe. He would put aside the gaming. He glanced around him. He would have to give up the house as well. He would put the town house up for sale and remove to his home in the country, where no one knew the source of his income. Everything about his life would be new and different.

With the last trace of his old life erased, he would be free to marry.

It would be difficult for the current servants, of course. Perhaps he could arrange for the new owner to take them on. Many of them had known this place as their home for much longer than he had. He would make it easy on them if he could. But it could not be helped. He could not bring Diana back to her own home, with the butler knowing its master's full history, and expect the facts to remain concealed from her.

And that same butler appeared before him now, in a state of agitation. 'Sir. The drawing room,' he said breathlessly. 'A gentleman. I could not prevent him…'

The tone of the last made it clear that in the opinion of the butler, the *gentleman* was no gentleman at all. Perhaps it was an acquaintance from the Fourth Circle. Dante Jones had never visited him, and few others would have the gall to follow him and learn his residence. But if someone had, it was all the more reason for him to leave this place behind and start a fresh life with Diana somewhere else. 'Do not concern yourself. I will deal with him,' he said, putting the poor man at ease. It was not the first time he had needed to clear the riff-raff from his doorstep, but he was certain it would be the last. He strode with confidence down the hall towards the drawing room door, flexing the muscles under his coat.

And when he entered, there was Stephano Beshaley, drinking by the fire as though he owned the house himself. He was arrayed in a tatty green coat with tarnished brass buttons, striped trousers, and had a bright scarf tied about his dark hair, and a huge gold ring gleaming from his left ear. Quite out of character for the neighbourhood. And for

Beshaley as well, he suspected. It seemed that he had gone out of his way to dress as a comic-opera Gypsy before forcing his way in through the front door.

Beshaley smiled at him as he entered, but did not bother to rise. 'Nathan. Old friend.' The bastard had the nerve to salute him with a glass of his own brandy.

'What are you doing here? You should know you are not welcome in my house.'

'Your house?' The Gypsy seemed to find this amusing.

'My house,' Nathan affirmed, giving him the same blank expression he used when at the gaming tables.

'Considering how long we have known each other, I did not think that your door would ever be closed to me.'

'Since you come here to threaten, you can assume that the door is closed. What do you want with me now?'

'Merely to congratulate you. I observed you in the park with Miss Price. Young love. Touching, Nathan. Truly touching.' The Gypsy gave a mocking sigh and put his hand over his heart. 'It did my soul good to see it.'

'You saw?' Nate's composure faltered. He had

seen no one on the path after his spectacular lapse in judgment. It had given him the false sense of security that had caused him to kiss her again.

'Did I see? Every moment of your time together. And heard your sad story as well.'

He had been a fool to promise her safety, while opening the door to public disgrace. Especially as he remembered the reason for the meeting. 'You arranged it all, didn't you?' Nate pointed an accusing finger at the man sitting before him.

'And how would I have done that?' Beshaley gave an innocent shrug that in no way matched his evil grin.

'You saw to it that I was delayed at the tables, gaming until past sunrise so that I would be late coming home. And then you sent Diana the note. You brought her to the park under false pretences. You led her to believe that I was interested in her.'

'If you are not, you have a strange way of demonstrating the fact. What gives her reason to hope has nothing to do with some silly note I sent her. You kissed an innocent chaperone in broad day light, in a public park where anyone might see. The poor girl would lose her position if someone told that old prig Narborough about it.' There was the barest hint of threat in his tone, although his expression had become benign.

'Do not dare.' Nate made no effort to hide the returned threat. 'If any harm comes to her because of your desire to meddle in my life, I swear by all that is holy, I will send you to the devil to answer for it.'

Stephano laughed. 'Do not think you can frighten me with the devil, Nathan. You are the one who needs to fear him. I mean no harm to the girl at all. I am only trying to protect her from you.'

'From me?'

'It is you who seem intent on harming her. You were the one who ruined her father. You were the one who kissed her today. And you are the one who is hiding your identity from her, lying about your proclivities, pretending to be more innocent than you are in all things.'

'I will tell her everything, when the time is right.' He said it without flinching, for it was almost the truth. Since there could never be a right time, the facts would die with him.

The Gypsy shook his head. 'Do not try to fool me with lies, Nathan. You have told her nothing. You mean to tell her nothing. I saw the smile on your face when she parted from you. You think you can escape what you did in the past by courting her like a gentleman now and lifting her from her circumstances. And that there will be no penance to be paid for any of it.'

'I have paid enough.' He said it softly, hoping that he could move his old friend and that there would be some way to avoid what he expected was coming.

'I will tell you when enough is enough. Perhaps it will be when Diana Price knows the whole truth.'

He would not allow it. For a moment, Nate's mind clouded with violent fantasies, the satisfaction of feeling Beshaley's words stopped by his own hands on the man's throat. He took a slow breath and fought for control. It would take icy calm to outmanoeuvre a man so adept at using the emotions of others to get his way. When he had convinced himself that this conversation mattered no more to him than any other game, Nate knew it was safe to speak. 'I will not beg for mercy, if that is what you seek. My own father went to the gallows without breaking. I can withstand a few idle threats. If you want reparation for old wrongs? I will give you anything you wish.'

'Give me?'

'How much do you want?'

'You think you can buy me off, do you? Because I am a Gypsy. Cross my palm with silver, and I will leave you in peace? I have money, Nathan. More than you. All I want is justice. For my family. For myself.'

'Then we want the same thing. My family was treated as unjustly as yours.'

'If your father was innocent.'

'It is always harder to find the guilty than it is to persecute the innocent, as you do.'

The faintest shadow of doubt passed over Beshaley's face. Then he smirked, and the moment was lost. 'If I treat everyone involved equally, than I am reasonably sure that the guilty parties are punished.'

'It is not fair.'

'But very efficient. First, I will finish with you. Miss Price as well, if you claim her for yourself. And then, I will find the rest of your clan. You are not the only living Wardale, you know.'

At the thought of his sisters, alive but in danger, Nate's calm evaporated. 'I do not know if you are mad or merely cold-blooded. But it does not matter. As you value your life, stay away from the women.' He reached for the letter opener on a nearby desk. 'Just now, I was thinking of using this on you, you bastard. But murder is messy and you are not worth the cost of a new carpet. If you are so eager to avenge your father, then do it. But let my blood be enough.' He pushed the knife into the Gypsy's hand. 'Cut out my heart and be done with it, you coward.'

The sudden change in him must have caught Stephano off guard. For he lost control as well, lunging forward, weapon in hand. But before he could strike, his body tightened and he jerked back as suddenly as a dog might when it reached the end of its leash. His arm went wide in a convulsive movement, flinging the letter opener aside. And then he reached up with both hands to cradle his own head. He dropped back into the chair, gasping for breath, and looked up at Nate, through pain-clouded eyes. 'I would if I could, Nathan Wardale. Long ago, I'd have finished you all. But it is not allowed.'

Nathan stood over him, arms folded in satisfaction. The attempt at violence had left his opponent helpless. 'Allowed?' He smiled, for the man in front of him was in such agony that he had not been able to hide the truth. 'I take it, it is not an English law that binds you?'

The Gypsy shook his head gently, as though to move it hurt him. 'You have heard the expression, *This hurts me more than it hurts you?* Not more, perhaps. While I might laugh as you ruin yourself, to kill you would hurt my poor head more than I can bear.' He lifted his face to stare into the eyes of his old friend. 'Here is your chance to strike, Nathan. I cannot stop you. If you wish, I will move to the flagstones in the hall, to spare your carpet.' Then he laughed. Nate had heard that laugh often. It was the ghastly, hollow sound a man made when he knew he was beaten.

And it made him feel as he did at the game table, when another poor sod had overplayed his hand and left himself open to ruin. He could not manage sympathy, or even mercy. But it filled him with regret at having to play a part in the downfall of another, no matter how deserved that end might be. Nate stared at the suffering man before him, and shook his head. 'I cannot kill you either. I am no more a murderer than my father was. If I can prove that to you, will you leave me and my family in peace?'

'After so many years, what can you prove?'

He did not know. But what harm could it do

to try? He had always suspected that Narborough had lied about the crime. But he'd convinced himself that the man was untouchable. If a confrontation now was the only way he might have Diana? Then what choice did he have but to hope? 'I do not know if I will find anything. But I intend to try. After so much time, you can wait a little longer for justice. I request a truce. You may leave here unhindered today, if you promise me two weeks without interference. If I can find evidence to clear my father, then you must go.'

The Gypsy considered. 'In exchange for my life today, you may have fourteen days.'

'And in that time, you will avoid Diana Price?'

Beshaley was still pale, and his brows drew together as though speaking was an effort. 'For two weeks only. But even if I lift the curse and leave you, you must tell her the truth. If you are innocent of blame and as worthy of love as you claim, it will not matter to her.

'If you are guilty, then you will suffer as a guilty man should suffer, knowing the thing you desire most is forever out of reach. And I will have found satisfaction. But whatever you mean to do, Nathan, you must decide in this fortnight. Or at the end of it, I will make the decision for you.' And with that, he rose un-steadily from the chair and left a stunned Nathan alone before the fire.

Diana returned to the house with a smile on her face, glad that neither of the girls was to spoil the joy of it. Just for a moment, what had happened was still her secret. And what a sweet thing it was. But once she saw the girls, it would be over. If they sent the note, then they must know what had happened and she would need to upbraid them for tricking her into committing an indiscretion, even if it was a pleasant one.

She was sure she had guessed correctly. For the moment Verity looked up from her needle-work, her face changed from a mildly inquis-itive smile to a knowing grin. 'And how was Mr Dale today, Diana?'

She did her best to look stern. 'What would make you think that I saw him, I wonder?'

'The look on your face, of course.'

'There is nothing singular about my expres-sion, I am sure.' She gave a hurried glance into the mirror above the mantel, checking to see if the time spent behind the tree had disarranged her hair in some obvious way.

Verity was almost bouncing in her chair with excitement. 'Why Miss Price, I do believe you are blushing.'

'I am not. I would never…' But denying it would do no good. It was there in her reflection.

Verity stifled a giggle. 'Turning crimson. Honoria, come see,' she called to her sister, who was passing in the hall. 'Diana is back from her walk in the park. And the air must be particularly fine today. She is positively glowing with good health and high spirits.'

Honoria came into the room and glanced in her direction, and then looked again as though seeing her clearly for the first time. 'Who is he, Diana?'

'There is no one…'

Honoria let out a snort of disgust. 'An assignation. With Mr Dale, no doubt. And I do believe he kissed you. See the look in her eye, Verity? She has been kissed. I am sure of it.'

'Honoria!' Diana's best warning tone fell on deaf ears, for she doubted it could be heard over the sound of Verity's giggles.

Honoria was laughing as well. 'Really Diana. It is not so big a thing. We are happy for you, truly. For it pains us to think that we shall both be married and you will have no one for companionship. Now, tell us. What is it like?'

She looked sternly at the Carlow sisters. 'I have no intention of telling you such things. You will discover all you need to know about them when you are properly affianced.'

'But it was wonderful,' Honoria pressed. 'Was it not?'

And she had to admit, it had been. It was hard not to smile when thinking of it. Although now was the worst time in the world to smile, for it would give the girls the idea that such behaviour was acceptable. So she put on an even more stern expression and changed the subject. 'Never mind that. I wish to know what you know about this.' And she removed the note from her reticule and laid it on the table in front of them.

'It is the letter you received this morning, is it not? The one you would not show us.' Honoria examined it closely. 'And it was from Mr Dale, just as we suspected.'

Diana gave Honoria the disappointed look that normally broke through the girl's defences when she was concealing something. 'When I arrived at the park, Mr Dale knew nothing of the note. And I suspect you might have had a hand in this, since you are so eager to see the two of us matched.'

'He had nothing to do with it?' Honoria gave

a rather unladylike snort. 'What utter rubbish. Perhaps he is too shy to admit it.'

'He was most insistent about it.' She folded her arms across her chest and waited for the confession.

But Honoria's face showed nothing but a thoughtful frown. 'You have no way of proving that he is not lying, do you? You have never seen his writing.'

'Perhaps I have. When Mr Dale was first here, he left a note for your brother.' It was vexing to remember that now, when it was too late. She could have compared the handwriting before leaving. But she had blocked the note from her mind, not wanting to see what was right under her nose.

'Let us see, then,' Verity said.

'You may not see the contents of the note. It is not addressed to you.'

'And yet you have read it,' Honoria challenged.

The truth stung. For when had she become so nosey as to do such a low thing? 'Only to know if I should bother Marc with it, now that he and Nell are finally alone.'

'Or perhaps you wanted to know the contents,' Honoria waved a hand. 'But never mind. We will not look, if it makes you feel better. But get the thing and look for yourself. Then tell us if both are written by the same person.'

She went to her room to get the letter, realizing as she did so, that it should never have been there. Why had she thought it acceptable to put the thing anywhere other than on the desk in Marc's study? But she had taken the paper out of Nathan's hand and walked directly to her bedroom to read it, as though it were a personal missive to herself and not business for Lord Stanegate. She was overstepping herself in so many ways lately that it would take all her self-discipline to return to the straight-and-narrow path.

After examination of the purloined note, she had to admit that the two hands were nothing alike, and she felt even more foolish for jumping to conclusions. She placed the thing in Marc's study where it belonged and returned to the girls.

They were believing none of it, even with the evidence of the note. 'Mr Dale was there when you arrived,' said Verity. 'So the person who sent the letter knew his schedule. And since we have no idea how he keeps himself—'

'When he is not dangling after you,' added Honoria.

'Then it should be proof of our innocence. And this note appears to have been written by a man.'

'Although it would have been a marvellous trick, had we have thought of it.' Honoria grinned. 'It is a great relief to me that you are affected by the same romantic notions as the rest of the world, Diana. While you are an excellent example to us, sometimes I wonder whether I am as weak as my mother claims or if you are the one who is unusual. But never mind that. Let us examine this letter and see if we can guess the sender.' She snatched the letter away from Verity and held it up to the light, but there was nothing extraordinary about the paper. Then she examined the writing. 'Did you save the paper that the bank notes came in?'

It was an interesting thought, and Diana tried not to rush as, this time, the girls followed her to her room. She went to her wardrobe and withdrew the pile of money. But she had discarded the note around it as worthless, for it had had only her own address upon it.

'That must be it,' Verity said. 'If you had kept the thing and could compare it to this, you would see that the hands are the same. It appears that you have a secret benefactor, Diana. If it is not Mr Dale, then it must be someone else who cares enough to see you both provided for and well settled in a home of your own. You are most fortunate indeed.'

And while it was a wonderful thought, that after all this time, there was someone who cared for her well-being, Diana had no idea who that person might be.

Chapter Ten

Diana waited in trepidation on the pathway, the following Tuesday. Nathan Dale had sent her a note, reminding her of the meeting, just as he had promised he would. But it had contained none of the romantic foolishness she had been hoping for. Just a few words requesting an interview at ten o'clock. The brevity of it made the tone seem almost curt. Perhaps the walks were not as important to him as they were to her. Suppose he forgot? Or changed his mind and remained at home? If that was the case, she could console herself that there were no witnesses to her disappointment. She recognized no one in the park this early.

But promptly at ten, she saw him striding down the path towards her, with a slightly nervous smile upon his face. If he had been coming to meet one of the Carlow sisters, she would turn her practiced chaperone's eye to him, and decide that he wished to gain the favour of a lady. But he was acting as though he did not expect to succeed.

She tried to hide her eagerness. For it was good to imagine, if only for a moment, that she could afford to be capricious in her affections. Or that his winning her favour could ever be in doubt.

'Miss Price?'

She curtsyed to him, and he reached out and took her hand again, as he had the previous week. The gesture was both warm and familiar, as though he found nothing unusual about her hand in his.

But for her, it was strange and wonderful. Other than a few stray moments on the dance floor when she was seventeen, she could not remember a man bothering to get this close. And then he slipped her hand protectively into the crook of his arm, as though it were nothing, and not everything in the world. He walked with her, down a quiet footpath, to a bench where they could sit close, side by side. 'I was afraid you would forget me.'

How strange to hear her own thoughts, coming

from his mouth. 'And I feared you would not come,' she said in response, and with a bit of a smile.

'I promised I would.' He smiled a little as well, but with sadness. 'I should not have, I think. There are difficulties.'

'You had another engagement?' He looked so serious that for a moment she was convinced that there must be another woman who commanded his attention. But she could not have read him so wrong.

'No,' he confirmed. 'My time is my own. It is just that you should spend yours in the company of one more worthy.'

'You? Unworthy?' She laughed. 'Certainly not, sir. I am humble enough, am I not? I know better than to set my sights higher than my chances of success.' And now it did sound like she was trying to ensnare him. She blushed. 'That must sound like a slight to your character, or that I assume anything will come of our meeting. I assure you, neither is true.'

He gave her a strange glance. 'I certainly expected you might think something would result in our meeting. If you remember, when we last saw each other, I kissed you.'

She felt her cheeks burning to show just how

well she had remembered it. She had been able to think of little else for most of the week.

'I would not have done it, had my intentions not grown serious. And so very quickly.' He frowned. 'It was not what I planned to do, certainly.'

This must be the set-down she had expected from the first. She readied herself for the inevitable disappointment.

He was staring at the ground in front of them, refusing to meet her gaze. 'I meant to tell you this earlier, to make a clean breast at our last meeting. To explain my interest in you, and to make it clear why there can be no further meetings.'

No further meetings? It felt like she were falling from a great height. A rush of air and a frisson of nerves before the inevitable crash. She gave a shaky laugh. 'If that is to be the result, then I would prefer you not explain at all, thank you very much.'

He went silent on the bench beside her, as though he would be only too happy to stop talking. And now, she was the one afraid to look in his eyes, unsure of what she would see there. At last, he said, 'I am more than a little tempted to give in to your request, Miss Price.'

'It was to be Diana,' she reminded him. 'Last

week I was Diana. And I wished to call you Nathan.'

She heard him give a little sigh at the sound of his own name. But he responded, 'I am not fit company for you, Miss Price. There are incidents in my past that are—' he struggled with his words again '—dark. They are dark deeds. I hesitated to tell you, for I knew how you would react. And I did not wish to spoil what was happening between us.'

She tried to keep her tone light. 'Best not tell me all, then. If it means that I will not see you again, just as I wish to. You have changed for the better, haven't you, since the dark time? The events are well behind you?'

'I have tried, God help me. My worst mistakes are years in the past. And for you? For you I would cast off what vices remain. I would be yours to command, truly completely and forever, just as I wish you to be mine. But I cannot hide the truth from you any longer. For should you discover it later…'

And she reached out and put her hand over his mouth before he could speak.

He was still for only a moment, and she thought that he would push her away and blurt the truth. Instead, he reached up and took her gloved hand in his, holding it to his lips, and kissing it with such fervour that she could feel the strength of his emotions through the leather, and through her other clothing as well. She could imagine his lips pressing against her bare skin, and her body tingled with answering desire. And she knew, no matter what he might think she deserved, that she deserved this. To have a man, who she loved and respected, who loved her with such passion in return.

She thought of her own secret. Would she be able to tell the man who loved her about the bet her father had made? She had thought it no business of another, and intended to keep the secret to her grave. Though she'd told herself that it was no fault of hers, she felt stained by it. It was as though she had been married against her will. Whether she liked it or not, a bond existed, and she was not free to give herself elsewhere. Deep down, she still worried that someday Nathan Wardale would appear on her doorstep and demand a reckoning. But Nell had said he could well be dead. She need have nothing to fear.

'I have a secret as well,' she finally admitted. 'One that I do not wish anyone to know. Not even you. At one time, I walked away from my past as surely as you wish to turn from yours. And if each party wishes to keep a secret from the other, and knows that there is ground that they must not tread, for fear that it would break the heart of the other? But that we swear to each other, with our whole hearts, that what is behind us does not matter? Then perhaps it is almost the same as telling the whole truth when we do not speak of it.'

His eyes were still averted as he clutched her hand tightly in his. 'It would not matter? It would be as though you were promising yourself to half a man.'

She smiled. 'If it is to be the good half of you? Then yes, I would be more than willing.'

He looked at her, then. And she could see the emotion in the green depths of his eyes, like a storm at sea. 'My darling, Diana, I want to believe you. If we were the last two people in the world…or if I could take you far away, so that we might never see another soul that knew us. But it is not as easy as that. There is someone who wishes to expose me for what I am. I swear I have done him no harm. But he thinks that I deserve punishment for a matter that did not involve me. I fear he will try to discredit me with you. I am trying to find a way to prevent it,' he said hurriedly. 'But if you do not wish to hear the truth from another, then there is something I must do, soon, that will keep you safe from this man. You may think my actions now are just as distasteful as my past. But I swear to you, what I will do may seem terrible, but I am convinced it is just.'

'If there is anything you need, I will help you.'

He smiled so very softly then, and shook his head. 'You do not know what you are saying.'

'That is for me to decide.' She wanted to be a part of his life, in any way that she could. 'How can I help you?'

He looked at her, speculatively. 'It will concern the Earl of Narborough.'

'And what does that have to do with you or me?'

'He is your employer,' he said. 'And you count the girls as friends, do you not?'

'Of course.'

'Suppose it were possible for me to bury my past, but it resulted in the downfall of the Carlows. What might you say then?'

This did not sound at all like the actions of a man she could love. 'You would ruin the family for your own gain?'

He shook his head. 'If what I suspect is true, Narborough dishonoured himself years ago. I would only be uncovering *his* secret to keep my own secrets safe.'

'After all that we have agreed about not looking back for unpleasantness, you would do to another, what you do not wish for yourself?' It was both mysterious and disappointing.

'This is quite different, I assure you. While I will admit that my past is shameful, I have not caused the death of any person, directly or indirectly, as a result of my actions. But George Carlow is responsible for at least two deaths, one by his own hand and one through the betrayal of a friendship.'

'Lord Narborough?' She almost laughed. 'He is a feeble old man.'

'And likely to go to his grave with the truth, if I do not act soon.'

She shook her head. 'He has never been anything but kind to me, nor have I seen him mistreat another.'

'Not recently, perhaps. But people can change for the better, with time. Twenty years ago, he might have been quite different, and you would not have known.'

'Twenty years is a long time,' she agreed. 'But surely, something so long ago could have no importance.'

'For some, it is as fresh as the day it happened,'

he said. 'You would do well not to belittle another's pain.'

She gasped, surprised by the vehemence of his reaction. 'Perhaps it would help me to know just what it is that you are talking about.'

'The murder of Christopher Hebden, Lord Framlingham, and the hanging of William Wardale, Earl of Leybourne.'

'You think that Lord Narborough was in some way involved?'

'I am sure of it. Hebden died at his house. And it was he who made the accusation against Leybourne.'

'But the earl was guilty.'

'How can you be sure?'

'If he was innocent, then why was he found with the dying man? Could he have done nothing to stop the crime? Knowing the Wardales as I do, I would believe them capable of anything.' The words flowed easily out of her. It surprised her, for she had not meant to come so close to revealing her own past.

He stared at her in disapproval. 'You can know nothing of that family. They were turned out of their home in disgrace and no doubt underwent hardships that were not in proportion to the crime. Think of it, Diana. A mother and three children. Two of them girls. Lord knows what happened to them. And if the father was innocent, all along…'

And for a moment, she put aside her own story, and thought of Marc's bride, Nell, *Helena Wardale*, and the past that she was so careful not to speak of. 'Perhaps you are right. Some members of the family have suffered unjustly.'

'How gracious of you to admit it.' Again, she was surprised by his passion on the subject, and his harsh tone stung her. Then he seemed to realize how he sounded, for he calmed. 'Please forgive my outburst. It was uncalled for. Even if the matter was important, you are right that it is the distant past. It hardly concerns us.' And for a moment, his face took on a funny cast. 'But the events of twenty years ago are about to return to haunt the families involved. I came to speak to Marc Carlow to offer a word of warning that the truth was likely to come out in the near future, and to be on his guard. But it would be better for all concerned, if Narborough had any part in what happened, that he admits the fact so that his family might prepare themselves for it.'

'But what makes you think this is the case, and what does it have to do with you?'

'I can explain very little, I am afraid. Other than

that I am sure of my facts. And I mean to gather the evidence necessary to prove them.' He squeezed her hand, as though wanting to assure himself that she was still his. 'Is that so very wrong?'

'If Lord Narborough is truly a murderer? Then I suppose it is not. But Nathan?' She squeezed his hand in return. 'He is not guilty. I am as sure of that fact, as you are of his guilt.'

And suddenly, there was a strange light in his eyes. 'Then you would have to prove it to me. If he is as innocent as Leybourne was, I would be making a horrible mistake in accusing him. If there is some way that I can be sure… You are an intimate of the family. If you have a way to assure me, other than conjecture…'

She pulled her hand away. 'Are you asking me to spy on my friends?'

He looked alarmed. 'Certainly not. And I never intended to suggest such a thing. It was an idle thought, nothing more. I meant what I said at first, when I refused your help. It would be too difficult for you. And possibly dangerous, should it turn out that I was right. I would be asking you to face a murderer in my stead. It makes me uncomfortable enough to know that you live with them. For all your confidence, I am not sure of their intentions.'

'You think they are a threat to me? Surely not. Lord and Lady Narborough have been nothing but good to me, as has the rest of the family.'

He touched her shoulder to reassure her. 'My problem is not with the rest of his family. They are no more to blame than the Wardales were. Those girls were no different from Honoria and Verity. Little more than babes when it all occurred, and God knows what happened to them.'

She thought again of the haunted look in Nell's eyes when she had first come to them. 'If their father was innocent, they deserved better than they received.'

His face clouded. 'You deserve better as well. A life of ease and not labour. But you are content, because your work is honourable. Perhaps it is true of them as well.'

'Or perhaps not,' she said, and watched as his expression became even more glum. And suddenly, it occurred to her why he might be so interested in the Wardales. He must have some knowledge of Nell's sister, Rosalind. A *tendre*, perhaps? If she was part of the secret he did not wish to share, it must have ended tragically. Did he blame himself? Perhaps the mysterious stranger he mentioned was their brother, Mr Wardale.

'I think I can see why you are obsessed with the crime and its aftermath.' Though she had vowed to him that she would not be suspicious or question him about his past, she wondered all the same. If her surmise was correct, she feared a visit from the mysterious stranger, almost as much as Nathan did. 'And now that you have put the idea in my head, I doubt I will be satisfied until I know the truth about the Earl of Leybourne. Although I am sure that Lord Narborough did them no harm. And I think there is a way I can assure you, that will do very little harm to anyone.'

He hesitated, and then said, 'No harm? Because I would not put you at risk.'

'What risk could there possibly be to me? I will be taking the girls to the Narborough's country house shortly, to visit their parents. Today, I meant to tell you that I would be gone for some days. In case you had been considering another meeting.' She gave a little dip of her bonnet to hide her face from him, for it embarrassed her to have him know how she had looked forward to their walk this week and that she was already planning for the next one. 'We will be leaving tomorrow. But once I am at Stanegate Court, I will have a chance to disprove your claim.'

His hand tightened on her shoulders. 'I would not have you snooping through drawers and searching the attics like some common thief.'

She smiled. 'That will hardly be necessary. Lord Narborough has kept a journal for most of his adult life. The full books are clearly labelled in a small library. Lord Narborough uses the space as his study, but I would hardly consider it private. No one will think twice if I go there in the afternoon to read. And once there, I am sure it would not be difficult for me to borrow the journal that corresponds to the year that Christopher Hebden died. If I find evidence that supports your claim, I will tell you.'

'You would do that for me?' He touched her face. 'I am not trying to turn you against your employer. Nor do I expect you to follow me blindly. I have not known you long enough to have earned your trust. I only wish you to exercise your judgment and objectivity over anything you might discover about the events in question. Look at it as a stranger might. If you find that I am wrong, then you have every right to correct my assumptions. But if there is any shred of evidence at Stanegate that proves me right? You would not be disloyal to your employer, if he did not deserve loyalty.'

There would be nothing to find, for she was sure that if the journal contained anything but the most mundane information, it would not be sitting out in a common room. If she looked at it, she could assure Nathan that she had done her best. But what if he did not believe her? Supposing his insistence was some mad obsession on his part and that he insisted on more and more searches?

As if he read her mind, he said, 'I give you my word that I will trust your findings, if that is what worries you. No matter what you discover, I will ask no more of you. That you would even consider helping is more than I deserve. I trust you would not conceal the truth from me, for I believe, after our few conversations, that you are an honest and fair-minded individual. Nor will I bother you further, if you arrive at the house and change your mind about this. I will go my own way, and you will see me again when I have satisfied myself on the matter of Lord Narborough.'

And this, more than anything else, decided her. For she was enjoying his company too much to give it up so quickly. If she looked at the book, she would be guaranteed at least one more meeting with Nathan when she returned to London. 'It will do no harm just to look at a book. They are kept in plain sight and easy reach.'

'You are too good, Diana. And your help and friendship are more than I deserve.' He took a deep breath, and looked all around them, as though making sure that there was no one to observe them. Then he smiled at her, and there was a merry twinkle in his eyes. 'But enough of this talk of the past. We promised ourselves that we would look only forward, did we not?' And very carefully, he raised her gloved hands to his lips, and kissed the knuckles again. 'It is a beautiful day, and we will not see each other again for some while. Let us enjoy what time we have.'

Chapter Eleven

The trip next day to Stanegate Court was as it always was, an exhausting experience, even though it was not a long journey and the roads were good. The travel would have been quite pleasant, had the attitude of one of her companions been better. Verity was no trouble, as even-tempered and cooperative as ever. But Honoria approached the trip with the enthusiasm of a condemned prisoner. She overslept, dawdled over the packing—taking first too little and then too much for a week's stay. Once in the carriage, she spent the time in sullen silence while Diana attempted to cheer her by pointing out land-marks that they had all seen dozens of times.

She could not really blame the girl. Despite the frequent corrections she received from Marc and herself, London held nothing like the censure

Honoria would receive in the company of her mother. Even when she was on her best behaviour, it was unlikely that she would find as much praise as her younger sister did. Lady Narborough's continual criticism would make her behaviour on their return to London worse rather than better.

Diana reached out a friendly hand and laid it upon the girl's, which were folded neatly in her lap. 'I know you do not wish the trip, Honoria. But think of the good it will do for your father.'

The girl sighed. 'I will do it for Father, of course, if it will cheer him to see us.'

'I am sure it will.'

'But we will not stay long, will we?'

'Not long.'

But once they had arrived, Diana worried that they would be lucky to manage even a short trip. The trouble began from the moment they entered the house. Lady Narborough greeted both girls warmly, commenting on their looks and demanding to know in detail about each dance at each party and every sign of interest from a gentleman of the Ton. But where Verity was congratulated on her good sense for her refusal to make a decision, Honoria was gently upbraided for being a flirt. Verity's dress was most flattering today. But Honoria's was a trifle too loose, was it not? And horror of horrors, her slippers were scuffed.

Diana felt a bit guilty for recommending the ensemble. For she had informed both girls that a trip to family hardly required their finest. And since Honoria exhibited a perfectly normal tendency to be active when in the country, it was better to add fresh scuffs to an old shoe than to ruin a new one. But Diana had long ago learned to hold her tongue in these situations. Lady Narborough meant nothing by her comments, and it was not Diana's place to explain to her how they hurt her eldest daughter.

After the grilling delivered by their mother, it was time to visit Lord Narborough. He was no longer confined to a sickbed, but according to the letters they had received in London, he rarely left his rooms. Diana had to admit that his colour was poor, and it appeared his appetite was as well. The contents of his lunch tray were nearly untouched.

Guilt, she wondered? And then checked herself. For the thought had never entered her mind that his failing health might be more than a normal weakening with age, until Nathan had placed it there.

'And how are my fine girls, Miss Price?'

Narborough's eyes sparkled at the sight of them, and for a moment, he seemed more his old self. But she could see by the way Lady Narborough hovered at his side that she feared any shock might finish him.

'Well, sir.' She gestured the girls forward and they greeted their father warmly, assuring him that the time in London was happy, and regaling him with stories of the balls and dinners they had attended and the people they had met.

And Honoria's behaviour was exemplary, just as Diana knew it would be. The girl made her time in London sound innocuous and glossed over the more rambunctious adventures with such good humour that her father laughed out loud. Even her mother could not have complained for the positive change her visit wrought in the earl.

When she was sure that she was not needed, and that the family was as happy in their time together as they were ever likely to be, she excused herself. She walked quietly into the little room where the journals were kept. They were just as she remembered them, lined up neatly behind the glass doors of the bookcase, bound in leather with the dates stamped in gold upon the spines. They were the work of a man with pretensions of grandeur. Lord Narborough must think that his every thought was worthy of study by someone. Although who would wish to read them, she was not sure. She had never seen the books removed from the shelves in all the years that she had been in the household. Not even in reference by the man who had done the writing. His children, when faced with the things, silently rolled their eyes at the folly of an old man.

When she reached to open the cabinet, it became clear to her why the things never moved. The glass door was locked against casual reading. How strange. Did he fear discovery of something or merely wish to keep the things clean and organized?

She shook her head to clear it of suspicions. After her talk with Nathan, even the most common actions seemed fraught with guilt. Whatever the reason for locking the things up, she had no real wish to ask for the key and call attention to her interest, for she could think of no way to explain herself.

Fortunately, or unfortunately, such intervention would not be necessary. She carefully removed a pin from her hair, rearranging the curls to disguise its absence. Then she went to work on the lock with the bent bit of wire and a letter opener from the nearby desk. Now she would see if ten years of excessive virtue had dulled her skills as a lock pick. She had not had to behave thus since she was a girl and tried to get around her father and his gambling, searching for hidden money in locked desk drawers.

She felt the satisfying click of the lock's mechanism as the tumblers slid home, and then she pulled the door open and traced her finger back as though travelling back through the years to a point almost twenty year's distant, and removed the volume labelled 1794. This would have the information, if anything would. She set it aside for a moment, rearranging the remaining books so the gap in years would not be obvious. Then, she relocked the door and slipped the purloined volume into her pocket.

Before she left the room, she paused to listen for noises in the library, feeling less than comfortable with the relief she felt when she heard silence. If she was doing nothing wrong, then why did she feel so guilty?

The lock was the answer, of course. She had planned on simply removing a book from a shelf in a public room and sitting down to read. But the lock was a warning that the contents were not meant to be removed. So when she was sure that no one would see, she took the book to her room, closed and locked her own door behind her, and opened it to the first page.

What had been the day of the murder? Had Nathan even said? Best to begin at the beginning and work her way forward.

She flipped quickly through the first few months, surprised at how little the family had changed. There were stories of Marc, serious and quiet even as a boy, and the little scamp Hal. Honoria was not out of leading strings but had already gotten into a multitude of scrapes. Verity was still in the cradle, and there were detailed descriptions of the baby gifts that Lady Narborough still had on display in shadow boxes and glass cases around the house.

And then an entry in a shaking hand, as though the writer were consumed by emotion.

> *Don't know what's to be done with Will. His behaviour grows reckless. No better than Hebden. They are both detestable and I am sick to death of their company.*

He might have known a dozen Wills and Williams. It was not specific enough to connect with certainty to William Wardale, the Earl of

Leybourne. Nor did it explain what might con-
stitute reckless behaviour. She continued to read.

*The situation grows worse with each day. Hebden's
Gypsy brat now playing with my boys. Kit encourages the association. Seems to find it amusing to
see the dark lad and treats him as though nothing
is odd. I cannot believe that his wife, Amanda, turns
a blind eye to it all. But she is raising the boy as
her own.*

She struggled to remember what she had heard
of the scandal. Kit must mean Christopher Hebden. There was something about a lost child, after
the father's death. A bastard son, who was sent away.
And Amanda Hebden, prostrate with grief over the
whole affair. Diana flipped through more pages.

*A shocking discovery. No wonder Amanda does
not clean her house of the Gypsy filth. She is too
busy with Leybourne to care. How can Will dine
with us at the club, and then go off to tup Hebden's wife? And Kit is too busy with his whores
to care. They laugh and talk together, then go off
to their sinful beds as though it means nothing.*
    *They were the friends of my youth. But now I
feel unclean by the association.*

The book shook in her trembling hand, as she tried to imagine the frail man upstairs penning the angry words. Although he was most particular with his own reputation and that of his children, she had never seen him cross with anyone in all the time she had lived with the family. But perhaps he had been a different man twenty years ago. She paged eagerly on.

Another shouting match with Kit over the cipher business. Too much whisky on all sides and not enough sense. He called me a traitor. I called him out, told him to solve the damn cipher if he is so eager to find the spy in our midst. But he cannot. The thing is unbreakable.

Without Will there, we'd have come to blows. Very embarrassing. But nerves frayed all round. This cannot go on much longer.

Traitor? She had never thought of Lord Narborough as less than an honest man and proud defender of his country. But he did not deny the accusation. And then, another note, coming almost as a postscript to the last.

Hebden says he has cracked the cipher. Now the truth will out. There is no stopping it.

And all that was left of the next page was a ragged tatter. Someone had seized the thing and ripped it from the book. She ran her fingers along the place where the pages should be stitched, and counted the little bits of paper: one, two, three pages missing. And at the top of the next page, a single line, hanging as though forgotten.

Dear God, forgive me.

Her pulse quickened. It proved nothing. But whatever had happened was worse than she suspected. Accusations of infidelity and treason on both sides. The missing pages, as though someone did not wish the truth to be known.

And that last statement, which could mean anything, but appeared damning when taken with all the rest. What was she to do with the information? It appeared that Nathan might be right. And it left her with a difficult choice to make. She'd lived in ignorance of any problems in this family and known Lord Narborough to be nothing more than a fond old man, caring deeply for his wife and children. But his health had worsened after the appearance of Nell and then the Gypsy. Was this because he feared the truth being revealed?

Had she found this information even a week ago, she'd have been tempted to turn her back on it. Better to let the matter rest and put the book back upon the shelf, instead of stirring up old troubles that could hurt more people than they helped. But now?

She took the book and set it in the bottom of her valise, and then covered it with a pile of folded stockings. She would pray that no one noticed its absence during the visit, and then she would take it back to London to show Nathan Dale. If he felt a pressing need to know the identity of the Hebden murderer, she would help him. It did not matter whether it was to avenge a lost love or free himself from the harassment of the same man that haunted her own past. She would do it, because in only a few weeks, she had grown to love and trust him beyond any loyalty she might feel to her old friends.

Because her objective opinion on past events, based on the contents of the little book, was that the truth could be every bit as bad as he assumed.

Chapter Twelve

During the week that Diana was away, Nathan could think of little else but her return. Although it was unlikely that he'd have seen her until the next Tuesday, even had she remained in London, he had not realized the comfort he felt in knowing that a chance meeting was possible. Now that she was gone, each mile between them was a hardship.

He went to the tables each night, just as he always had. But he played listlessly, paying little attention to the desires of men and women across the baize. Where once he would have watched without emotion as his opponents bankrupted themselves, now when games got out of hand he could no longer contain his disgust, with them or himself.

As yet another broken fool began rooting in

his pockets for some treasured heirloom to cast away, Nate stood up from the table, hours earlier than normal, proclaiming loud enough for all to hear that he would rather play cards with the kitchen cat than to watch another soul publicly shame themselves at his expense.

As he pushed his way through the crowd, he heard the ladies muttering amongst themselves that, while they still found Mr Dale was quite attractive, of late he had not been nearly as diverting as they had hoped.

He smiled to himself at this. Her absence had convinced him that there was only one woman in London that he wished to entertain. But was it better to initiate contact, or to wait until she was returned and was ready to see him? Surely scrawling a line or two to welcome her back to London would not be seen as forward. But had she even returned from Stanegate? He did not know. When they had parted, she had been able to give him no firm date of return. As always, her schedule was at the mercy of the Carlow family.

He quietly damned them all for their hold over her life, and damned himself for placing her in the situation. A week without seeing her had seemed like an eternity. It had given him too much time to relive the previous meetings and imagine possibilities for the next. Assuming that there would be a next meeting. What if she had decided not to follow through on their plan, and realized that it would be better to remove herself from him? It was no less than he deserved. Perhaps she had found some other gentleman whose company she preferred. Or maybe the next meeting was assumed, and he would find her waiting in the park on Tuesday.

There were so many possibilities that he could not choose and was driving himself mad with trying. At last, he decided there could be no harm in going to the park for a walk on the normal Tuesday, and went so far as to forgo his Monday evening at the tables so that he might be rested and waiting for her in Hyde Park on the following morning.

He arrived on the usual footpath by the Serpentine promptly at ten, to find Diana Price pacing the ground ahead of him in obvious agitation. Not only had she come, but it thrilled him to think she had arrived early, as though she were afraid she would miss him. He frowned. Unless there were some other reason for her anxiety.

When she saw him, she looked up with a relieved smile, and he hurried to her side. He clasped her hand, to assure himself that she was safely returned and not just a vision of what he wished to see. 'I was not sure you would come. Perhaps you were still travelling, or had decided that my last request was too forward? But I decided to wait here each Tuesday until you returned.'

'I hoped you would.' She gave a relieved sigh. 'But if you did not come, then at least you would not see me waiting for you.'

He grinned. 'I thought the same.' So she had been eager to see him. All of his previous concerns for her safety, and worse, her constancy, evaporated. 'Come, let us walk.' He offered her his arm.

'That would be delightful.' She took the offered arm, her fingers giving it a light squeeze that warmed his heart. 'And could it be somewhere secluded, if possible? For I have something to show you.'

He gave her a vague nod and set off with her, down the path and away from the other early walkers, laughing at his own foolishness. For a moment, he had quite forgotten the real reason for their meeting and had heard only what he longed to hear. It had sounded quite like she wished to be alone with him for no other reason than that they might share a moment of intimacy.

But then he remembered the journal and the need to keep it a secret.

Devil take the thing. He still wanted to see it, of course. But he had not realized just how much he had wished to see its bearer, until he had spied her on the path before him. When he was sure they were out of sight of prying eyes, he pulled her into the shade of a nearby outbuilding and drew to a stop.

Then, she slipped the small leather volume from her pocket. 'I think this will be of interest to you. Read it, starting from where I have marked. And notice the missing pages? I fear that a lack of evidence may be as damning as an excess of truth. For what reason would he have had to remove the page, other than that he regretted what he had written about the night in question?'

Nathan was turning quickly through the book, scanning the pages eagerly, shocked at the vitriol of some of the posts. George Carlow had been no true friend of his father's, to be sure. The entries sounded as though any bond between them had been severed in the months before Hebden's death.

Then he came to the missing pages, fingering the ripped paper scraps at the binding. The full story should reside here. Had it been torn out in anger? Shame? Guilt? It could be any reason. But it seemed plain that Carlow had not wanted the full truth known, so had disposed of the evidence.

He looked up at her, excitement on his face. 'There is a secret of some kind. It supports my suspicions, does it not?'

'I fear it does.'

'And now, I must decide what I will do with the information.' He frowned in distaste as a possibility occurred to him.

Lord Keddinton had risen far since the days when he was humble Robert Veryan and eager for a chance to dine with the Wardales. His help with the prosecution of the Earl of Leybourne had earned him his own title, just as it had taken Nate's away. 'There is a man who might help, if he had a mind to. He is an old acquaintance of my family.' He smiled bitterly. 'And I believe he owes me a favour. I will take it to him and see what he makes of it.'

But Lord Narborough would surely hear of an investigation and would punish anyone he thought disloyal. Nate gave Diana a worried look. 'But before I do anything, I must help you to get away.'

'Away?' She almost laughed. 'Away from what, sir?'

'From the Carlows, of course.'

'I am safe in London with Verity and Honoria. I have nothing to fear from them.'

'But I think you will, if the information in this book becomes public and they understand how I came by it.' He reached out and took her by the hand. 'And I would not, for all the world, have anything happen to you, my darling Diana.' The endearment slipped easily from his lips, and he saw the sweet look of surprise as it registered on her.

And then, he was drawing her further into the shadows, and cupping her face in his hands. His hands strayed to the ribbon that held her bonnet, and she batted them away. 'What are you doing?'

'Being very impertinent, I think.' He returned to his task and untied the bow that held it in place, then reached up to lift it gently off her hair. He leaned closer to smell the soft scent of her, and whispered, 'I have been dreaming of seeing the sunlight on your hair. Would the lights in it be gold, I wondered? But I was wrong. They are the deep red of Spanish wine.'

'Oh.' Her voice was breathless, and her hands still rested lightly on his wrists as though unsure whether or not to stop him.

He traced the curves of her ear with his tongue, and his teeth caught the lobe, sucking it gently into his mouth. She was soft and sweet and wonderful. And she had no idea how the simplest mysteries of her body would affect a man. She had kept them all hidden, even such small treats as this. And the way she sighed in response to the slightest nip on her ear boded well for the future.

'We mustn't,' she managed, after a few more delicious moments. But the tone hinted that, while she was sure she mustn't, she wished for much more.

'Do not worry,' he whispered. 'We won't. Not yet, at any rate. But do not blame me too much for doing this.' He pulled her close to kiss the side of her throat, turning her so that he could reach the nape of her neck, and he felt her ribs moving under his fingers, for the kisses to her throat made her breath release in shallow gasps. 'And do not fault me for wanting to take down your hair, so that I might run my fingers through it. To see it free as it lies on the pillow, and tousled as it is when first you wake.' He touched her very gently, so as not to disturb her coiffure. The silken smoothness of it made his fingers itch for more. 'Maybe I could take a single pin. It could be a curl blown loose by the wind, or caught in a ribbon and disarranged. An accident. Nothing more. But no. Once I start, I will not be able to stop.'

For he was sure it would not be enough to take down her hair. Next he would be laying her down in the new grass, and begging to make love to her where they could smell the first scents of spring. It would be sweet disaster, but it would bind her to him in ways that would make her rejection impossible, should she learn the truth of his character.

He made to release her, for her good and the sake of his own sanity. But she reached up and took him by the chin, squirming against him until she could force his lips to meet hers. She rewarded him with the kiss he longed to give her: open mouthed and passionate, innocent and inexperienced. Utterly delightful.

And so, he gave himself up to the pleasure and did not release her until he had marked every bit of her mouth as his. He heard the distant thump of her bonnet dropping to the ground and let his empty hands move over her, from shoulders to back to bottom, moulding her body to his, feeling the pressure building within him.

She should struggle, or argue or give some sign that she wished him to stop. If she did not, he did not know if he would be able to save them both from this madness. But instead, she wrapped her arms about his waist, clinging to him, letting him support her as he took all he wanted.

It was her total surrender to him that gave him the strength to break the kiss and push her gently away. He shook his head as he smiled to reassure her, then gave a quick look about them, to be sure that they were still alone. 'Oh, my sweet, I am foolish to risk you in this way. What will you think of me, when your head clears enough to realize how we have carried on?' He reached down and picked up her bonnet, which was looking rather scuffed after being crushed between them and then cast upon the ground.

She took it, and concentrated on straightening the flowers and fluffing the lone feather, and he wondered what had hurt her, his forwardness or the suddenness of his rejection? 'It is perfectly all right, Mr Dale. I was well aware of what I was doing.'

He scoffed. 'Throwing yourself away on a wastrel, without care for your reputation. And the only defence I can offer is that you have bewitched me with your beauty, Miss Price. One disapproving quirk of those very proper lips and I am lost to all propriety. I must have them. I must have you. I swear, the frown on your face right now is more delightful than a hundred smiles from another woman.'

There was the slightest smile on her lips as she finished with the bonnet, which he feared would never be quite the same, and placed it back on her head, tying it in a firm bow. 'Your praise would be more convincing, Nathan, if it were not so fulsome.'

He leaned back against the building, eyes closed and hands behind his head, and laughed, waiting for the beat of his heart to slow and his reason to return. 'Thank you, dear Lord, she is calling me Nathan again.' He opened an eye and peered at her. 'And smiling. The blush on that cheek is more perfect than any rose.' Then he said, softly and slowly, so that she might believe him, 'Forgive me my excessive praise. I have never been in love before, and I am rather at a loss as to how to go on.'

Love. He had said the word aloud to her, and now he would see what she made of it. Suddenly afraid, he went on talking, leaving her no time to respond. 'Give me time. I will grow into it, I am sure. And I will find a manner of praising you that suits your practical and modest nature. If you prefer, I will compliment you on your generous heart and your excellent manners, and remain silent with my suspicions that you are Venus herself, hiding behind a prim facade.' He patted the pocket that held the journal. 'When this is taken care of, we will have no need to sneak about in the woods, stealing kisses and tempting fate. I will take you away with me. And when I do, I mean to keep you safe and make you happy. I will make it right again, you shall see.'

She looked puzzled at his last words. And he realized that they made no sense. For why would Nathan Dale wish to make amends for her past, if he'd had no part in it? He waited to see if she understood. If she questioned him, he would tell her the truth and go where it led.

Instead, she said, 'I would like that very much.'

He was still free of the past, if there was freedom in hiding. But what did it matter, as long as she wanted him? And while she had not offered love in words, he had heard the truth in the response of her body to his. It would be all right between them, somehow. He smiled at her. 'I have much work to do. To secure our future.' He reached out for her, kissing her fingertips before linking her arm with his. 'Will you allow me to escort you home, Miss Price?'

'Gladly, sir.'

Chapter Thirteen

Nathan came back to the Fourth Circle that afternoon, flushed with the success of his walk with Diana. He had escorted her to the very door of the Carlow town house, and bid her a proper farewell. It had seemed the most natural thing in the world, and not an endeavour fraught with risk. He had pushed aside the hundred worries in his mind about his mending his tattered reputation and her preserving her spotless one, and enjoyed the little time they'd had as he should have done. Caution was all well and good, when kept in its place. But if he wished for a future that was a tenth as happy as this morning had been, it was time to act, even at the risk of failure.

Dante indicated with the barest nod of his head that he would find the Gypsy seated at their usual table. Nathan approached slowly, to assess the mood of the man. There was no sign of the headache of two weeks ago. And with a doxy on his knee and a drink in his hand, Stephano looked almost at ease. It seemed he had taken the two weeks as a holiday from his quest, as well. His usual dark mood was gone, and as Nathan watched, he leaned back his head and laughed at something the girl had whispered to him. It sounded nothing like the sour mirth Nathan had heard from him, when gloating over the misfortune of his victims. The girl responded with a kiss, and then tossed her head and laughed as well.

She was rewarded with jealous glares from the other women in the room, who were looking at the Gypsy as though they would gladly change places with his chosen *inamorata*, the moment he lost interest in her.

For a moment, it was as if Nate's old friend had grown to adulthood and sat before him, ready for a game of cards. Then Stephano looked up, and his good mood evaporated, as though it had not existed. The merriment disappeared and a cynically smiling mask covered his handsome features. He muttered something and pushed the girl from his lap, then raised his glass in a sarcastic salute. 'Nathan.'

Nate dropped into the chair opposite, noting the absence of a surname in the greeting. The Gypsy had not yet decided if he had earned the right to hide behind the name Dale. He said nothing in response and placed the journal on the table between them.

The Gypsy raised an eyebrow. 'What is this?'

'Proof enough for you to leave me alone. The entries in this book show Narborough to be no real friend of my father, nor of you. If you wish for justice, get out of my chair and go to bother him.'

Stephano opened the book at the marked page and began to read. When he came to the missing pages, he looked up. 'There is nothing at all here about the night of the murder.'

'Is that not strange? Was the event not significant enough to record in detail? Or perhaps George Carlow wrote the whole truth in an impetuous moment and then thought the better of it and tore out the pages.'

Stephen closed the book and offered it back to him. 'When you bring me the missing pages, I will tell you what I think.'

'Until recently, I would have been unable to get this much information. If you want the missing parts? Then find them yourself. I have given you more than enough reason to doubt.'

Beshaley gave him a sceptical look. 'Why would it matter to me what they say?'

Perhaps it would have mattered to the man who had been sitting here as he had arrived. So Nate appealed to him. 'For a moment, let us ignore the nonsense of your mother's curse. Stephen Hebden, if you care who killed your father, then this journal could make us more allies than antagonists.'

The man across the table from him did not respond, staring in response to his old name as though Nate had not spoken.

'All right then. Stephano Beshaley.' Then he continued. 'If my father died for a murder he did not commit, do I not have as great a reason as you to be angry? I lost a father, a title and my reputation, just as you did. And my family as well. You seem to have found a new one, when you returned to your people. But my sisters are lost to me.'

A shadow flitted across the face of his old friend, and then it was gone.

'I have no love for the Carlows. I've proved as much for you. Can you not lift the curse from the Wardales?'

'I tell you again, it is not for me to decide what happens. The curse is a test, Nathan. I have been called to administer it. You will pass or fail, according to your nature. If you are innocent, then nothing I do will truly harm you. There will be a period of hardship, and all will come right in the end. And perhaps it will bring me closer to my goal.'

Nathan laughed bitterly. 'I knew you once, Stephen Hebden. For that is who you were, though you wish to reject it. And I liked you. You were a kind boy, a good friend, and had things been different, you would have grown to be a good man. And now you are willing to destroy my life on a *perhaps.*'

The Gypsy shook his head. 'You give me too much power, Nathan. Only God can truly destroy a man, just as he created him. If I am not doing his work, then I cannot hurt you. It is up to him to decide your fate.'

'Small comfort. I will only meet my end if God thinks I deserve to. Any number of horrible things have happened to me when we were young. And I did not deserve a one of them. They made me into the man I am, a person I take no pride in being. Now, after life has driven all the goodness from me, you seek me out and hope that God will find me wanting, so that I may be punished further?'

The Gypsy gave him a wry smile. 'I'll take no

joy in it, if that is the case. For once, I liked you as well. But take heart, Nathan. Whatever might occur, it will be over soon enough. For both of us.' He reached to pocket the book.

Nathan held a hand out for it. 'Here, then. If this will not end things between us, then give that back.'

The Gypsy shrugged, but returned the book. 'What do you mean to do with it? Confront Narborough?'

'That would make me no better than you. If you think my fate is in the hands of God, then I will take the thing to the authorities and see if they can make anything of the contents.'

Beshaley snorted. 'Because English justice has treated you fairly in the past?'

'Because it is the right thing to do. And what my father would have done, if he were alive.' Nate straightened his back. 'If I truly believe that he was innocent, then I had best start behaving so. If I think there is truth to be revealed, then I do not mean to skulk in the bushes like a common criminal. I will go to Lord Keddinton with it and let him use the information as he sees fit. He knew both our fathers and is well placed in the Home Office. He will have the power to follow through on this, if anyone does.' The idea had been but a stray thought when he'd mentioned it to Diana. But spoken, Nate knew the rightness of it. For suddenly, he felt more like the true Earl of Leybourne than he had since the day his father had died.

But Stephen was unimpressed. 'Good luck with it, old friend. I wish you success. I truly do. But if your father is innocent, you may find that the world is less interested in truth than you think.'

'I am Nathan Wardale. I wish to see Lord Keddinton, on a matter of business, please.' It had been so long since he'd used it, his own name sounded strange in his ears.

Perhaps the unfamiliarity showed in his tone. For the butler at Robert Veryan's country estate raised an eyebrow, as though doubting his word. Nate could offer no calling card to assure the man of his identity. So he stood his ground and gave the kind of cold stare that he might have given had he still been a peer, as though he was not accustomed to being kept waiting on the doorstep.

At least there was no sneering response to the name Wardale. The man was certainly old enough to remember the scandal, but too disciplined to show distaste for his employer's business. After a chilly pause, the servant stood aside to allow him entrance, taking him to a receiving room not far from the front door. A short time later, a footman came to escort Nate the rest of the way to Keddinton's office.

As he was presented, Nate resisted the urge to shift nervously on the carpet before the desk like an errant schoolboy called to the headmaster for punishment. Though Keddinton had been expecting him, now that Nate stood before his desk, the man kept him waiting in silence as the footman retreated, and continued to read the papers in front of him. It was a move designed to demonstrate that whatever business Nate might have, it could not be of sufficient importance to hold his full attention for more than a moment.

Nate smiled to himself and relaxed, as he recognized the gambit for what it was. While some might take it for a masterstroke of manipulation, it was really no better than the bluff of an inexperienced card player. When did a man with a good hand need to work so hard? Lord Keddinton was wary of him. Perhaps even frightened. And knowing that made the waiting much easier.

But what had Keddinton to fear from him? The man had been a friend of his father's at one time—long ago, before their disgrace. There had never been any indication that he was less than fair in his dealings before the trial or since. Surely an appeal based on that friendship would be heard.

Robert Veryan need have no fear of vengeance from him, for he had done nothing to earn it. Let Beshaley harass everyone involved with his Gypsy nonsense, if he wished. If Nate wanted things settled, he had best start behaving as though he were a rational gentleman with nothing to fear. Vindication after all this time could mean a return of the title and his good name in a way so public that it would regain him his family.

And lose him his love. If he was revealed as Nathan Wardale, Diana would hear of it. Perhaps a public attempt to clear his old name would show her that he had changed and meant her no harm. But at least he would be honest with her. And he suspected that the truth would be easier to accept if she heard it from the new Earl of Leybourne. She would certainly like that better than if it came from Nate Dale. Or worse yet, from the Gypsy.

So Nate waited patiently in front of the desk, and at last, Keddinton looked up from his papers, showing little interest in the man before him. 'Mr Wardale.'

'Lord Keddinton. I have news of an old matter.'

'I assume it concerns the disgrace of your family.' Keddinton pursed his lips, as though the matter was distasteful to him.

Nathan nodded. 'Fresh information has come to me concerning the death of Christopher Hebden.'

'Concerning your father's part in the events?' Keddinton leaned forward.

'My father had no part in the events, other than to place his trust in the wrong people. I think the same as I always have. There was a miscarriage of justice. My father did not commit the crime he was charged with.'

Keddinton leaned back again. 'And you have waited twenty years to come forward with it?'

'There have been difficulties that prevented me.' Would the man check his background and find the desertion? It was probably within his power. And from the disapproving look on his face, it was no different than he would expect from a Wardale. 'Recently, something has come to light that might change your view of the situation.'

He pushed the book forward, onto the desk,

so that Keddinton could see the title, in gold upon the spine.

The man stared at it without interest. 'And what might this mean to me?'

'Read it. Particularly the pages leading up to and following the day of Christopher Hebden's death.'

Keddinton opened the book and paged through it, stopping as he got to the marked page, then pausing to read. Then he looked up, his expression unchanged. 'And you think there is significance in this?'

'I should think it would be obvious. George Carlow's friends suspected him of being a traitor. And he says nothing to deny the claim.'

'An innocent man would not feel the need.'

'The missing pages imply guilt.'

'Or spilled ink. Or damage by mice. Or nothing at all. For all I know, you removed them yourself before bringing me this, in an attempt to shift your father's guilt on to Lord Narborough. Did you ask him to explain them?'

'Of course not.'

'He did not give you this book, then?'

'Why, no. I…'

'Then how did you come by this?'

Caught in the sudden barrage of questions,

Nate understood how Lord Keddinton had gained a reputation as the most crafty of spymasters, for he was a difficult man to distract. 'That is not important.' And damn him if he hadn't tipped Keddinton to how important it must be by saying those words. But it had not occurred to him, when he had come here, how quickly blame might fall onto Diana.

As suddenly as the questions started, they stopped. The other man pushed the book aside and sighed, his sternness evaporating into sympathy. 'I understand, Nathan, that you are eager to clear your father in the murder. You lost much by it and must wish to escape the disgrace. You loved him, as a good son should, and do not wish to believe him capable of evil. But I have seen no evidence, in twenty long years, that there was anyone else at work against the crown. Although you do not wish to believe it, the activities of the spy stopped conveniently after the death of your father. You must also understand that I cannot act on guesses and assumptions. I will look into the matter, of course. For if we were wrong, and the traitor escaped?' He shook his head. 'That would be a most serious thing, indeed.'

He paused, watching Nathan for a bit, as though weighing out choices before speaking further. Then he leaned forward again and said, 'When you came to me, I had hoped…I should not even tell you this, for it is a fact that few know and a matter of state security. But you had no part in this crime. And I would like to believe you would help, if you could, whether your father was involved or not. You would put the good of the country before your own needs, would you not?'

'Of course, sir.' And again he wondered how much Keddinton might know of his time in the Navy, for would he have so easily trusted a deserter?

Keddinton paused again, still observing his reactions. Then he nodded, as though what he had seen satisfied him, and said, 'At the time of Kit Hebden's death, we were having a problem with confidential information being leaked regularly to our enemies abroad. The messages we intercepted were being transmitted in a code so difficult that only the most skilled cryptologist could have cracked the thing. Without knowing the key to the cipher, there was little way to even tell how to begin. We put Hebden to work on it, hoping that there would be progress. He had a keen mind and a fascination for such things.'

'Perhaps he was the spy,' Nathan suggested. 'If the problem stopped after my father's death, it could as easily have been because Hebden was gone as well.'

'True, I suppose,' Veryan conceded. 'But Hebden assured us all, when last we saw him at dinner the night before he died, that a solution was forthcoming. If he had been guilty, then why would he have bothered? He could have stalled indefinitely and told us the code was unbreakable. We'd have been none the wiser.'

Nate tried to contain his impatience. 'So there was a code, and Hebden had cracked it. What is that to me?'

'Possibly the key to it all, Nathan. I knew both men. I doubt that Hebden would have made a false boast that night. He did not speak the whole truth about the code because he felt the traitor was in the room with us. Perhaps he wished to give the man warning, expecting him to end his life with honour or flee the country. We were all friends, you know. I doubt he'd have wanted to see a friend hang.'

'Then he was softer than the rest of you,' Nate responded. 'You and Carlow had no problem watching my father die.'

The memory must have been a difficult one. For the implacable Keddinton almost seemed to flinch at it, before regaining composure. 'It was harder than you know, Nathan. But Kit Hebden was like a brother to us as well. What else could we do?'

'You could have believed my father, when he said he was innocent. And while I might believe that it pained you to watch him die, I do not see the brotherly feeling recorded in George Carlow's journal.'

Keddinton made a helpless gesture. 'These are the private rantings of a much younger man. And Carlow had a bit of a hot head, back in the day. He was a man given over to impulse.'

'All the more likely that he was the killer.'

Keddinton shook his head. 'Every man with a hot temper does not turn killer. I see nothing in the journal to persuade me otherwise.'

'Then what would convince you?'

'If you should turn up the code key, it would tell us much. I searched for it that night, expecting it to be on Hebden's person. But there was nothing in his pockets that might be a key. If your father stole it—' Keddinton held up a hand to forestall any argument from Nathan '—he would not have had time to destroy it. Carlow was there within moments of the blow being struck. And I searched the grate. The fire was still unlit and with no fresh ashes at all.' He looked seriously at

Nathan. 'Surely your father had secret places, in his study or somewhere else in the house. If he had concealed it upon his person, he might have had time to hide it, before they took him to Newgate. Or maybe he gave something to your mother. Perhaps he slipped it between the pages of a book. I doubt it would be more than a single sheet of paper. Perhaps only a half sheet. Or even less, if the writing was small. Do you remember anything in his effects that might have seemed odd? An unintelligible thing, rows of numbers, or a language you did not understand?'

'It has been so long.' And very little existed from that time before it had all gone bad. 'I remember nothing that was as you described. The contents of the house were sold at auction, just after the hanging. How can you expect me…'

And then he remembered the torn pages of the journal. 'The only paper I bring to you is from Narborough's library. Maybe if we could find the missing pages, there would be some answer in them. Perhaps Carlow had written it there.'

Veryan shook his head again. 'I will make inquiries as to why the book is damaged, but I am sure they will come to naught.'

'But if they do not?'

Keddinton stood to show that the interview was near its end, and came around the desk to put a fatherly hand upon Nate's shoulder. 'I am as interested in the truth as you are, but for a better reason. The safety of England is at stake. Leave your direction with my servant. I will contact you, if anything is found, just as you must contact me if you discover what your father did with the cipher key. But until that time, you must trust me to proceed in the way I see fit. And that will be with caution, and sensitivity. If there is any fresh truth to be gained, after all this time, it will not involve purloining journals, or making wild accusations. Do you understand?'

In truth, Nate did not. What good did it do to employ spies, if they stuck at spying on the people they suspected? But he did not wish to lose the trust of so powerful a man. So he said, 'Of course.'

'Good day then.' Keddinton stepped away from him and signalled the footman to show him out.

Chapter Fourteen

Diana woke with a start to find the sun already high in the sky. She had overslept again. This made the third time in two weeks that she'd had to hurry her toilet to beat Verity to the breakfast table. It was little consolation to insist that this was most unlike her normal behaviour, for she feared that an error made three times must signal a change in character.

Of course, so much had changed around her in the last weeks that she might have reason to fear its effects. The journal had shaken her faith in Lord Narborough, which made prompt attention to the needs of his daughters less appealing to her than it had been.

And after the kisses in the park and all Nathan's talk of secrets, she'd found her own secrets had come back to haunt her. Her normally peaceful sleep was disturbed by dreams. Nightmares might be a better way to describe them, although she was not sure. She awoke more troubled than frightened, and sometimes rose in the night to check the latch on her bedroom door. In her dreams, the past caught up to her with a knock upon that door, and the silhouette of a dark man, pushing his way into her bedroom and whispering, 'It is time to pay the debt.'

Nathan Wardale. If the man was anything more than a ghost, she'd have heard something before now. Or his sister would have known his whereabouts. If he had not already come, he would not be coming and the dreams were nonsense. It was only her closeness to another very different Nathan that was making the old fears reawaken. And the knowledge of his kisses, which were turning some shameful part of her brain to carnality.

For though in dreams of youth, she had woken struggling against the bedclothes, fighting to keep the shadow at bay, the new dreams were different. Now, the dark man came to find her bedroom door unlatched. And when he grabbed her, she did not struggle. When he kissed her, she opened her mouth. And when he pushed her back upon the bed…

What would she do if things went the way she suspected in her waking life? Would she find herself married to one man and submitting to another, in her sleep, night after night? And worse, that she might enjoy the dreams. For she awakened from them with only vague memories of what had occurred, but a licentious desire to close her eyes and escape back into them.

Thank God she had awakened before the end. Suppose he had stepped out of the shadows as the grasping little man that her father had described to her. In reality, he would be ugly and pale as the underbelly of a rat, and he would laugh as he took everything she had, with no thought to her happiness or her future, just as he had with her father.

To dissolve the terrible image from her mind, she rose quickly and splashed the cold water from the basin on her face. A good wash and a cup of tea would clear the foolishness from her head. And perhaps a brisk walk in the park, before breakfast.

It was not her usual day for a walk, of course. It was not Tuesday. She smiled at the secret, and put her fingers to her lips to hide the fact. In all her years of work, she had never longed for her free day, during the other six. In her time with the

Carlows, the things she had done on it were rarely any different than the things she did while working. Perhaps it was because she enjoyed the company of the girls, and they did not mind her taking time to herself during the week, as she needed it. She doubted Verity would miss her overly, should she go out on her own this morning.

It was only since the arrival of Nathan Dale that she had felt a need for privacy or a desire to be secretive about any of her actions.

And perhaps that was why she felt a tingling sensation at the base of her neck as she walked along the path this morning. Was it the memory of the dream that still lingered, or of last week's kisses? Or perhaps it was guilt over the theft of the journal.

She did not like to think on that. It could not have been such a terrible thing to take a book that had been untouched in the library for years. If Lord Narborough had wished the secrets hidden, surely he would have burned the thing.

Or perhaps he had just destroyed the pages that contained the worst of it. That book had been one amongst many. If he had elected to destroy it, then its absence from the set might have been an even easier clue to find.

There was certainly something wrong at the

heart of the Carlow house. Maybe her feelings of foreboding were not the result of her own actions, but the creeping suspicion that troubles that were likely to fall upon the family as a result of what was occurring.

Or perhaps… She darted a glance to her side. Had the man by those chestnut trees been looking in her direction, only to suddenly turn away?

Nonsense. But she quickened her step and took the less popular fork in the path, assuming he would continue straight down the way, and she would know that she was being foolish.

But instead, she saw him again a short time later. He was still behind her and closer to her than he had been. When the same thing happened at the next turning, she admitted the truth: The man was following her.

He was of average height, slender and dark, with a gold hoop in one ear, and determined smile upon his lips. It was the Gypsy that Marc had warned her about, making no effort to hide himself from her, stalking her like a fox might stalk a hare as she walked amongst the trees.

What had Marc expected from this man? She was not sure, but she hoped he was not a mortal threat. The turn had been a mistake, for the way she had chosen was not well travelled. Without thinking, she had wandered farther away from help, should she need to call for it. She glanced around her, looking for anyone who might offer assistance, should the man try to take her purse or physically accost her. But the path was empty.

The Gypsy must have guessed her thoughts. He smiled at her, teeth startlingly white, hands held at his sides, palms open and facing her as though to show he meant no harm. 'Miss Price?'

She turned to face him. 'How do you know me?'

'Suffice it to say, I do know you. And I mean you no harm.'

'I have been warned about you. By Lord Stanegate.'

'What I have to say to you has nothing to do with Marcus Carlow or his family. It concerns you alone.'

She felt a sinking feeling in her stomach. She could think of several reasons why a stranger might want to talk specifically to her, and she liked none of them. 'Why should I believe anything you might say to me?'

He laughed. 'It does not really matter to me, either way. If it makes you feel more at ease, I will not approach closer. If you do not gaze at me, no one need know that we are even speaking, should they view us from a distance. I have some information for you. Nothing more than that.'

'Then give it and be gone.'

'There is a man, come recently into your life. He is not as he appears. Do not trust him.'

'You are the man come most recently into my life, sir. At your own advice, I had best not remain here.' She made as if to go, but the route home would take her closer to the Gypsy, if only to pass him.

Realizing her dilemma, he stepped off the path to give her room. 'Very well, then. But I came to you because we have a common enemy. Did your father ever tell you of Mr Wardale?'

She swallowed her shock at hearing the name, and said nothing. But her steps slowed to hear what he might say.

'You are right that you have no reason to listen, even if I tell the truth. But if you pay an unexpected visit to your old home, everything will be clear to you.' He turned and walked away into the trees, leaving the path clear for her.

She went slowly, one foot in front of the other, knowing that when she left the park, she would hail a cab for Hans Place and do as the Gypsy suggested. She did not know what she would do if she found Nathan Wardale in residence there.

But she had to know—one way or the other—if the man was alive.

And as to the Gypsy's warning about a man come recently into her life?

A possibility occurred to her that was too horrible to contemplate.

Nate sat at the desk in his study, chewing on his lip and absently rearranging the items listed on the paper before him. Although he should not tarry over the execution of the duties, there was no reason that he shouldn't tackle them in an efficient order. And much as he might like to go haring after Robert Veryan's mysterious cipher, it was ranked at the bottom.

The important thing was that he take action. Any kind of action at all. He would not spend another day sitting at this desk, drawing pictures, sketching on the blotter as his life passed away. After years of hiding and remorse, it would feel good to be doing something. He could almost feel his mind stretching for the possibilities, as though waking from a long sleep. He had lain down as Nate Dale. But he would arise as Nathan Wardale. And a glorious morning it would be.

Should he go to the Admiralty first? It would ease his mind considerably to know that he need not fear arrest, nor was he likely to find himself locked in some hold and on his way back to America.

Once he was safe from the Navy, he would place an advertisement in the *Times*, seeking information on Rosalind, Helena and their mother.

And on the very next Tuesday…

No. It would not wait so long. Although he feared the response, Diana Price must be the very first thing on his list. He would write to her immediately, and explain in detail who he was and what was about to happen. He would bare his soul to her before proceeding, so that nothing would come as a surprise. She would be angry, of course. And possibly frightened of him.

But Diana was not without a heart. He had looked into her eyes and seen nothing but love. She had said the past was not important. Now, he would see if she could overlook it, once the worst was known. He would tell her, let her judge. He would promise to wait each Tuesday morning, in Hyde Park, until she returned. Then he would wait. His entire life, if necessary. And one day, he was sure that she would come to him.

There was a commotion in the hall outside the study, growing closer as the people involved neared the door. The butler, Benton, had raised his normally placid voice in a greeting—and then in argument. And a woman was protesting.

And as the door opened, he realized his plans were useless, for he had made them a day too late to save his future.

'You.' She was framed in the doorway, bonnet askew and coat disarranged, as though she had hurried to confront him with little care to lady-like decorum. The composure that he so often saw in her features was collapsing into a mix of anger, tears, fright and disgust. '*You* are the gambler my father warned me about?'

'Diana.' His voice choked on the word. 'I can explain.' But of course, he could not. There was no explanation for what he had done. No defence.

'I think it is quite obvious what happened. You discovered my position in the Carlow household. You wanted to discredit Lord Narborough, just as you said. So you used my growing affection for you to manipulate me.'

'I did not. I had no idea I would meet you when I came to that house. And I could not anticipate how things would end.'

She sneered. 'I find that hard to believe, sir. You played me like a harp. You enquired after my past and my future. Then you used my own needs and desires against me.'

'I asked you about yourself, because I wanted to know. I did not intend…'

It was plain on her face that she did not believe him. 'Why did you need to be so cruel? Did it amuse you to arouse feelings in me? Why did you not simply use my father's note to gain my cooperation? You must have known I'd have done anything to retrieve it.'

'I hoped you had forgotten by now.'

'Forgotten?' She put her hand to her mouth as though she was about to be ill. 'My entire life has been routed around that night. What I am. Where I am. Who I am. You thought I would forget that a gambler holds my honour like it was cheap coin?'

'Because your father bartered it away.' He had not meant to say the words, for he was sure that the bluntness of them would hurt her. But why must he be the one to pay when fools came to play with him?

There were tears welling up in her eyes now, and he felt the pain of them in his own heart. 'He could not stop himself from playing. And you took advantage of his weakness, just as you have taken advantage of me. You tricked me into turning on a family that has shown me nothing but kindness for years.'

'I did not trick you into taking that journal. You volunteered. And when you read the thing, you agreed with me.'

'Only because you planted the seeds of doubt in my mind. You promised that we would be together, once it was settled. And I?' She laughed. 'I foolishly convinced myself that you meant something honest with those words. I had no idea that if you wished for *togetherness*—' she shuddered '—you had but to produce my father's note and demand to receive it.'

'But you understood me correctly. I intended to offer. What you suspect? It was not what I meant at all. Here.' He fumbled in his pocket. 'If it means so much to you, then take the damn letter from me, now.'

'You carry it on your person? You have had it with you, all along?'

And how could he explain that to her, when he could not explain, even to himself, why he had not thrown the thing in the fire on the first night. 'Yes.' He held it out to her again. 'Take it.'

She reached out a hand for the paper, and her fingers trembled as though she thought the contact would burn her. And then she stopped, her hand still inches away. 'You are toying with me, aren't you? What do you want in return?'

'Toying? Certainly not. Take the thing back.'

'Because I can give you money. Not much…'

And again, her words pushed him to the brink of anger. 'Think what you will of me, Diana, for I deserve your contempt. But do not tell me that your virtue can be measured in money. Even if it were, it would be worth more than thirty-four pounds.'

She fell silent, as the meaning of his words sunk in. And as the silence wore on, he wished that he could call them back and start again. Perhaps then he could make something he'd intended as a noble act seem less common and thoughtless.

Then she said, in a voice barely above a whisper, 'That was you, as well. There has been no one but Nathan Wardale interested in me. All along.' And she said it like it was the worst thing in the world.

'I meant to help.'

'I thought I knew the extent of my debt to you. And now I find it is everything I am, *plus* thirty-four pounds? What a fool I was to spend some of it. I will have to dip into what little savings I have, to return the full amount to you.'

'You misunderstand me, Diana. I do not want money…'

'Then there is only one thing you could want from me.' Her gaze felt cold upon him. But there was nothing cold about her. Her eyes flashed, her skin was flushed a healthy pink, and the trembling of her lips made them all the more kissable.

He could feel his gambler's nerves trembling in answer beneath a facade of calm. Her disdain for him aroused him as much as it angered him. He could remember the feel of those lips, her hands on his face, her look of concern when he told her of his past. When he'd held her in his arms in Hyde Park, she'd been eager to forgive him anything and ignore his flaws. Was he so different today?

He threw his hands in the air. 'All right. I admit it. All of it, Lord help me. I never wanted the letter in the first place. I begged your father to stop before it came to this. And when he would not, I thought to shock him to his senses with a bet no sane man would take. It was a mistake. It does no good to bluff a madman. And Diana Price, your father was too mad with cards to care about his own daughter's honour.'

She covered her ears as though the truth was something she did not wish to hear.

'So I did an unthinkable thing. But I did not seek you out. Not once in ten years. And when I found you, quite by accident, I had no intention of acting upon this letter. I gave you the money hoping to assuage my guilt, which has been acute.' He laughed at his own folly. 'And it seemed to help. I even thought, for a time, that all was forgiven. I'd convinced myself that it would be possible to offer for you honourably and hide what I had done. You would have been happy with your fantasy of Mr Dale. I would have made sure of the fact.

'But then, the Gypsy threatened to tell you the truth, and I was willing to do anything to prevent it. And he has gone and done it anyway, hasn't he? For how else would you have found me?' He silently cursed Stephano Beshaley, and his own folly for believing that there was any mercy left in the man who had once been his friend.

'You have come to this house, which once was yours, to demand the truth. I will no longer deny it. I am Nathan Wardale, the man who ruined your father and your life. And I want you. Totally and completely. In ways that you cannot imagine, and that cannot be encompassed by this foolish bit of paper. The sight of you, the sound of you, the taste of you. Your sweet face, your soft skin, the way you tip your head to the side when you are thinking, and pretend to frown while smiling, so that you can appear to be the stern old chaperone, and not as young and lovely as the girls you watch. I can hardly breathe when I think of you. And the kisses we shared in the park?' He gave a slow shake of his head. 'The memory possesses me.'

'You villain.' She reached out a hand to strike him, but he caught it easily and pulled her body to his. The kiss, when it came, seemed both expected and unfamiliar. He opened her mouth and drank her in. She was as sweet and good as he'd remembered, her body warm and inviting. And he felt as she returned the kiss, her tongue moving in his mouth and her arms reaching out to circle his waist.

And then she pushed him away, wiping at her mouth as though her own actions disgusted her. 'I hate you.'

'You do not even know me.' He held out a hand to her, hoping that it would soften her mood. 'But I would like you to. We could forget the past. Start fresh, as we planned.'

'Not while that marker exists.' She swallowed.

'Here, then.' He put the paper into her hand, and curled her fingers about it. They were so cold, almost numb, that he feared she would drop the thing once he released it. And for a moment, he thought it was over. She had the note and he did not. That was what she had come for. Now they could start again.

But then, he saw the look in her eyes. She was still suspicious, waiting for the catch, the snare, the string that came attached to the paper. There was no good way to convince her that he did not expect a reckoning. If he left her alone, she would live waiting for it. And if he did not? Then it would be all she could think of, on their first night together.

'What do you want from me?' she said, her tone dry and empty.

And so he answered her. 'What do you think I deserve?' If she thought him such a demon, the least she could do was tell him so. Damn him to hell and call him unworthy.

She went to the sofa by the fire and lay down upon it, fumbling with her skirts, spreading her legs.

'Stop that immediately.' She had dropped the paper upon the floor. And without thinking, he picked it up again.

'I do not wish to live a moment longer with an unpaid debt upon my conscience. Knowing that you could come for me at any time? It has been unbearable.' Though she did not rise, she pulled away from him as he approached her, as though the thought that he might take advantage of what she was offering was almost unbearable. Her face showed such pain that he could hardly stand it.

'I asked you.' He pointed a finger at her, in accusation. 'I asked you if you were happy in your job as companion. You assured me you were all right. You were happy. And that it had all turned out for the best. Were you lying?'

'That was before I knew who you were.'

'And now that you do, it is all changed. I understand that you cannot be happy with me. But it appeared you were growing quite fond of Nathan Dale. Was that a lie as well?'

'It was a mistake.' She lay still upon the couch, her bosom heaving and skirts so disarrayed that he could see the slender ankles and shapely calves beneath them. Every movement, every breath, seemed an invitation. But she was looking at him with those wide, innocent eyes. And although the affection in them was gone, there was not a trace of guile. He had been sure that she wanted him, and yet she swore that she did not.

'Then it is a mistake that is easily corrected. Nathan Dale, who you loved, is gone, never to return. And between you and Nathan Wardale, there is nothing?'

She hesitated. It was less than a breath. Less than a fraction of a second. But it was there. And then she said, 'There is nothing between us but the writing on that piece of paper.' And when he looked into her eyes again, he saw it: the bluff that he had been hoping for.

He had broken her heart with his carelessness. She was disappointed and angry and afraid. But she was not afraid of him. She feared what she was likely to do, should he touch her again. And she hoped that a single, weak lie could make him throw down his cards and leave the table.

There was much more between them than she would admit. But if he allowed her to escape, she would never understand. He took a shallow breath, and read the paper, as though the words were new to him, but of little consequence. Then put it back into his pocket. 'Then I lied when I said I did not wish to redeem this. If that is all I am to you, if there is no love between us, then what reason do I have to yield it unpaid?' He patted his pocket. 'It is still on my person, as it has been for ten years. And during that time, I made no effort to hurt you, to hunt you down, to humiliate you with it. And so it will remain, if you wish to walk out of my life. But if it is so important to you, then you must retrieve it from the table beside my bed. Return here, at eight tonight. We will settle what is between us. If you wish to leave afterwards, the marker will go with you and you may do what you like with it. I hope you are happy together. But once you go from here, you will never see me again. Good day, Miss Price.'

He left her, striding out of the study and up the stairs to his room. She was still sprawled on the couch, and if he remained one more moment in her company, he would give in to his desires and fall upon her like the animal she thought him to be.

After what he had suggested, she would not dare to follow. His own words had shocked him. For what gentleman would ever say such to a lady? Especially the woman he loved. But if she did not see his self-disgust, then she could assume what she wished. And since she seemed to expect the evil seducer, that was what he would give to her. He would play her game—and beat her at it, for if he was nothing else, he was good at games.

And what was love, after all, but another game of chance? He was sure she would come back to the house, prepared to make the ultimate sacrifice to conclude her business with Nathan Wardale. But when the door was closed and the lights were out, it would be a different matter entirely.

She had loved him before this morning. And if he had lured her to his rooms two days ago, and asked as Nathan Dale for what she was now willing to barter, she would have given it willingly. If she had the nerve to return to him, he would make her face the fact that she wanted him in the same way that he did her. He would give her the sort of night that any man would be proud to offer the woman he loved. And then, he would see if she was so willing to leave him.

Chapter Fifteen

How could she have been so stupid?

The words echoed endlessly in her mind as Diana sat with Verity and Honoria in the white salon, mechanically jabbing the needle in and out of her embroidery. Had not her father warned her against just such a day as this? Had not she spent the whole of her adult life on guard, always suspecting that someday there would be a knock on the door and a man would come who would know far too much about her past?

Of course, Nathan Dale had not come as a seducer. He had come to speak to Marc and seemed surprised to meet her there. But his initial curiosity should have been a warning. Who would have reason to be interested in a paid companion? It was her own vanity that had led her to believe he fancied her. Nothing more than that.

Of course, her father's description had been totally different from the man who had come to her. He had described Wardale as little better than a boy. Pale of skin, thin of body, and with cold dead eyes. And having met Nell, she'd assumed a greater family resemblance between them than existed.

If Nathan Wardale's life had been as hard as the one that Nathan Dale had described to her, then the person her father had seen was but a shadow of the man to come. Whether he'd enjoyed it or not, life at sea had put muscle on him, changed his colouring and his gait. And hardship had made him serious, and sensitive to the feelings of others.

But those thoughts sounded almost like sympathy in her mind, so she pushed them away. His appearance did not matter, nor his reason for coming. He was still the person who was responsible for her current condition, and she had hated him for years.

Her inner turmoil must be reflected in her face. Verity had put down her work and was looking at her with concern. 'Are you sure you are all right, Diana?'

'I am fine.' Her voice sounded brittle in her own ears, and her smile must look as false as it felt. For now Honoria was staring at her with the same worried expression. 'Well you certainly do not look it. Perhaps this evening, it would be better if we attended the party without you.'

The party. She had forgotten, in her rash promise to Nathan Wardale, that she was already engaged to attend the Carlow girls at a musicale. And now, she must lie to free herself. 'I think you are right. It is probably just the beginnings of a megrim. I should make an early night of it. But that would leave you without a chaperone. And I would never…' She let the thought trail away, waiting for one of the girls to take the bait.

'We will be safe in the company of Lord Keddinton, I am sure,' said Honoria. 'And I promise there will be no ill reports of me tonight, for it would hardly be fair to worry you.'

Verity nodded. 'We will give you no trouble, and will be very quiet when we return, so as not to disturb your sleep.'

Or notice her absence, if she had not yet returned herself. 'Thank you,' Diana said with a smile, ignoring the pang of guilt she felt at how easy it was becoming to deceive her friends.

It was Nathan Wardale's doing. All of it. Until he had appeared in her life, she had worked so hard to resist temptation. But a few short weeks later, she was lying, stealing, and preparing to sneak away from the house, coldly contemplating the loss of her virtue to a man she detested. How many other sins would she commit before he was through with her? And did uncontrollable anger count against the total of them?

For she felt angry now. She had never been so angry in her life. Not even when father had lost their house, and sat her down with the tearful explanation of why they must go so quickly. And why she must, at all costs, avoid contact with a man named Wardale.

When that had happened, she'd felt shock. And fear. And for a time, she had been upset with her father. But it had been tempered with love and forgiveness. For what good did it do her to be angry with Father, when his behaviour never changed? She had learned to put anger aside as impractical.

But now? There was no sympathy in her heart for either of the men that had brought her to this. Had she meant so little to Father that he could not put down the cards? And that he would lose her to Nathan Wardale, of all the people in the world. He had become a man she could have loved and respected, had the past been different. Had it not been enough for him to know that he owned her body? Had it been necessary to win her heart as well?

Her response to him was infuriating. She had melted under his kisses and longed for the touch of his hand. Even this morning, when she was furious with him, he had managed to turn the heat in her brain to passion. It was like a red light, burning in her mind, obscuring rationality and smothering the calm and reasoned response she would have encouraged for anyone else. She wanted to hurt him. She wanted him to suffer as she was suffering.

And it was in her power to do so. The red light faded, and in its wake there was a horrible calm, as she saw the weapon of torture, plainly in her grasp.

She knew the location of Helena Wardale.

Had she mentioned the woman's name to him at all in their discussions? Obviously not, or he would have commented on it. If he had even suspected, he would have inquired in an offhand manner, about the birth name of Marc's bride. She had seen the hungry look in his eye as he had told her about his family. If he'd known how close he was to the solution, he'd have dropped his charade and begged her for the truth. He'd have done anything to know, just as he would make her debase herself for her freedom tonight.

But now? She would use his only weakness to her advantage.

She waited until the girls had gone away with Lord Keddinton, accepting their concern with a wan thank you, and a promise to rest well in their absence.

And as soon as the door latched behind them, she went swiftly to her room. She threw aside the dress she had worn as simple Diana Price, lady's companion, and pulled out the green silk gown she had bought with the money he had given her. Blood money, meant to salve his conscience.

She fastened herself into the dress and turned to admire it in the mirror. It was indecently low and the deep green of his eyes. Her breasts all but spilled out of the bodice, creamy white and beautiful. He would want to touch those breasts, she was sure, and felt a shiver run through her. She went to work on her hair, loosening the pins and freeing braids until the curls seemed ready to fall about her shoulders at the least urging. Another way to trap him, if his talk in the park was true.

She had always imagined herself, should she be forced, going to Nathan Wardale as a virgin sacrifice. But now? She would go as a conqueror. When he tried to take her, she would take from him as well. She would tempt him with her body.

When he thought his moment of triumph was near, she would ask him what lengths he was willing to go to, to regain his sister.

And then they would see who was master. And who was slave.

Her preparations complete, she pulled on her cloak and crept down the backstairs and out onto the street to hail a cab. Once under way, she settled back into the squabs, revelling in the cruelty of it. How best to hurt him? If she attacked immediately, the shock might prevent the rest of his plans for her. If she offered to trade the information for the marker, she was sure that he would cave to the demand.

Or she could savour the moment, letting him think he was controlling her, all the while knowing that she held the true power. Perhaps she would never reveal the secret at all. She could tell him that she knew, but that he never would. Give hints of the truth, but no more.

She would let him suffer as she had, balanced on the knife's edge for years, never knowing when or if the revelation would occur. Withholding of good news would be as bad as the suspending of catastrophe.

The hired cab pulled up in front of the building that had once been her home. She wrapped the cloak tight about her body, pulling the hood up to obscure her face from the driver, signalled him to wait, stepped down into the street, then hurried up to the front door. Benton answered to her knock. He was the same as she remembered from childhood. He had been unable to contain his joyful, 'Miss Diana!' when he'd opened the door for her earlier in the day, as though her anger with him and Wardale could not extinguish his happiness at seeing her well.

Tonight, she said, 'I am expected.' And he answered with a dispassionate nod.

She gave him no other explanation, but he must have guessed what was about to happen. The shame of it took her in a wave, for it was as though her own father had survived to see her disgrace. He reached for her cloak, but she pulled away from him, as though even the slightest touch were an invasion.

Benton cringed at this, and his hands dropped to his sides. Then he muttered that he would get his master, and led her to the sitting room, closing the door against prying eyes.

The house seemed strangely quiet, for other than the butler, there was not a footman in sight, nor maids, nor any other sign of a servant. But it only took one set of eyes to see her enter the house. It would not be possible to keep the secret, once it got below stairs. How many people would know of her fall, by the end of this night? Could she ever go back to what she once was, after stepping across this particular threshold of her life?

Not possible. Less than a week ago, she had been a woman in love. That feeling seemed a distant memory, compared to the loathing she felt for the man now.

And the house gave her muddled emotions a nightmare quality. Everywhere she looked was familiarity. She knew the rooms as well as she knew her own hand. But it was all wrong. Here was the little marble-topped table she had played under as a girl. But that had been in the upper hall. How had it come here? Where was the chiming clock that had been upon the mantel? The bowl of fresh flowers that stood there now was quite attractive, but shouldn't it be in the foyer?

It was as though her childhood had been altered with time, as the tide might change the sand on the beach. It was wrong, all of it, and nothing like what she had pictured on the few times she had imagined returning here in triumph to oust the usurper.

It was not *her* parlour. But it was a lovely room,

all the same. Under different circumstances, she might have found it comfortable, and the fire in the grate and the flowers above it would have seemed more welcoming than the cold ticking of a clock. She frowned. She had expected to feel more, somehow. Happy, or sad or more likely, filled with righteous anger at the man who had taken her home and worked to wipe the traces of her from it.

Instead, it was as though some portion of her anger was wiped away with the change. This was not her home any more. Even if she returned, a simple rearrangement of the furniture could not bring back the past. Nor could it change any of what had occurred.

The door opened, and Nathan Wardale entered, unannounced. He smiled at her, as though nothing had changed between them. 'Welcome, Diana.' He held out a hand. 'Benton did not help you with your cloak? Here, allow me. And then perhaps, a glass of wine?'

Rage simmered fresh within her. How dare he pretend that this was a normal visit, or that she wished his hospitality? 'Wine will not be necessary. Let us complete our business,' she said through gritted teeth. 'My cab is waiting, and I wish to return home before ten.'

'You told the driver to remain?' He gave her an odd look and then a pitying smile. 'I will go and send him away again. I would send a servant, but I have dismissed most of them for the evening. I assumed that you would prefer it.'

'The evening?' The insolence of the man was astounding. 'You misunderstand the amount of time I will devote to this enterprise.'

'And you misunderstand the amount of time it will take.' There was the smile, again. 'It is obvious that you have managed to retain the loan's collateral, for you are quite naïve. You must allow that I am more experienced in the events that will transpire tonight, and permit me to set the timetable.'

Before she could speak, he stepped out of the room, closing the door behind him. She drew back the curtain and glanced out of the front window to see him offering a bank note to the driver before waving the man off. The view of the street was just as she remembered. But the red silk that framed it was nothing like the green she had been expecting. She closed her eyes against the dissonance, and tried to decide whether his high-handed behaviour made her angrier or just nervous. It definitely added to the sense of disquiet she felt, as she waited for him to return to the sitting room.

It had been easy to plot against him, when not staring into those deep green eyes. And so easy to forget that the man was a master gamesman, adept at disguising his true feelings while parting others from their valuables. She needed to be on her guard. For if she began to think of him as legitimate master of this house, what right had she to be angry?

When he returned, he was smiling again, as though he found her impending downfall to be faintly amusing. 'On this night, of all nights, you wanted to hold the cab, as though you were running an errand. I am curious. Just how long do you expect this to take?'

She wondered if the question was an attempt to draw out the action, or did it have some logical purpose? But then, she'd wondered the same about all his other questions, since the day they'd met. 'The minimum amount of time necessary. It has taken ten years of my life already. I do not wish to spend a moment longer than I must.'

She had meant the words to sting, but if they did, it did not show on his face. Instead, he shrugged. 'It will take as long as it takes. Not so fast as you might like. Nor as long as I would wish. If I were ham-fisted, selfish or cruel, I could have had you back in your waiting cab before now. We could conclude our business here, on the rug or against a wall, without even bothering to undress.'

He looked at her again and his gaze grew as soft and warm as it had been on their walks together in the park. And for a moment she weakened, wishing the man in front of her could ever again be Nathan Dale. Then he said, 'I have heard tales of Sultans in seraglios, taking days, even weeks over this process. The slow baring of the flesh, the destruction of inhibition, the readying of the minds and bodies of both participants, the evoking and sharpening of each sense to appreciate the final consummation. It is not a thing to be rushed.'

The timbre of his voice dropped, and his pace slowed to linger on each word, each image forming in his mind. Was it her imagination, or could she smell incense, hear the exotic music and taste dates on her tongue? She could see herself lying back in silk cushions, the height of decadence as he bent over her, caressing and perfuming her skin.

She caught her breath, trying to find her anger again, for the image had been strangely pleasant.

She saw his half smile change again, as though he knew what she had imagined and it pleased him. 'I will have you home by dawn. Not too late to save your reputation, if you have managed to conceal your absence.' He paused again. And then said, 'If you still wish to go through with this, that is. I have no intention of forcing you to do something you find abhorrent.' He paused once more time. 'It is not too late to change your mind.'

'No. I am resolute.' But her voice did not sound that way in her own ears. He had given her the chance to get away. Why did she not take it and run? Or take it as her moment of victory. She had but to say the words, 'Touch me and you will never see Helena,' and the evening would be at an end.

But when she should have spoken, her traitorous mind had been wondering how the impending process could possibly take weeks. She had missed her opportunity.

Perhaps time was an illusion. Because he was progressing so methodically that each thought, each smile, each word from his mouth, seemed to take hours to reach her. Several more heartbeats passed before he said, 'Very well. Then let us begin.' He touched her shoulders with his hands, brushing the cloak out of the way, and draping it gently over a chair. When he turned and caught sight of her dress, he froze in place for a moment, and she could feel his eyes travelling over her body, lingering on the exposed flesh.

She waited for the pounce. The rough grasp and the shock of his ravenous mouth against her breast.

'So beautiful. But too much, too soon,' he whispered. 'You are like a feast, and I am a starving man. You come to me like this, knowing that, other than by accident, on the very first day, I have not felt the touch of your ungloved hand?' He reached for her again with tenderness, beginning at the shoulders and letting his fingers trail down until they barely touched her own, and then he took both her hands, and brought them to his lips in a gesture that was more reverence than kiss. Then, one at a time, he tugged gently at her fingers until he had pulled her long white gloves down, baring the flesh of her arms inch by sensitive inch. The gloves dropped to the floor and he brought her hands to his face again, rubbing them with his closed lips, binding them together with his fingers about her wrists as he kissed the palms, turning them so that they were cupped before him and he could taste each fingertip in turn before settling over her pulse point, his tongue flicking against the skin in time to the ebb and flow of her blood.

From somewhere deep within her, there came an unexpected shudder of delight.

He smiled. 'This is why it must not be too quick. We must not squander this night. Do you understand?' He held her by the fingertips, walking backward, leading her through the door and toward the stairs. 'I have so much to learn.' He never took his eyes from hers as he went, drawing her after him, up the stairs and down the hall, to the master suite.

She went with him, powerless to resist, as though the kisses on her hands had bound her to him more tightly than any shackles. She glanced about her as they walked, and saw that, in ten years, the decoration of the corridor had changed. Colours, furnishings, the hangings on the walls, all different or rearranged. It was a different house than the one she had left, just as she was a different person.

And Nathan Wardale was a different man from the one she expected to find here.

No. The same. He was the same man that had ruined her father, and she must not forget it. Nathan Dale's stories of hardship and loss meant nothing to her. They were not justification for what he had done to her. Other men had suffered, yet they did not buy and sell innocent girls over a gaming table.

And yet, he continued to stare at her in wonder, as though none of that had happened. He looked as she imagined a man in love might look, as though no past or future existed outside of his lover's arms.

They had crossed the threshold to his room, and he released her, closing the door to shut them away from the rest of the world. And for a moment, she wanted to reach out to him, to cling for support. Or run away. The world had gone mad and would take her with it if she thought too closely about what was happening to her. Then he came back to stand very near to her, and he kissed her on the back of the neck as he had in the park. It was sweet and soft, not like she had imagined the kisses of her despoiler to be. 'I wish to touch your hair.' There was a faintly wistful quality in his voice, as though he thought she could deny him.

She moved to the mirror above the tall dresser and pulled the remaining pins from her hair, ready to shake it free. And then she caught sight of him, watching as though mesmerized by the sight. She basked in the warmth of it, for his gaze was as gentle as the touch of his hands had been, when bringing her here. Though his words had been seductive, everything about his actions calculated to reassure and not threaten, to coax the responses from her gradually. Her anger faded as she watched him, and he felt it go. And then he paused to look into her eyes, and breathed, 'Let us undress.'

The anger came flooding back, and anxiety along with it. She did not see the note that she had come to retrieve. And how much longer did she wish to play this game, before bringing it to an end? Shedding a few hairpins and a pair of gloves did little damage to her honour. But she could not very well strip to her chemise before springing her trap. Or perhaps she could. For it was difficult to see the man standing so reverently in front of her as a true adversary. She took a moment to gather her courage, and reached to undo one of the tiny hooks at her back.

He shook his head. 'Let us undress each other.' And he caught one of her hands in his, rubbed the knuckles across his lips until he felt her fingers begin to relax, and then placed them on the end of his cravat.

She paused for a moment, unsure, still waiting for the move on his part that would give her reason to strike back. And then she took hold and gave a gentle tug, watching as the elegant knot dissolved into a wrinkled strip of linen and dropped to the floor.

His neck was bare. It had never occurred to her to look at a man's throat before. She was so used to seeing them covered. She reached up and touched him. He was soft and smooth, close shaven though it was late in the day. Perhaps he had done it for her. And without thinking, she undid the neck of his shirt and let her fingers linger in the hollow of his throat.

His eyes closed as though he were sleeping and lost in some very pleasant dream. And then, he leaned forward and kissed her again, one hand cupping the back of her neck. He was bolder this time, opening her mouth and letting her feel his hunger as he slowly licked into her and drew her tongue into his mouth. She should not enjoy this. And yet she did. Her hand still rested against his throat, and she could feel the way his pulse increased as he grew more passionate. He pulled away, to kiss the hollow of her throat, bending her back to lay his cheek against her exposed chest and press his lips to the upper slopes of her breasts. As a counterpoint to the dizzying feel of the contact, she felt the barest touch of fingertips at her back. And when he withdrew, her dress was open and loose against her body, the sleeves slipping off her shoulders.

He touched her face, then, placing his fingers under her chin and tipping her lips up to touch his. And he whispered, 'You are beautiful tonight. Even more beautiful under the silk you wear. And I swear by all that is holy that if you give yourself to me, you will not regret it.' He kissed her again, pressing his lips to her cheek, her hair and her neck, and wrapping his arms around her body.

He was warm, and it took away the chill on her back, so she nestled close to him, putting her arms around his waist under his coat. After a time, he whispered, 'Would you help me off with my coat, please?'

It was not such a hard thing to run her hands up his body until they reached his shoulders and to push the wool away from him. The coat fell to the floor. She glanced down at it, ready to bend and pick it up, for it would become wrinkled if they left it in a heap.

But he sighed, 'Unimportant,' against the shell of her ear.

And when he used that tone, it did seem so. He was making her feel as if she was the thing most important to him in the world. She laid her head on his shoulder, and felt how different it was. Now that the coat was gone, she could feel more of the man and less of the tailor. And she felt a strange stirring, as the outlines of his body were uncovered to her.

His hand was on her back, fingers spread to span it, and he rubbed gently, his other hand stroking her neck and her hair. And the buttons of his waistcoat were poking against her chest, so she undid them, one by one, and pushed it out of the way.

His breathing quickened and he kissed her again, running his tongue along the seam in her lips until she opened them again. The taste of him amazed her. It was wine and spice, and she could not seem to get enough of it. When she stopped for breath, she found that they had pushed her gown out of the way, until it hung from her body at the hip, and his waistcoat had followed his coat to the floor.

He looked down, and gave a shaky laugh. 'My valet will be appalled.'

'Oh, dear.' She looked in the direction of the changing room.

He gathered her to him again. 'I am teasing. Do not think of it. We are alone, remember? All alone.' He put his hands on her hips and pushed her dress the rest of the way off her body. 'No one will see. No one will hear. And not a word shall pass from my lips over this.' Then he reached around her and undid the knot of her stays.

She had a moment's fleeting longing for his first suggestion, that they do it quickly without bothering to remove their clothing. It was all getting out of hand, and her thoughts swirled into focus and away again. She would put an end to this. She would stop him, soon. Another minute. Perhaps two. But it felt so wonderful as he worked slowly to lay her bare. And to put her hand on his shoulder and feel muscle through the linen of his shirt was as exciting as feeling his fingers on the small of her back, with a bit of cotton lawn as the only protection. Without thinking, her hand moved on his body, and she could feel the softness of hair, the smoothness of skin and the hard flat nipples on his chest, resting just below her fingertips beneath the fabric.

He smiled at her, and then closed his eyes and sighed. 'Your touch is so gentle. I am not accustomed to gentleness.'

She wondered if he meant that he wished her to be more bold. She surprised herself, for even caring what he wished. There was nothing in their agreement that required her to act, only to submit.

He opened his eyes again. 'Touch me as you wish to be touched, so that I may know what gives you pleasure.' And he mirrored the position of her hands on his body, placing his fingertips against her nipples, but making no effort to do more.

It was maddening. The skin beneath his hands tingled in expectation of his movement, and her nipples peaked as though her body could imagine the brush of his fingers and the increasing roughness of his touch.

His face relaxed into a lazy, seductive smile, and he leaned forward to kiss her, catching her lower lip with his teeth and sucking gently upon it.

Her breast ached in answer to each tug upon her lips, and she moved her hands experimentally over his chest, rubbing her thumbs against him.

In answer, he moved his hands on her, and kissed her again, his tongue tracing designs upon her lips.

Desire stirred within her. That was what she wanted. To feel him touching her, possessing her. She circled, rubbed, palmed and pinched. And he did the same. She pulled away from his kiss and buried her face in his shirt. She pressed her lips to him, licking softly against the linen until it grew wet and clung to his skin. She bit at him, sucking hard, doing her best to draw the little bud into her mouth.

He took a deep breath, and she could hear his heart, so near to her ear, beating faster. His hands on her breasts grew more forceful, tormenting her body as she did his. Then he took them away, and cupped her face, pulling it up to his mouth, and kissing her with the same demanding strength, pushing his tongue into her mouth, thrusting until she could feel the penetration deep within her body. He trailed down her throat, marking her flesh with the force of his kisses until he settled over her breast. He paused for a moment, letting his breath warm her, then took the cloth-covered nipple into his mouth. The sensations grew in her, and she dug her fingers into the muscles of his shoulders, as though she feared that the force of her feelings would rip her away from his body.

When it seemed all but unbearable, he released her and began again on her other breast. She gave a tiny laugh of relief, for she had forgotten that there was still more to feel. The same feeling of expectation was building, compounded with the excited nerves that he had left behind.

And the sudden knowledge that he could begin it all again, on naked skin, with no chemise as obstacle.

In response to her grip on his shoulders, his fingers dug into the flesh at the side of her waist, pushing her petticoat down and pulling her hips tight to his. And she remembered that what they were doing was nothing compared to what they would do.

Then the sensation broke over her, and she was gasping for control, her body shuddering, her muscles clenching as though they wished to hang on to the feeling, to take it inside and keep it forever. Nathan gave another pull upon her breast, as though he knew how to prolong her reaction, until she had experienced the last drop of the pleasure, before letting it slowly fade, leaving her weak and in his power. When she could manage to speak, she whispered, 'What is happening to me?'

He lifted his head and smiled up at her. 'Nothing that should not happen. And nothing that will not happen again. It is the reason that I did not think it necessary to retain the coachman. I had no wish for a few minutes alone with you, while I took without giving.' He dropped to his knees in front of her, letting his hands trail down her body until they touched her ankles. And then they progressed slowly back up her leg, touching her stockings until they reached the top. 'I recognize the sacrifice you make by doing this, and I mean to be worthy of it.'

His fingers were undoing her garters, and occasionally, some part of his hand would brush the bare flesh of her leg. Each time, she felt a fresh shudder go through her, as though her body remembered the release she had experienced as he'd kissed her breasts. But now, his face was settled between her legs, and she could feel the heat of his breath, pooling there, stroking her as gently as his hands were touching her legs. He drew each stocking down to her ankle, with long smooth caresses. And then he lifted each foot to remove slipper and stocking, and as she offbalanced, her body pressed close to his face for a fleeting kiss through the lawn of her shift.

The trembling within her was almost continual now, a strange fluttering that was a precursor to her body's surrender. Before he could kiss her again, she reached for the linen of his shirt and pulled it over his head, distracting him and leaving his chest bare for her admiration. He was still kneeling before her. And for a moment, she imagined him helpless before her, as though she were in the seraglio he had described and he existed only for her pleasure. Experimentally, she lifted her bare foot and ran it up the inner seam of his trousers, feeling the muscle of his thigh jump at her touch. He cupped her ankle and drew her leg higher, until her knee rested against his chest and her foot at the apex of his legs.

He stroked her instep, making her laugh, letting her foot struggle to escape the tickling. She nuzzled it against his body, stroking it against his member. Feeling him grow as she touched him, and watching his face contort with the strain of control. He positioned her against him, holding her there, showering her knee with kisses, his breath coming as a moan of desire against her skin.

Suddenly, he pushed her leg down and rose. He bent and caught her easily behind the knees, scooping her up into his arms and striding across the room to the bed, tossing her in a heap onto the pillows piled there. The skirt of her chemise rode high on her legs, and he stared down at her—thighs sprawled open, breasts straining against the damp fabric. In a scant hour with the man, she had become a wanton.

And she enjoyed it. He was staring at her body. She reached for the hem of her shift to pull it higher in invitation.

He held out a hand to stop her, then leaned against the bedpost, pulling off boots and stockings, and reaching for the buttons on his trousers. 'Do you understand what you are doing to me, Miss Price? A little more play, and I will spill my seed without ever touching you. And we shall have to begin, all over again.'

Her body gave an answering shudder, welcoming an idea that would have been abhorrent to her this morning.

He was naked before her now, fully aroused. He knelt upon the bed, between her legs as she pulled the last garment over her head, casting it aside and settling back into the pillows to await what she knew must come.

But instead, he covered her with his body, kissing her mouth, her eyes, her chin, and then slowly down, lingering over her breasts until she was nearly mad with desire, and then moving lower, to kiss between her legs, massaging her thighs with his palms, opening her with his tongue until she had no defences left and her body was wracked with wave upon wave of ecstasy, desperate to be filled.

And after he had claimed her with his mouth, he took her, when she was too lost with need to feel the pain, plunging over and over, while she shook with joy, tightening against him, welcoming him in. He shook as well and moaned her name. And then his body went still against hers.

He pulled her close, and rolled to the side, never leaving her, caressing her back and kissing her face as they lay nestled in the pillows on his bed. He reached to draw a counterpane over them, and whispered, 'My love.'

And from there, it was too easy, just to fall asleep in his arms.

Chapter Sixteen

Where were her gloves?

On the floor, where he had dropped them? She fumbled over the carpet of the darkened sitting room. The candles had burned away and the fire as well, leaving her cold in the predawn light.

'Are you all right, Miss Diana?'

She started, instinctively reaching to straighten her hair, her dress, anything…her hands fluttering over her body as uncontrolled as birds, desperate to assure herself that nothing on the exterior had changed and that the letter of debt was still secure in her pocket, where she had tucked it before creeping from the bedroom to find her cloak.

The voice had come from behind her, in the hall. The butler, again. If he did not guess the purpose of her visit when she arrived, he could have no doubt now.

She turned to him, trying to smile, pretending a composure that was not possible. 'All right? Of course, Benton. I am fine.'

He continued to stare at her, without judgment or disapproval, but with an unusual amount of concern. 'Are you sure, Miss Diana?' A cloud passed over the old man's face. 'He did not hurt you?'

And suddenly, she was sure that she had but to raise her voice in alarm and Nathan would be dragged from his bed and beaten bloody by his own servants.

She gave the man another false smile. 'Hurt me? Of course not, Benton. You have nothing to fear on my account. But if you wish, you may help me find a carriage. I would like to return to Lord Narborough's town house. Discreetly, if possible.'

'Very good, miss. Mr Wardale's carriage is at your disposal. I will see to it at once. And the other glove is under the side table. Allow me.'

He retrieved the thing for her, escorted her to the front door and stepped outside to arrange for her transport.

Once inside the carriage, she collapsed on the seat, her legs weak with relief. She was glad that her father had not lived to see this day: his only daughter turned whore to the man who ruined him. But there was some comfort in the remaining loyalty and discretion of the servants. She could see by the look in Benton's eye that he liked this no better than she did, and his sympathy did not lie with his new master.

Nathan Wardale was still asleep in his bed, with no idea that one of his sisters was alive and well. She had told him nothing, not even the evil hint meant to torment him. Just a few hours ago, she was taking great satisfaction in the fact that she controlled the degree of his suffering. But now, she had become equally to blame for anything that had happened between them. She could pretend that it had been forced upon her by a wicked man who deserved whatever misery she could provide. The first time, perhaps.

But what had happened, after…

She felt her legs go weak again. Without parting, they had dozed together for a short time. And she had awakened, restless, all thoughts of vengeance gone. She had pushed at his shoulder, playfully, and then rolled so that he was beneath her. She had kissed his lips, wrapped her legs around his body, and thrust her hips into his.

He'd returned her kiss. But he made no effort to hold her, although she could feel him growing hard inside her, again. So she'd sat up, straddling him. She'd rocked against him, and he'd bent his knees behind her, supporting her back, then lain back in the pillows and watched her give in to the needs of her own body. He'd guided her fingers, encouraging her to touch herself until she was a slave to the sensation. And then she had ridden him wildly, for her own pleasure. After wave upon wave of ecstasy, she'd clenched her thighs on his body until he'd responded with short, hard thrusts, smiling as he drove himself to exhaustion.

It had made her feel powerful, to watch him fall asleep beneath her, strong in a way that had nothing to do with vengeance. If this had been a battle, she had emerged victorious. He was conquered. And if she wished, she could celebrate the victory by having him again.

And then the doubts had begun to creep back in. When she was sure that he would not awaken, she had climbed carefully out of the bed, dressed as though nothing had changed, and taken the IOU. It was at the bedside, just as he had promised. She had closed the door as quietly as she could and started down the stairs.

And begun to fall apart. Benton was helpful. The carriage driver was polite and the trip short.

She had crept back in the Carlow town house, successfully avoiding both servants and family. And now, she was on her way to her room. It was so late as to be almost dawn. She could lie down for a few moments. At least she would stay long enough to muss the bedclothes, so there would be no question of where she had spent the night. And then she would rise, wash, and go about her life as though nothing had happened.

But first, she would throw the accursed, life-changing piece of paper into the fireplace and watch it burn. She would poke it until there was nothing left but ashes, and then she would poke the ashes until they were dust.

And finally, she would be free.

She closed the door behind her, then took the paper out of her pocket, staring at the shaky writing of her desperate father. And she knew that she could no more throw it away than Nathan had. It held no power over her. Perhaps it never had. It was a nothing, a jot, a scrap. It was not a true debt of honour; there had been no honour in the giving of it, or the taking.

It was a strange, sad reminder of the night when everything had changed. That was why Nathan had kept it, she was sure. Not as a threat, nor a punishment. And never meaning to find her and call it in. He had kept it because he did not wish to forget what had happened, for he did not wish to repeat his mistake.

It was her own imagination that had turned the paper into a nightmare and turned the man that held it into a monster.

She turned it over in her hands, folding it along the old creases. Now, it was she who did not wish to forget. This paper had brought her to Nathan Wardale. To his life—and his bed. It would be eminently foolish to go back, now that she had left him, to devote herself to an unrepentant gambler who was no better than her father. But she did not wish to forget her time with him, nor to repeat the mistake of falling in love with a man so utterly inappropriate.

She took a deep breath, remembering the rush of panic followed by desire, and the deep satisfaction of the previous hours. And the cherished way she had felt when he'd held her afterwards, staring into her eyes. While it had been terrifying, it had been sweet as well. How nice it would be, to have a life full of moments like that.

But more likely, if she returned to Nathan Wardale, her life would be full of lonely nights, squalling children and an angry and distant husband who cared more for cards than he did for her. She remembered what it had been like for her mother when her father would not leave the tables, and how she had cried when she thought no one would hear. Nathan's luck was bound to change eventually. And then there would be debts, the men who collected them and eventual ruin. Unless she was prepared to see another paper such as this, to be sold when her husband treated her as chattel or to see a daughter similarly treated, she could not go back to him. She need only look at the paper to know why she could never return.

She would put it away somewhere. In the wardrobe with the bank notes. Or perhaps she could tuck it between the pages of a book and it could lie forgotten.

There, on the bedside table, was the little book of poetry. And she did not need to open it again to realize where it had come from or to know that the ribbon that marked it was her own. He had taken it from her old bedroom and given it back to her. Without thinking, she had taken the thing up and begun reading where she had left off, all those years ago.

He had been trying to tell her the truth. Before the note, before she had sought the journal for him. Even before the first kiss. He had been seeking a way to tell her, as gently as possible, who he was and that she need have no fear. And she had been so set on who she wished him to be that she did not see what was before her very eyes.

God help her, even if she could not forgive him for what had happened before, he deserved some small credit for trying to find a way to be kind. He had earned a measure of kindness from her in return. It was in her power to end some portion of his suffering, and Nell's as well. But she had kept it from him.

It made her ashamed. Whatever might happen in the future, no good could come of keeping grudges or offering punishments for ancient mistakes. When Marc brought Nell home from Northumberland, she would find a way to tell her enough of the truth so that she could find her brother again. Diana need never see the man again, of course. That would be too painful for so many reasons. But whatever he had become, he and his sister had suffered in ignorance of each other for long enough. She would not be the one to keep them apart. It was the very least she could do, if she wished to clear her slate with Nathan Wardale.

So she tucked the note into the book, along with what was left of the money, and tied the whole thing shut with the ribbon, as though it were possible to close off this chapter of her life, perhaps to open it again on a day when the whole story was not so fresh and painful.

Nate started awake, as though the awareness of a lack was sufficient to disturb him. He had meant to close his eyes for no more than a minute. But he had slept soundly, and now she was gone from his bed. He felt the sheets next to him, trying to decide if they were still warm from the body that had lain beside him. The letter was gone from the dressing table. Damn the thing to hell for all the trouble it had caused him.

There was a noise in the hall, and he jumped out of bed and threw open the door, eager to catch her before she got to the front door. 'Diana, wait…'

The startled maid screamed at the sight of him standing naked in the hallway.

He stepped back and slammed the door again, muttering an apology to the girl through the oak panel. Then he requested, as calmly as possible, that Benton be sent to his rooms immediately. Embarrassed by his own behaviour, Nate returned to the bed, wrapped himself in a sheet and rang for his valet as well.

Did she not see, after what they had done together, that this was about more than a few words scrawled by her father years before they met? He had done everything in his power to show her, to love her with his body and prove that his words were not lies.

Yet, she had ignored it and left him. And he felt more desolate than he did after a night at the tables, as though there was nothing and no one in the world to erase the loneliness.

As the valet dressed him, Benton explained that Miss Price had left before dawn and in rather a hurry. She had requested that he bring the carriage around for her. She had insisted that she was fine and that there was nothing to be concerned about.

Of course she would. She was always insisting that she was fine, needed nothing, and was perfectly happy. She needed no one. And she did it so convincingly, so placidly, and with not a drop of excess emotion that it took a professional gambler to see she was bluffing.

The old butler said it all with a distinct air of disapproval. As though it were not clear enough that he found his master's actions towards the young lady near to reprehensible.

As did Nathan. Damn his own pride for thinking that his skill as a lover would have been enough to hold her. She had made it plain that she detested him and would never forgive what he had done. He must be as base as she thought, if he assumed that she would throw over her deeply held beliefs after a few hours in bed with him.

And damn again to his promise that he would not seek her out once she left. If he had the honour he claimed, he could not go back on his word. Better to have begged forgiveness at the start. He should have gotten down on his knees before her and pled for another chance. It would have been easy enough. For when he had seen her, resplendent in a pool of green silk, her mouth the same Cupid's bow, and her eyes wide and innocent, he had been a willing supplicant. And then, she had toyed with him…

Was she an angel or a tormenter? It did not matter. She was perfection. He never should have let her escape.

As if to reinforce the opinion, his valet tugged so tightly upon his cravat that he was near to choking before the tying was through. It was hardly fair, for the man had not even been a servant of the Price household. He had arrived here along with Nate. But it was clear that he'd chosen to add to the silent chorus of contempt that had been building in this house since the day he'd met Diana Price.

All the more galling that he deserved what he got from them. Every arch look, every small shake of the head. Every indictment of his character. Every sniff of disapproval. They took his money easily enough, when it was time to collect their salaries. And he continued to play, telling himself that they depended on his gambling to pay their keep. It was his responsibility to continue.

But how much did he need, really? It had been almost honourable, when he'd had a mother and sisters to protect, however best he could. But once they were lost? He'd gathered enough winnings to support himself in luxury for the rest of his life. Gaming had become nothing more than a way to pass the time until the moment when some loser at the table decided to put a ball through him.

No more. Perhaps he could not stop going to the tables. For without Diana, what more was there left in his life? But he could stop keeping score. He glanced at the box on the dresser, full of signets, fobs, and bits and pieces of the lives of others. Each one a memory of a life he had changed.

And none of it all his fault. He had played and won, of course. But they had played as well, knowing that losing was all but inevitable. Did they not deserve some responsibility for their actions? If it was not his fault, then why did he keep the things? What earthly good did it do him to hang on to trinkets that meant nothing to him? *And the damned letter.* If he had refused it, or given it back? Then he would not be in the mess he was now.

He might never have met Diana.

But perhaps that was a good thing. For neither would he have lost her over nonsense. He was tired of being the sin eater for half of London. 'Benton, bring me paper. And string. Some small boxes, perhaps. I wish to post some packages.'

He gathered up the box and sat down at the writing desk in his room. It was not hard to remember the owners of the things. In many cases, the names were engraved on the items. But the loss of each was firmly engrained on his memory. Here were the diamond studs of a duke, who had sworn he would shoot himself over the loss. And the ruby necklace of the marchioness. She had thought to bargain her favours for another hand, and had stamped her feet and pouted when he'd demanded the necklace instead.

And now, she could have it back. They could

all take the bloody things back. He cared little whether it might be blessing or curse to receive them, so long as he need never see any of it again. His heart felt lighter after each package. And when the box was empty, there was but one thing left.

He looked up at the butler and grinned. 'Benton. Go to the safe in my study. Bring me the deed to this house.'

The butler looked rather alarmed at the prospect, but did as he was told. When he had returned with the paper, Nate signed it over, with a flourish—to Miss Diana Price. Then he folded it carefully, sealed it, addressed it to the Carlow house, and put it in the stack with the rest, ready for the morning post.

Chapter Seventeen

The few hours of sleep that Diana managed to steal had done nothing to refresh her. The girls must have been out almost as late as she, for when she rose at nine she did not hear them stirring. It was a comfort, for it gave her some small time to prepare for the day, to wipe any traces of the night's activity from her mind. She looked into the mirror, smoothing her expression and her clothing, jabbing the pins into her hair until it was tight and smooth, with not a strand out of place. When she was through, she was sure that there was not a hint of awareness to give her away to the girls as anything less than the same proper, controlled woman who had watched over them for years.

As she pushed the last pin in place, there was a sharp rap upon her door. It was Peters the footman, coming to tell her that Lord Stanegate wished her presence in the study, immediately.

Marcus, here? Had he arrived while she slept, or had he come in the night, before she had crept into the house? She should have recognized that returning to the house without incident was almost too fortunate. Her luck could not hold forever. It now appeared that she would face an interview with her employer's son, on this of all days, when she needed just a few more hours to understand the changes in her life.

When she came down to the ground floor, the house was abustle with the sudden arrival, as though the staff feared that their exemplary housekeeping was somehow at fault. They were behaving as if to placate a man in a temper.

She'd have understood it in another house. But here it was most unusual. And that the person who had frightened them into the boughs was Marc Carlow made the situation even more unusual. She hurried to the study to see the reason for it.

She walked through the open door and felt the change in him almost immediately. He was no longer the happy newlywed who had left London such a short time ago. Instead, he glared at her and snapped, 'Shut the door, Miss Price. We must speak in private.'

She did as she was told and went quickly to the desk where he sat. 'Is something wrong, Marc? There is nothing the matter with Nell, I trust.'

'I left her in Northumberland. This matter concerns you, Miss Price, and your behaviour in my absence.'

'I cannot think…' Which was a lie. She could think of several things she had done in the last few weeks that would upset him greatly.

But then he reached into his desk, and removed the journal that she had taken from Stanegate Court. 'Do you know what this is?'

'Y-yes.' And she was sure that the stammer was enough to give away the truth.

'And can you explain to me why it is not sitting with its mates on the shelf in the study off the library?'

Now that she knew him as a Wardale, Nathan's obsession with the thing made more sense. But it was horrible to think that he had taken the book and rushed back to confront Lord Narborough on his sickbed. 'Where did you get it?'

'That is no answer to my question, Miss Price.' And there was her surname again, used against her as though she was a stranger and not a trusted friend. 'I received this from a family friend who works in the Home Office. I suspect he received it from a man who is a sworn enemy of my family. The same man who caused my poor Nell so much grief. How did this book leave the house, Miss Price?'

But how had the Gypsy come by the book? Was Nathan a friend to him? Had he worked without knowing, to harm his own sister? Why had she not spoken when she'd had the chance? For it was too cruel…

'Miss Price, I await your answer.'

There was little point in dissembling. He knew she was the thief. He'd either guessed, or he could read it in her eyes. 'When I took it from the shelf, I had no idea…'

Marc shook his head. 'That statement says it all. I could forgive you the theft, Diana. And the damage to the book—'

'But it was already—'

He went on, ignoring her interruption. 'It seems I have left my sisters in the protection of a woman who is easily gulled by just the sort of man I wish them to avoid. If you are working with the Gypsy? Even if it is without intention to harm?' He shook his head. 'Leave this house immediately, Miss Price. Your services are no longer required.'

'But I can explain.' She had so much to tell him. But it was even more important that she explain it all to Nell, who would be much less judgemental if she heard the details.

'I imagine you can.' The look in his eyes was sad, for it signalled the death of their friendship. 'But it will not move me from my decision.' He was staring at her now, as though reading a book himself. And she was convinced that the thing she most wanted to hide from him was written plain on her face. Then, he said, 'Your heart is involved, is it not?'

'Yes,' she whispered, letting him assume what he would. For now, it was better that he suspect the Gypsy than the man who was now his brother-in-law.

'Then you have made your choice in this matter. I have known you long enough to realize that you would not give your affections lightly. But through no fault of our own, Miss Price, my family is at war. You have chosen a side. And it is not ours. Please. Go to your rooms and pack your things. I will explain to my sisters. You are dismissed.'

Dismissed. She walked slowly towards her room. After all these years, that was all. She had done a better job of safeguarding the girls' honour than she had her own. She had thrown that away on a man who was unworthy. She was a thief and a liar. And worse.

What could she possibly say to Marc that would make things any better? It was bad enough that he suspected her of the theft. But if he believed she was unchaste? What kind of reference could she expect then? Why had she not realized that Nathan Wardale had been talking about the Gypsy, when he said an enemy would reveal his past? He was as trapped by the man as the Carlows had been.

She reached into her wardrobe, and removed a portmanteau. Then she set it upon the bed and began stacking her small clothes in it.

There was a shadow from the doorway, with the sound of Marc's shouted, 'No, Verity,' ringing in the background.

'How could you, Diana?' Verity gave a shuddering sigh and then burst into tears. 'I thoughtyou would never…And with father so ill…'

Honoria appeared at her side, reaching out to take her sister in her arms. 'We treated you as a member of the family. You were like a sister to us. And this is how you have repaid the family. Come, Verity.' She said the words loud enough for Marc to hear, and then turned back to her, and with an expression that conveyed the urgent need for secrecy, she held out a letter.

Diana snatched it from her hand, and gave a small grateful nod and a wave of farewell.

The girls nodded back, as though they understood as best as anyone could, that things were not as they appeared. Then Honoria pulled her sister from the room in a cloud of muttered remonstrations.

Diana returned to her packing. Even if the last scene had been a sham, Verity was right. Lord Narborough was too ill to face this latest problem, and it pained her to be the cause of it. Perhaps he was at fault for Hebden's death. Or perhaps only for a false accusation against Nathan's father. Whatever had happened, he was to blame for the fate of the Wardale family. Because of him, Nell had suffered, as had Nathan. And in his suffering, Nathan had struck out at her family, and she had struck back. And now, the misery was woven through their lives like a thread through a tapestry.

Marc had been right when he'd accused her of choosing a side. Without meaning to, she had given her heart and her loyalty to Nathan Wardale. However much she loved the Carlow family, she did not wish to stay with them until the truth was known.

She walked slowly to the wardrobe and looked down at the small pile of possessions that had accumulated during the course of the years she'd lived there. This was the sum total of her life, after all this time. It had felt very significant, and very permanent, just a day ago. And now it seemed as if she had no roots at all.

She began stuffing gowns into a carpet bag, thinking little of what the casual arrangement might do to the fabrics. She picked up the beautiful dress she had worn on the previous night and shuddered. It had been very foolish of her to squander a portion of the windfall on something she had no reason to wear. But at the time, she had been happy and in love, and giving no thought at all to what would happen after. And then, her hand fell upon the little book, at the bottom of the wardrobe.

All that he had given her could be tied neatly in a package. It was but a small part of her small life. But it was not quite all he had given, for there was still the letter that Honoria had just handed to her. She was sure it came from Nathan.

She reached out to where she had set it, on the bed next to the portmanteau. It felt thick enough to be an apology, but not so thick as to be the pile of bank notes that she would probably need, now that she had no position.

She wished that she had the strength to fling it into the fire, to show him and the world what she thought of the gifts of a man such as him: a gambler, a liar, a betrayer of women...

She closed her mind to the anger. For while some of the accusations might be true, they did not tell the whole of the story. And while she was not sure how angry she had a right to be, she could not afford to be a fool. If there was any chance that the letter contained more money, she would need to open it. His last gift had more than equalled what she had accumulated after ten years of work. He had seen that this day might come, and it was as if he had given her a gift of time. A year, perhaps, in which to plan what she might do next without worrying about her expenses. She cringed at the sight of the letter, because if there was money there, it would feel like a payment for the previous evening. But she needed all the help that she could get at the moment. With the options available to her in this crisis, it would not do to be too proud.

She steeled herself to read the actual words. They would hurt whether they were entreaties of love, apology, or the gloating comments of a rogue. They did not matter to her, for all were equally unimportant.

But the paper was blank, just as the first had been. And then, another paper fell out on the floor in front of her.

Her hands were shaking as she picked it up. The deed to her father's house. With her name written upon it, plain as day. After all this time, he had given it back to her.

There were at least a dozen reasons why she should return the thing immediately. He could not mean to give it without strings or obligations, for it was too large. It was too valuable. This was too much to grasp. Something would have to be exchanged for it. Although she suspected that he had been pleased with the activities of last night, her pragmatic mind would not flatter itself into thinking that anything she had done was worthy of an entire house.

He was trying to draw her back to him.

And it was working.

As though sleepwalking, she stood up, turned and exited the room, leaving her possessions behind her. She went down the stairs and out the front door of the Carlow home, not bothering to tell anyone why she was leaving. It hardly mattered any more that she was going out. Marc had made it clear that he wanted her gone. How and where would not be so important as when.

It could not be wise to go back to Nathan Wardale. And so soon after leaving him. But she had to know the reason for this latest gift. Did he expect her to live publicly as his mistress?

Surely not. She hoped not, at least. She had almost convinced herself that such behaviour was beneath him. But why had he given her the deed? Whatever he wanted from her, she must return it to him, or she would be no better than the opportunist the Carlows thought she was.

Her feet carried her home, from Albemarle Street to Hans Place without even thinking of it, although she had long avoided the neighbourhood because of the painful memories it brought. And there was her old front door, no different than it had been ten years ago when she had left it, or this morning when she had left it again. She reached out with hesitation, and took the knocker in her hand, letting it fall once against the wood of the door with a satisfying clunk.

Benton opened for her, and in a move totally inappropriate to his station, reached out to her and pulled her into the house, encircling her in a fatherly hug before she could speak. 'Miss Diana. You are finally home. When he told me what he had done, I hardly dared hope. But you are here now.'

And then he released her. And straightened. And said, 'Ma'am,' with a respectful bow and a slight twinkle in his eye.

'I don't understand.' Which was perfectly true, although it was clear that she had at least one friend left, no matter what might happen. She straightened as well, so that she did not appear broken by her circumstances. 'I wish to speak to Mr Wardale, please.'

'That is not possible, I'm afraid.'

'If he is from home, than I shall wait.'

Benton shook his head again. 'It will do no good to wait, Miss Diana. He made it quite clear to us when he'd finished his business this morning, that he would not be returning. He said you were the mistress of the house and we were to obey you as we had him. Or better.'

The realization staggered her, and she would have fallen, had Benton not pulled her the rest of the way into the house and helped her to a chair. 'He has gone. And left me the house.'

'Yes, Miss Diana. He said to me, "It was hers all along." And he sent back all the things he had won from others as well. If he knew the owner of something, he bundled it up and shipped it off with the first post. And then, he left with the clothes on his back and a single bag.'

He thought the house was hers? She had wanted a house, of course. A cottage. A small place where she could live in security, answering to no one. But this house? It was nearly a mansion. Far too large for a single person. Even when she was small, she had heard her parents say it was far too much to keep for two people with a single daughter. With all the bedrooms, it was a better space for a much larger family.

A family she would never have. She looked helplessly at the butler. 'I cannot do this, Benton. It is too much. The size of the house. The servants. I cannot afford to keep you. I am little better than a servant myself.'

He patted her hand. 'Do not worry on that account. Mr Wardale set the place up, from the first, so that it very nearly runs itself. The household accounts are so well stocked that we have run for years at a time without the master present. I suspect we can go even longer for you. Your needs are likely to be simpler than his. In any case, do not worry. For now we are all safe and warm, and I have a better knowledge of what it takes to maintain the house and staff than you do. Even without cash in hand, there are things left, from your father's time, that are worth a pretty penny and would have been sold to keep the place afloat, had not the old master gambled them away to Wardale. But they are yours again, to do with as you please. You will find a way. And I will help you.'

She smiled sadly. 'But I cannot keep it, Benton. I simply cannot. It is too much, too soon, and I do not understand Nathan's gift, nor do I wish to take the house back from him. It would be like admitting…' She shook her head, and tried to rise, but it was as though all the stress of the week had hit her; she might as well have been asleep and dreaming, as sitting on a bench in a hall in the middle of the day. 'But for now, I need someone to go back to my old place of employment and fetch my things. I will stay here until it can all be sorted out. It has been a most trying day, and I simply do not have the strength.'

'Ma'am.' He gave a curt nod. 'I will send a footman to get them, and they shall be brought to your old room. You must have some tea, I think. And a light lunch and a nice dinner to celebrate your return. I am sure that Cook still has the menus from when you were a girl. If your tastes have not changed, she knows what you will enjoy.'

'Cook? Still here?' A wave of warmth and comfort swept over her, as her happier childhood memories returned.

'You will find many familiar faces, miss, once you have become used to the place. Mr Wardale was not with us much.' Benton cleared his throat, as though making a final effort to protect his master's secrets. 'Travelling, I think. And even when he was here, he was often away from the house. During that time, the running of the place was left to his man of business, who did not see fit to change the staff any more than was necessary. But now? I shall bring the tea. There is a fire laid in the sitting room.' He moved to open the door for her.

'Benton.' She called him back. 'What was he like?'

'Mr Wardale?' The butler seemed surprised that she would ask.

'Yes. I knew him for such a short time. It was all very confusing. What was he like?'

The older man gave her a thoughtful look as though trying to decide what he owed to a man who no longer employed him. 'He paid regularly. He was courteous to the staff. Although he kept irregular hours, he did not require that we do the same. In food and drink he was temperate, as he was in dress and decorum.'

'That is what he was like as a master. But what kind of man was he?'

'He was—' Benton frowned. 'Not what I expected. I have met men in his line of business before.' He cleared his throat softly. 'When working for your father.'

'My father had other enemies?' She did not remember any. But she had been young, and he had sheltered her from the worst of it.

'Yes, Miss Diana. For he lost more than he won. There were questionable gentlemen who gamed as a diversion, who would come to the house and take a note, or a ring, and then leave him in peace. But the men who took gambling as their sole occupation? They were the sort that would just as soon take a pound of flesh as let a debt go uncollected. Rum 'uns, to the last man. Coarse. Hard. Not fit to come in by the front door of a house such as this, much less to live here. They were men without honour. And I saw them too frequently at the end, for—you will forgive me for saying it, miss—your father was not one to let common sense stand between him and the gaming table.'

She had forgotten the truth, but truth it was. She had put the blame for her father's ruin squarely on Nathan Wardale's shoulders for so long, it had never occurred to her that he was not the first to threaten her father with the poor-house. Nor could she accuse him of using under-handed means to lure her father into the game that had finally ruined him. He had gone will-ingly at any opportunity.

Benton's frown deepened. 'But Mr Wardale was different. Perhaps it was because he was brought up as a gentleman before his family's troubles, which were no fault of his own. He knew life from both sides. He was deeply con-scious of the effect his gaming had on others, and it troubled him. I doubt he spent an easy night in this house, knowing how he had gotten it. In a word Miss Diana? He was unhappy. He had no friends and many enemies. He did not seem to take satisfaction in his endeavours, but it was the only life he'd found that would suit him. It is only recently that I have seen a change in him. Of late, he seemed lighter of spirit.'

Because of me? She thought of the walks in the park and the way her heart had quickened from the first moment she'd seen him. And she won-dered: had it been the same for him? Or had it been harder? For if there had been true feeling on his part, he had been forced to sit opposite her in the White Salon at the Carlow house and in the carriage, knowing who she was and what she would think of him should she learn his true identity. And now, she understood the awkwardness of their first meetings and the reason for the curious way he had behaved. He had treated her with the utmost care and concern for her welfare, without giving anything away. He'd opened himself to her gradually, knowing how it would most likely end.

She remembered him, as he came to her last night. When he had said, 'I have not known gentleness…' She had given him that, and he had been glad of it. And she had taken it away again.

Suddenly, she was overcome with need of him, and the desire to be gentle for him and gentled by him. To stay together in the bed upstairs, and to sit before the fire together in the drawing room for as long as life would allow.

When the butler went to find her refreshment, she moved listlessly through the house, haunted by memories of her past. Mostly happy memories: of mother and of youthful innocence. But there were touches of her father, here and there. The chair he used to love was still in the parlour. Although it appeared that Nathan had favoured a different one, for the seat closest to the fire was not one she knew.

And here was the study. She took a deep breath, and then pushed open the door. For whoever had left his mark on this room, there were likely to be memories of a man she wished to forget.

The walls were the same dusty gold colour, and the desk and shelves were just as she remembered from her youth. But the contents of the shelves were different. Her father had favoured atlases, poring over them as though he wished to escape. But it appeared that Nathan Wardale had had his fill of travel. The maps had been replaced with local histories and books on art and drawing.

She turned to the desk, where she had learned the importance of picking simple locks while trying to find enough money to pay the bills. The surface was clear of papers and more orderly than she remembered it. Her father's old glass inkwell had been replaced with a heavy silver desk set. And here was the little locked drawer where Father had kept his purse and his memories of Mother. There had been letters, a miniature in a silver frame, and a lock of her hair, bound up by silk thread.

Without thinking, she pulled a pin from her hair and set about bending it to the shape of the desk key. Then she inserted it into the lock, and gave a jiggle and twist, feeling the mechanism turn, just as it always had.

What had she meant to do, she wondered, other than to prove that she could? There was no need to go through Nathan Wardale's desk, if he'd left his money in the bank for her. Perhaps it was the same curiosity that had led her to keep his note to Marc. Though she might claim that she wished no more from him, she still wanted to know the state of his mind.

The drawer was empty, except for a deck of playing cards. In that, he was not so different from her father after all. In the place where her father had hidden his most precious possessions, Nathan kept nothing but cards. She picked up the deck and stroked it, feeling sad for the man that had owned this house. Then she sat, shuffled and went to lay out a game of patience.

And stopped as she turned up the first card. Apparently, Nathan was something of an artist. He had transformed the cards, drawing little pictures around the pips. The clubs grew in flower gardens, dogs and cats played amongst the diamonds, the spades had been turned into fish.

And the hearts. Her breath caught in her throat. The hearts were her. She was sure of it. The likeness was not expert. But there she was, in her old bedroom, reading a book, with hearts floating around her like memories. And here on the five was the bonnet she had worn on her visits to Hyde Park, with hearts hidden amongst its flowers. On the ten, her hand was outstretched, to hold one of the hearts in her palm.

And as she looked at it, the conviction grew in her that it was his heart she held. If he'd said it to her face, she'd never have believed the words. But when he was alone in his study, with nothing to prove to anyone, what reason would he have to lie?

She cradled the card in her hand for a moment, and then gathered up the deck and thrust it back into the drawer, so that no one would see. It was a precious secret, and deserved to be kept safe. Then she ran out into the hall and called for the butler.

The man came hurrying to her side, probably fearing an emergency, for the tone she was taking. 'Miss Diana?'

'Benton. Where did he go? If I meant to find him…'

'That would not be wise, miss.'

'So few things I have done recently are. But I

mean to do it, anyway. Please, tell me, Benton. Where is Nathan Wardale?'

'If he is not here, I expect he is where he always is, Miss Diana. He has returned to the gaming table.'

Chapter Eighteen

Nate stared down at the perfectly arranged cards in front of him, and the shocked expression on the man across the table. Then he gave his usual cold smile and said, 'Another hand?'

'One hand too many, I think.' His opponent gave a shaky laugh. 'I should know better, Nathan. You and your damned luck.' And then he smiled. 'Next week, perhaps?'

Nate smiled and nodded, gathering the stakes into a neat pile before him. 'Perhaps,' he said, relieved the game was over. The man in front of him knew when to push himself away from the table, and might return as a diversion. Or he might not. But he would not reappear with a driving need to avenge himself or with a score to settle. Would that there were more like him, for Nate could take tonight's winnings in good conscience.

As soon as the chair was empty, another man seated himself. Nate looked up to see the Gypsy, darkening the table again. He smirked. 'And who are we today, then? Hebden? Or Beshaley?'

'As you prefer.' The Gypsy gave a bare nod of acknowledgement.

'I prefer that you leave. Both of you. But if you must stay, then let us play for something that has value to you. I should like to see you suffer, when you lose it.'

'Taking vengeance, Nathan?'

'If I can.'

'And how did your meeting with Keddinton go?'

'Just as you suspected. He was not impressed with the evidence, and had no real desire to help me. He expected me to work for him, as a matter of fact, in further smearing my father's name. I mean to take matters into my own hands, to go after George Carlow, once Diana is forever safely out of that house.'

'Revenge is not an easy course. I speak from experience when I tell you it takes as much from the wronged as it does from the cause.'

'Fine words from you, Beshaley. And meaning-less. You speak as if you care for my future, after all you have done to me.'

The Gypsy gave him almost a clinical examination, as though he could see the spirit as well as the body. 'Nothing has changed then? Your luck holds?'

'As it always does,' Nate said. 'No thanks to you and your kind.'

'So the curse did not break.' The Gypsy seemed surprised at this.

'Did you think it would?'

'As a matter of fact, I did.'

Nate frowned. 'Perhaps the luck was my own then, and this has all been nonsense. If so, I hope you are through with me, for I have no wish to part from it. I should think, taking the father, the family, the house and the girl would be enough to satisfy your mother. You have ruined the better part of my life and left me with no hope for the future. Leave me the cards at least.'

The Gypsy held out his hands in a gesture of finality. 'For my part, you have paid enough. You are released in any way I can release you. What is left, lucky or unlucky, is up to you.'

'Too little and too late. But it is something, I suppose.'

They played in silence for a while, and the stack of coins in front of Nate became larger. Then he said, 'And what of you? Are there others who will receive your *gift*?'

The Gypsy rubbed his temple, as though his head ached. 'Unfortunately, yes. While this business may be through for you, it is far from done for me. Until then?' He shrugged. 'The shadow moves where the sun commands. I will go where fate leads me. And it will be done when it is done.'

'And if you find proof that Narborough knew of my father's innocence?'

'Then he is my father's murderer. Despite what you may think, his debt to me is greater than to you. It will end in blood.'

'If you can prove George Carlow's hand in this, tell me of it. We will finish him together.'

The Gypsy's mouth quirked. 'Together, as friends?'

'To call you friend goes too far, after what you have done. Ally, perhaps. Let us say we have a common goal.'

Stephano raised his glass. 'To honour and justice for our families.'

It was impossible to tell by his expression which family he meant, the Hebdens or the Beshaleys. And so Nathan responded, 'For our families. Whoever they may be.'

The Gypsy let out a bark of laughter. 'Very well. If I have information to give, you shall have it.' And then, with a sidelong glance, 'If, when the time comes, you are still so eager to throw your life away on the past.' He tossed his cards on the table and stood up. He waved his hand in a strange gesture of blessing, and said, 'God keep you, Nathan. May I dance at your wedding.' He moved quickly away, so that he could not hear Nathan's responding curse to such a sarcastic parting.

Nate rubbed his temples, wondering if the Gypsy's headache was contagious. The air was oppressive, heavy with tobacco smoke and the smell of too much whisky and too many over-heated bodies. He longed for the fresh scent of the park, the feel of the cool breeze on his face.

And if he were honest, the feel of a small hand in his. But he did not dare go back. For suppose he was to see her? She could have the park and Bond Street, along with the house. Half of all London would be hers, if it meant that he would not have to see her again. There was nothing left he could offer her. He had given everything he had, and there had been no response. He must accept it. This was home. Hyde Park was a million miles away from the room he was in, and as dangerous a journey as a trip to the Indies. It would be too painful to risk another meeting.

He heard ribald laughter from the front of the room, and then the crowd parted, as a woman timidly approached his table.

'Diana.' The cards slipped from his hands. He gathered them quickly and shuffled in a skilled, nonchalant manner, so that she might not see how her arrival had unnerved him. Why had she come here, just as he was trying to reconcile himself to the loss of her? He had to fight with all his might against the urge to jump to his feet, hide the cards behind his back and stammer an apology for being caught in so low a place.

But it would do little good. If she knew to seek him here, there was no way to present this to her as an isolated occurrence. He could not pretend that he was any different than what he was, a habitual gambler, as at home here as she was sitting before the parlour fire in his old home. And so, he composed himself. 'I beg your pardon. Miss Price.' He rose to honour her properly, and offered a bow and a smile that was courteous, but would give no indication to those around him that she was anything more to him than an acquaintance.

'Mr Dale.' She looked nervous. Was it just the gaming hell that made her uncomfortable or was it his presence? He had longed to see her again.

But the sight of her unhappiness was even more painful than her absence had been.

'Mr Wardale,' he corrected. 'If you please.'

'You have decided to use your real name, then?' Her lips formed what might almost have been a smile of approval.

He nodded. 'It is time, don't you think? In the end, the alias proved to be more bother than it was worth.'

'What of your troubles with the Navy?'

'I mean to see to it that they are the Navy's troubles with me. They took me unjustly. They must acknowledge the fact.'

She nodded. 'It pleases me to see you are ready to face your past.'

And what good did it do him, that she was pleased? 'I assure you, it is hardly a magical transformation of my character. No matter my opinions on the past, the present is likely to stay just as it is.' He gestured around the room to remind her of their surroundings. 'I did not expect to see you again, certainly not in such a place as this. I trust that you will not think it a breach of my promise to leave you in peace. I will quit the city, if my presence in it is a problem for you.'

'No. No, of course not. That will not be necessary. It is a very big city, is it not?' She sat down at the empty seat across from him, fussing with her skirts. She was wearing the green silk dress that she had worn to seduce him; he wondered if that had meaning or was merely her attempt to blend with the gaudiness of the surroundings.

She leaned forward, almost confidentially. And he doubted, from the innocent look in her eyes, that she realized what a fascinating thing it did to her décolleté. 'There is more than enough room in London for the two of us.'

The two of them. If for once his life had turned out the way he wished, they would have needed very little space at all. He stared fixedly back at her, reminding himself that a gaming table was no place to show emotion. He looked directly into her eyes, waiting for her to speak.

Then, without a word, she removed a wad of folded bills from her reticule and set them upon the table, pushing them to his side. 'I believe these are yours.'

'Not any more. At one time, they belonged to your father. I no longer wish to retain them.'

Her returning smile to him was surprisingly cynical. 'If you meant to repay what my father lost to you, then it is not enough.'

He shrugged. 'There were expenses.' Then he

pushed his night's winnings towards her across the table. 'If you wish more, then take. Or I can write you a bank draft.'

'That is not why I am here. I come to return what you have given me, for it was fairly won.' She reached deeper into the purse and removed the deed. 'And this as well.'

'It is yours.'

'*Was* mine. My father's actually. In the distant past. But it has not been in the family for some time.'

'How fortunate that you have it again,' he said, pretending that the matter did not concern him.

'I no longer wish it. That is why I have been trying to return it to you.' She was staring back at him, her kissable mouth fixed in a resolute chaperone's smile.

'Nor do I. That is why I will not take it back.'

'I understand what you are trying to do by re-turning it to me. But you do not have to. It is kind of you to wish a different life for me than the one I had, but it is too late. While you might learn to live with it, you cannot change the past, Nathan.'

She had called him Nathan. The other words in the sentence paled to insignificance, leaving only the sweet tone of her voice and the sound of his name. For a moment, it gave him some small bit of hope. 'If there is some way to soften the memory of them, I wish to try. Or to make you forget altogether.' He frowned. 'Although there are some things, one night in particular, that I wish you to remember in every detail.'

There was not a trace of blush upon her cheek to reveal that she understood him. Perhaps she had lost the ability, after the previous evening's activities. Or maybe it was a sign of rare composure and her ability to maintain an even keel, though the waters were rough.

She ignored his hint and went on. 'Your life was more difficult than mine, and you have been less content. There is much I would not change. More than one night, certainly. It does not do to put too much emphasis on the actions of a single day, whether they be good or bad.'

Did she mean their night together? Or his night at the tables with her father? Or perhaps both. For then she said, 'Whatever the past between us, giving me the house and the money means nothing. They are not what matters. They do not indicate whether a person's character is changed or constant.' She pushed them back across the table.

He glanced at the papers and gave a shudder of revulsion at the sight of the deed lying in front of him on the baize where it had been so many years before. 'My character has changed for the better from what it once was. If the change is insufficient and you do not like it as it is, then I am sorry. And if you do not believe me to be constant, then tell me what I can do to prove it to you.'

'You certainly do not need to do—' she waved a hand over the deed '—this.'

'And yet, I have.' Her stubbornness over the thing made his head ache, and he wished that she would take it and leave him with what little peace he had, instead of coming to give him a fresh reminder of how unsuitable he was. 'I will not take it back. I wish I had given it to you on the first day, the moment I realized who you were. It and the damned letter, and anything else I could think to give. And then I could have walked away from you before speaking a word, with a clear conscience.'

And that had an effect on her, at last. Her eyes grew round with shock and hurt. He could not help himself and hurried to soften the blow. 'Do not misunderstand. My acquaintance with you was pleasant. More than pleasant. But it was a mistake. For now it hurts me to think of even the most pleasant moments, knowing they are all in the past. And the association hurt you as well. I could have spared us both so much grief by tearing up your father's note on the night he gave it to me.' He gestured to the money and the deed. 'This is all I have left to give you. Please, remove them from the table. If they are not stakes in a game, they do not belong here.'

'Stakes.' Her eyes had a stubborn sparkle. 'That is all these are to you? Nothing more? Then I...I wish to wager them.'

He laughed. 'You have no idea what you are talking about. And you know nothing of cards or gambling.'

'On the contrary. I may know nothing of cards, but I know more than you think about gambling and gamblers. And I know exactly what I am doing. You will accept this challenge from me, because you cannot help yourself. It is like a madness, isn't it? You have no control over it.'

Too true, although he did not like to admit it. But he could master it if he tried, he was sure. It was just that there was seldom a reason to try.

'You did not stick at winning the house away from my family the first time it was offered. Are you afraid that you will not succeed a second time?' Her voice was no longer the prim and proper tone of a paid companion, but the low, sultry murmur of the cards and the dice, cutting through his resistance.

The men gathered around the table gave a laugh. She had just called him a coward. He would have called out any man who said the words. He could hear the beginnings of mutterings, as a crowd began to gather to see the spectacle of the strange woman come to challenge the infamous gambler. And he could not very well let the insult stand. But neither did he want to play against her. 'It is just that I do not wish to take from you unfairly.' What had sounded like surety in his head, sounded overconfident, arrogant and dismissive as he said it to her.

'Since when have you turned away a game?' She was sweet and cajoling now. Intoxicating. If she were calling him to bed, he'd have gone in an instant. 'It is hardly unfair to play me in a game of chance. Unless you mean to cheat, of course.'

The crowd gasped. She had insulted him again. Even if it came from a woman, he dare not let that pass. 'Very well.' He'd said it more sharply than he intended, his fever for the game momentarily overcoming his fever for the woman. He spoke again, more calmly, 'What do you wish to play?'

She bit her lip, considering. 'What would you suggest?'

He groaned. 'Miss Price, the first lesson you must learn is not to allow me to choose the method of your destruction.' He shuffled quickly, giving the cards an elegant flourish, hoping that his dexterity would frighten her away. Then he dealt out the cards for a hand of Macao. 'I assume you are at least slightly familiar with this game? Let us make this interesting. Your house and money, against the contents of my purse.'

'I think that will be satisfactory. Thank you.'

Damn. If he'd had any intention of winning, the bet would have been unfair beyond words. Why did she not cry off? It would serve her right for insulting him if he took the things back, for she was too ignorant of the ways of the table to have any idea what was happening to her. If he was able, he would throw the game to her. And if not? At least it would be over quickly. 'Shall we begin?'

He had prepared himself to play as inexpertly as possible. But it was hardly necessary. For a change, his incredible luck was not with him; the cards would not go his way. She was most fortunate in the hand he had dealt, and as the game progressed she beat him easily. He smiled, relieved that he would have no further guilt upon his soul. Now she could take the things he had given her, knowing that she had earned them. He emptied his purse onto the pile of bank notes already on the table. 'There. You have bested me. The house and the money are yours, fairly won to do with as you wish.'

She frowned at the money in front of her, and her expression was no different from the people he had beaten over the years, as dissatisfied with winning as they were when they lost. 'But you did not try.'

'It is not enough to play your own hand but you must play mine as well?' He responded a little tartly to her criticism, for in the end, he had not been able to persuade himself to lose. He had played the best game possible with the hand he'd dealt himself and had still not been able to beat her. 'I tried hard enough against a player as inexperienced as you are. Enough so that you might have a chance of winning, if luck was with you. Which it was. And that is the end of it.' He pushed the pile of notes back to her side of the table.

'You insult me, sir. If you do not bring your full skill to the table? It is little better than cheating.'

There was that word again. 'Cheating? I?'

'Since the object is to win and you were attempting to lose, yes. I demand that we play another round.'

'Hand,' he corrected. 'And I do not cheat at cards.'

'Another hand, then. And if you do not cheat, then you are not as good at this game as I expected. Deal again, Mr Wardale.'

'The deal passes to you, Miss Price. Which should help to convince you that I do not cheat at cards.' He said it loud enough so that all could hear. 'I swear, I have never had such trouble over losing a game.'

Everyone laughed as she went about the painfully slow process of shuffling the cards to her satisfaction and carefully counting out the hands. She glanced up at him. 'I mean to bet all I have.' She pushed her pile of winnings back toward him.

'Then I shall put up something of equal value, this time, to prove to you that I am trying.' He thought for a moment. 'I have a country house as well as the town house. I meant to retire there. But you shall have it, at the end of this hand.'

'If you lose,' she said. 'But I expect you to do your best to defeat me.'

'My best?' She still did not understand what she was asking of him.

She nodded. 'Do not insult me. Play the game, as you would against a stranger, and let fortune decide the winner.'

Let fortune decide? He might as well take the house back now and not bother with the game. The last hand had been a fluke and he did not expect another. 'If you will force me to bankrupt another Price at this table, then you do not understand what the last game cost me.'

She looked back at him, her eyes tranquil. 'You will not bankrupt me, because unlike my father, I have the sense to stop playing, once I am satisfied with the results. You will leave me as you found me, with a small savings. Which was not such a bad thing, really. I have been behaving most strangely of late, and I date the change to the moment I opened your first envelope.'

She thought that the money was what wrought the change in her? He had hoped that it was more than that. For it would have been most flattering to think that she had felt changed on the day that they first met, as he had. He sighed. There was no way to leave her as he found her, if she wished honesty from him. And in comparison to that, the money was a small thing. 'If losing the house again is truly what you wish, I am sure another hand will do the trick.' And he bent over his cards in concentration.

And he lost again.

It was not unheard of, to lose two hands in a row. Uncommon for him, of course. But not impossible. She had been right. It was a game of chance. Anything might happen. And he had barely tried, on the first hand, so it should not count against him.

The woman across the table was livid. 'How dare you, sir? You are trifling with my…my…my patience.'

He stared at the cards, which had picked a most unusual time to betray him. 'I am doing nothing of the sort. I was quite fond of that house. If I'd known that the hand would not go my way, I'd have bet something else. My stable. Matched bays, a phaeton and a curricle. All on the table, Miss Price. Please do me the honour of keeping your original stakes. But give me a chance to regain the country house.'

'All or nothing, sir.'

'Damn.'

She drew in a sharp breath at the oath.

'Your pardon, Miss Price.' He glared at her, which probably spoiled the apology for his rudeness in swearing. But the temptation to let her win had dissipated. It was one thing to give up the London house, but to have no home at all was not what he had intended for penance. After all the years he had played here, it galled him to lose it at cards to a green girl. And at Macao, which was hardly worthy of his skill. He had a reputation to consider, and their play had drawn quite a crowd of onlookers. They would not let him forget it, if he cried off now.

But his luck was sure to turn on the next deal, just as it always had. 'All right then. If you insist. My stable against your houses.' He dealt the cards.

As he stared down at the unplayable mess in his hand, he bid a silent goodbye to the horses, and the houses as well. She set down her cards without joy, and called out 'Macao' as though it pained her to say the word. If she must beat him so thoroughly, the least she could do was take joy in it.

He glared at her again. 'Do not dare say that I arranged that for your benefit, Miss Price. It would give me more credit than I deserve.'

She looked up at him, alarmed. 'If not for my benefit, then why is it happening?'

'I have no idea. Deal the cards.'

'Certainly not. This has gone on long enough, and is not working at all the way I planned.' She rose to go.

'Sit!' He said it far too sharply, and she dropped back into her chair as though he'd yanked her into place. He struggled to control his emotions, trying to remember a time when he had been flustered at a gaming table. Embarrassing displays of temper were for his opponents, not for him. He took a deep breath. 'I beg your pardon. Please. Sit. You must give me a chance to break even in the game, at least. Another hand, please.'

She shook her head. 'I suspect that that is what my father said, when he gambled with you. He assumed, until the very last hand, that his luck would turn.'

That was what all his opponents thought. But they did not know what Nate did: There was no hope for any of them to win against him, until the curse was lifted. And this game would not go on much longer. Another hand and things would change in his favour, just as they always had.

Unless…

'Please,' he said urgently. 'One more game, Miss Price. For the sake of my curiosity, if nothing else. The contents of my bank accounts, against all that you have.'

She gave him an amazed smile. 'And what would that leave you, should I win?'

'Very little, I expect.' He grinned at her. 'And it doesn't matter a jot to me.'

'But how shall you live?'

'I shall find someone to stake me, and gamble again with someone else. As long as I have anything left of value, I shall return to the tables and wager it, Miss Price.'

She stared back at him, horrified. 'You are mad, sir.'

'I would have to be, to make my living as a gambler. Once begun, it is almost impossible to stop. But I have not enjoyed it.' He looked at her very seriously. 'The only true happiness I have felt has been most recently. And that, I fear, was a transient thing. It seems the feelings I had for a young lady were not reciprocated. She disapproved of my profession.'

'It is a most disreputable profession.'

'I know that. And I wish, most heartily, to have a provocation to end my gaming, just as your father did. It was only when he had reached the point where he'd lost all and was bartering with precious things he had no business offering, that he realized what he had done and changed his life. And from what you tell me, he was repentant, even to the end.'

'He was.' She said it softly, as though it had

never occurred to her that she had been the cause of his change.

'I suspect it was his stalwart devotion to you that affected him. There is much about you, Miss Price, that might cause a man to change his ways. Now if you please, deal the cards.'

Her hands were trembling as she pushed the rectangles of pasteboard to his side of the table. And it was just as he'd hoped. There was not a useful card in the hand, nor any hope of bluffing her to think otherwise. He smiled, relaxed in his chair and prepared to lose the hand.

She became more and more agitated with each trick she took. 'Do not grin at me so. I find it upsetting.'

He smiled all the more. 'But it does not seem to be spoiling your play.'

'It is pure luck, and you know it.'

'Since I have never seen it on the other side of the table from me, I hardly recognize it.' He tossed his cards down on the table. 'That is it, gentlemen. The lady has ruined me.'

But the poor girl across the table looked to be near tears. 'I did not mean to. I only wanted to give you your money back. I thought this would be the easiest way.'

'I am afraid, darling, that things are never easy

between us. I have made your life difficult, right from the beginning. And I am most sorry for it. What has happened here is divine justice, plain and simple.' He stacked the deck and began to shuffle again, glancing up at the proprietor. 'Bring me pen and ink. If the lady will play one more game, against my marker, we will see if my current luck holds.'

'No! I do not want this. We have played enough. Let me go.' She was drawing away again, and he would have to be gentleness itself to keep her.

He put down the cards and placed his hand on hers, before she could push away from the table. 'Diana. I beg you. Do not go. Not yet. There is one last thing I have to offer. Although, I dare say, you have it already. And if it is yours, no ill can come to me by gaming with it.' He took the pen and scratched at the edge of the paper for a moment, trying to remember the words.

'To Diana Price, I promise you, in the event of losing this game, that with my body I thee worship, and with all my worldly goods I thee endow.' He looked up. 'Although I seem to have done that last already. But no matter. You get the gist of it.'

'Nathan Wardale, do not mock me.'

'I do not, darling. My heart is yours whether you wish it or no, just as my possessions are. I will lay them all at your feet, if you let me. But if you doubt the sincerity of my gift, then pick up the cards I have dealt and win it from me.' He looked at the people crowded around the table. 'Anyone here can vouch for me. As long as I am gambling, my word is good. If you win again, you may walk away from this table and I will follow, abject to your every whim.'

She was staring at him in a most odd way, and he feared she did not want him or his heart. She did not even want his money. And now she would prove it to him in front of all these people. She would push aside the cards and walk away and everyone would know him for a fool. Her gaze was fixed on him, searching his face for a bluff, trying to break his concentration, as he had done to opponents for years, and he could feel himself start to perspire. He wanted to blink and turn away from her scrutiny, ready to cry out that she should have mercy and be done with him if she didn't want to play. She could take the pot and go, and he would pretend that he had never made her the offer, and never bother her again. That he was sorry to have bothered her in the first place. Or her father, for that matter. Or anyone else in the room.

And then she said, 'You would leave the table?'

He blinked. 'If you wish.'

'And never return?'

His mouth opened automatically, ready to protest. But the thought that he could stop had never occurred to him. There had never been anywhere else to go. And now…

She went on. 'Because I would have no use in my life for a gambler, Mr Wardale. And certainly no desire to attach myself to a man who would bring ruin upon us both.'

Suddenly, it was clear to him how hard it must be for her to come to him and how fearful she must be that her married life would be a repeat of her mother's.

And he knew he was standing at a crossroads. He could keep the life he had known and spend the rest of it financially safe at the tables he detested. And he would spend his nights alone. Or he could go with Diana today, into the unknown, with no guess as to how he would make a living for her, if the money he had was not enough for a family. Did he have skills, beyond cards and dice? He knew he was not a sailor. And he could not be an earl. But other than that, he had no idea who or what he might be. Until he found his way in the world again, every day would be a gamble.

But then, he had always been a gambler. He smiled. 'This building has been more church to me than any other, for many years. When I am at the table, though I might bluff, I do not lie, I do not cheat, and I never welsh on a bet. If you win, I will walk away from here and I swear there will be no returning.'

She shook her head ruefully. And then she smiled, and reached for the cards. 'Very well then. It is a game of chance, after all. There is no guarantee of the outcome. And you are said to be very lucky. Let us see how the play goes.'

He looked down at his hand and knew that he could make nothing of it, and felt the swelling sense of relief that ultimate failure would give to him. 'I think I am very lucky indeed.'

She looked down at her own cards, and did nothing to disguise the little moue of surprise on her face that he might have used to his advantage had he thought himself up to bluffing her. The play continued, and as she had with the previous hands, she beat him easily. She stared at the note on the table and blinked up at him in shock. 'I won.'

'You did.' He grinned at her, feeling a lightness of spirit that had been missing since childhood, as though some great burden had been lifted from his back.

'But does that mean…do you still wish…' Poor, sweet, sensible Diana was at a loss.

'Very much so. Miss Price, would you do the honour of accepting my offer? You would make me a very happy man. And I will do everything in my power to be the husband you might wish.' He stood up from the table and came to her side, offering his hand to her.

'I…I…Yes. I accept.' She was still looking at the cards, and then at him, as though the suddenness of it was quite overcoming her.

So he pulled her out of her chair and close into his arms. And then he kissed her. Gently at first, and then slowly, ardently, passionately. And he felt her kiss him back, first with hesitance and then as she had on the night they'd been together, as though she did not wish the moment to end. When they parted, she looked up at him with a twinkle in her eye. 'Mr Wardale, really. We are in a public place. This is most improper.'

He laughed. 'The place is most improper as well, Miss Price. My actions suit my environment. But if you wish to remove me from it, then perhaps my behaviour will moderate. Come, let us re-enter polite society. If you wish, I shall become the sort of lacklustre, milksop who would never dare to take you in his arms and kiss you senseless.'

She reached down to the table and scooped her winnings into her reticule. And as an afterthought, took his marker, folded it carefully and tucked it down the bodice of her dress. 'I should certainly hope not, Mr Wardale. For both our sakes.' And then she smiled. 'We have much to talk of. There is the matter of Nell, for instance.'

He smiled back, puzzled. 'And who might that be?'

She seemed surprised at his reaction, and then said, 'Perhaps you know her as *Helena*, although she does not favour that name.

'Helena?' His mind clouded for a moment, with distant memories. 'How could you know her? Or what she favours? I swear, I have said nothing.'

She touched his arm, and leaned close to him, whispering in his ear. 'She is safe and well. Married to a dear friend of mine. Although a full reconciliation might be difficult, given recent events. But considering what has transpired between us, anything is possible, is it not?'

'My sister, found safe?' He took a breath, and steadied himself as a feeling of relief hit him that nearly knocked him from his feet.

'There is much I need to explain,' she rushed to tell him. 'And I am sorry to have kept it a secret. For I knew how important it is to you. But for a time, I wanted you to be hurt, and then… It is all so very complicated…'

He stopped the words with a kiss. 'Do not trouble yourself. I am the last person to berate you for withholding a difficult truth from me.' He kissed her again. 'If Helena is safe, that scrap of knowledge is a gift. You can tell me the rest in good time. But we will have all the time in the world, soon enough. Marry me, Diana Price, and I shall truly be the luckiest man in England.'

Nate glanced up at the shadowy figure standing near the door and put a protective arm around his bride-to-be.

The Gypsy stared back at him, dark eyes unreadable. And then, he gave the smallest nod of approval, a shrug and a gesture that might have been a salute of farewell. And he was gone.

Epilogue

Diana walked down the hall of her old house, to the study of her new husband. He spent much time here, poring over old papers, still searching for anything that might lead him to the true killer of Christopher Hebden. If not that, then he was sending discreet inquiries as to the whereabouts of his sister Rosalind, or penning hopeful notes to Nell, while trying not to upset her with suspicions about her new family.

She hoped for success in this. But what little news she had managed to glean on the subject did not bode well for the Carlows. Although the girls had been forbidden to communicate with her, Verity had ignored her brother's command and sent several brief notes, urging her to seek a speedy reconciliation. In Diana's absence, Honoria was growing increasingly reckless. While Diana could not return as chaperone, perhaps the steadying influence of an old friend would be all that was needed to set things right.

It was some comfort that it troubled Nathan as much as it did her, that another family would be thrown into chaos over what he might find. Were it not for his soft heart, he would be no better than the Gypsy. It would do him good to see what she had found, no matter how unpleasant it might be. 'Nathan,' she reached out for his hand from the doorway. 'Come with me. There is something I wish to show you.'

He smiled at her, as he always did, and followed her up the stairs. She felt the warming of her blood as he paused, and she had to tug him past their bedroom door. 'Later,' she whispered.

His eyebrow arched in surprise. 'Of course later. But now is nice as well.'

'Later.'

'If not there, then where are we going? For you are wearing a green dress and you know the effect that it has on me.'

'It is a day dress and not particularly special,' she cautioned. 'And I often wear green because you claim to prefer the colour. If it troubles you, I will change.'

'I'd hardly call it trouble. My feelings on seeing you are most easily remedied. But if you wish to change, I will make a suggestion. You are very fetching in a green dress. But you will be even more fetching out of it.' He grabbed at her, and she wondered how she could have ever feared that he would prefer gambling to a wife and family. His preference for her was obvious. And his enthusiastic attentions made family almost inevitable.

She let him catch her, for a while. Then, she put his hands firmly to his sides and said, 'Definitely later. First, there is something you must see.'

He sighed. 'Your tone is rather dire, my dear. I suspect you have put on the green dress to soften some kind of a blow.'

She gave him a worried look. 'I fear you may be right. But I know it is something that will interest you, and now that I have found it, I must tell you. There are no secrets between us, after all.'

'None,' he assured her.

She led him to the end of the hall, to the stairs that led to the attics.

'And what reason do we have to go here?'

'I got the keys from Benton, and went searching. I thought that perhaps there were things that I remembered from my own youth that might be pleasant to see again.' She tried to sound casual at the suggestion, for she did not wish him to think she was dwelling in a past that she had promised she would forgive.

But he nodded in perfect understanding. 'If you wish to see them, I will not have you traipsing round the lumber room in melancholy. And if you are adamant that you do not wish to re-decorate the house…'

'I do not. It is lovely the way it is. And very much in tune with your character.' Perhaps that was why she liked it so. While it was not the home she remembered, it was the haven of the man she loved above all in the world.

He smiled, and there was a glint in his eye that made her think of Christmas. 'Then I fear we shall have to move your heirlooms to a place where you might enjoy them more fully.'

'The country house?' They had honey-mooned there. It was just as lovely as Hans Place. And while she enjoyed the novelty of riding or walking through the fields, without seeing a single soul, it seemed very far away from everything she was used to.

He gave a small shake of his head. 'I was thinking, perhaps we could find a cottage. There is a place I know of, in Hammersmith. A few rooms, only. But there is a lovely garden and the deed is already in your name. If you wished to house your treasures there, you might visit them whenever you liked.'

'A cottage,' she said, confused. 'For me?'

'And me as well, if you would allow me there. Or not, as you choose. In any case, it is secured as yours, legal and proper.'

'How did you know?' For hadn't this been exactly what she had dreamed of?

He smiled again. 'Along with my other quests, I have been searching for a worthy wedding gift. And since I know very little about what a proper young lady might appreciate, I might have inquired of my sister, who might have asked the Carlow girls, who seemed to think you would be in favour of the idea. And considering my history, it does make sense, does it not? While I have no intention of backsliding into the gambling rogue that I was, let this gift be proof to you and those that love you that you will never be left homeless because of me.' He reached into his pocket and removed a most ordinary-looking key, which he placed in her hand, closing her fingers to wrap them around it. 'Does it please you?'

She swallowed back tears of gratitude, and

threw herself into his arms, kissing him most passionately. And then she whispered, 'As long as there is room enough for the two of us, it pleases me very well.' She dropped the key into her own pocket, and whispered, 'We shall visit it, soon, I think. And when we do, I shall wear green.' And she watched his eyes go dark in response.

'But first, there is something I must show you. And I fear it is not so pleasant as what you have done for me.'

She felt the slightest hesitation in his step, as he followed her. But considering what his life had been, he had no desire to seek more misery, though she was sure he would do it, if she asked him to.

She led him to the back room she'd found and the small trunk under the window with the initials NW carved into the leather at the top. 'In searching for my own past, I have found a part of yours.'

He stopped, staring at it. 'I had thought it lost, after all this time.' He looked at her, worried. 'Do you know what is there?'

She nodded, for curiosity had caused her to lift the lid. 'It is better to face it, is it not? And there are papers.'

'If I wish to prove my father's innocence, then they are all I have.' He smiled at her. 'But I am glad that I do not need to do this alone.' He leaned forward to kiss her, putting his warm arms about her and holding her close so that he could rest his chin against her temple. 'Together?'

'Yes.' And she sat upon the floor beside him, as he examined the little chest.

He stroked the wood, and let his fingers trail along the brass fittings. 'I have not seen this in years. It was all I had left, before I was forced into the Navy. I cannot even remember bringing it to the house. But obviously I did.'

'Benton put it away, when you did not return. It has been waiting for you.'

'I am glad I did not know. But if the thing Veryan wants still exists, then this is the only place I would know to look.'

She watched him steel himself, and unlatch the chest.

And there, at the top, was the real silk rope. He put his hand on it again, after all these years. It looked no different to Diana than other ropes. It was black, not the gaudy colours of the Gypsy's imitation that he had shown her. She reached out a finger and prodded it carefully. It was soft to the touch, for it was silk.

Nathan gave her as sad smile. 'As though it would be any better to be hung gently. I wonder if the person that had come up with the plan to hang nobles in silk recognized the irony of it? Or did they seriously think it was a last sign of respect?'

She shuddered. 'It is disgusting, in any case.'

'But better to keep it, than to see it cut into bits and sold to collectors. This is the only entail I was left to offer our children.' He picked it up and set it deliberately aside, so he could get to the things beneath.

There was a loose collar stud in silver, engraved with a small L. A penknife, and pipe. He picked them up, and brought the pipe to his nose to get a whiff of the stale tobacco. 'Father's.' He gave a sentimental smile, and she rested a hand on his shoulder in support.

'And mine.' There was a tiny lead soldier discarded beside them. He picked it up, and put it to the side with the other things.

And then, there was a sheaf of paper. 'And this is what we have come to see.' He quickly sorted them into two stacks, by the hand they were written in. '*These* are the things written by my father. I do not see anything written by Hebden amongst the rest. I fear our quest is in vain, just as I thought it would be.' He riffled quickly through them. 'I must have read them all at one time, seeking comfort. And I don't recall anything that made me think of a code.' He shrugged. 'Of course, I was very young. Most everything that adults wrote might well have been a code to me, for all that I could understand of it.' He folded his legs, tailor fashion, and piled his father's letters into his lap to read by the light of the attic window.

He was silent as he read, lost in his own past. And there was little for Diana to do, so she contented herself with reading the rest of the stack. It made her heart break to think of the poor little boy who had gathered everything he could find hoping to preserve the few remaining memories of his father. Here was a tailor's bill. And here a note of thanks from a long-ago friend, concerning a weekend of shooting at the Leybourne estate. And then, a note in a woman's hand.

She read. And then said, 'Nathan, this is from Amanda.'

She saw her husband flinch at the name. 'Kit Hebden's wife. You saw the journal. You must know what was said about them at the time. That note will do us no good, if I remember it for what it was. She wrote to him when he was in jail. I think she wanted him to confess. He passed me the letter, and bade me hide it from my own mother, because he said it would distress her. And so, I brought it back to hide amongst my things.'

She gave him an amazed smile. 'That is not what this is at all. But you were a little boy when you read it. You must have stopped after a line or two, then put it away. What did you know of such things? Tell me if you do not see it differently, now.' She held up the paper and began to read.

'"Tell them, William. My husband is dead, and I do not care who knows. There is no reason that you need keep secret what happened between us that night. Not if it means death for you. Kit would not hold it against you, for you know as well as I that he knew the truth and did nothing about it while he was alive. You might think there is honour in secrecy, but if it means that I retain my reputation only to watch you hang, then what good is my honour to either of us?"'

He looked at her, his expression puzzled. And she said, 'Can you not see it, even now? He was with her on the night of the murder. At least the first part of that night. That is why your father was so eager for you to hide this letter. He was trying to protect her, and your mother. And she says that Kit Hebden did not mind. So it was not a crime of passion. Whatever was on your father's mind that night, it had nothing to do with codes or keys or spying. He had no reason to kill his lover's husband. The arrangement suited them all.'

He read the letter again, and she watched the paper shake in his hand. 'You are right. My God, Diana. I think you are.' He looked at her in amazement. 'I don't know what Veryan will make of this, if anything. And I don't know if I dare show it to the Gypsy, for if he has any scrap of love left for his stepmother, then he will not welcome this news. But you are right. Nothing here makes my father out as traitor.'

She smiled. 'And you thought there would be nothing at all.'

He smiled back. 'It is but a scrap of information. But a scrap is more than I ever hoped to find. It is enough to build on, at any rate.' He rose and dusted off his pants. 'And it renews hope in me. My father was innocent, just as he said.'

'And if that is true…'

He squared his shoulders. 'Then whatever people may say of him, I am proud to be his son. I will clear my name, and his as well. And even if it takes me a lifetime, I shall make you the Countess of Leybourne, my dear.' He held out a hand to her, lifting her to her feet again, and led her down the stairs to their rooms.

★ ★ ★ ★ ★

Read all about it...

MORE ABOUT THIS BOOK

MORE ABOUT THE AUTHOR

DON'T MISS

Read all about it...

AN INTRODUCTION BY THE AUTHOR

When the six of us involved in writing **Regency Silk & Scandal** set about divvying up the characters, I was surprised at how quickly we snapped up our choices, and how little argument there was over who would write about whom. We all took a look at the family trees we'd created and were drawn instantly in different directions. Since Louise Allen had taken the heir to the Carlow family for the first story, book one, *The Lord and the Wayward Lady*, I chose Nathan Wardale for the second book, to see how the other half lived.

I was pleased to find that Nathan was not as hard and cynical as fate had tried to make him. He had a sensitive side that the sheltered Diana Price would recognise and be drawn to. And it seemed only natural that this gentle nature would manifest itself in a hobby of some kind. Since I doubted that gambling would ever be far from his mind, I chose transformational playing cards.

Although they were most popular in Victorian times, the first decks of transformed playing cards were printed in the early 1800s, just in time for Nathan to see them and to pick up the habit of sketching designs on his own decks for amusement.

"Ah Child, when I was at your Age, I never had occasion to go abroad for admirers, the young Fellows used to give me as a toast. Fanny the fair and prodigiously clever at all kinds of curious Work...that I was..."

"Lord Mamma, I have heard that so often."

The queen of spades from an 1810 deck of cards by Vincenz Raimund Grüner (Vienna)

Read all about it…

THE NEWGATE CALENDAR OF 1795

Excerpt from broadsheets collected in *The Newgate Calendar* of 1795, found in the effects of Mr Nathan Wardale:

The Short Life and Scandalous Execution of William Wardale: Last Earl of Leybourne, who brought disgrace to his family and country with the foul murder of his friend, Christopher Hebden, Baron Framlingham.

…as the villain Wardale was led from the gaol in shackles, he raised a hand to point at the crowd and cried, "Death to the King!", laughing in a most evil way, shaking the chains and frightening the good people who stood close around the platform, eager to see the criminal punished.

At the sound of his taunts, the widow of the murdered man wept and railed against him, finally having to be restrained by friends and escorted from the courtyard.

"He is dead," Wardale cried after her, "And I am glad of it. For it was I that struck the mortal blow! I watched his heart's blood run from him." Then Wardale waved away the Ordinary, swearing that he would go unrepentant to the Devil and be glad of it, "for the lecherous bastard had it coming to him and I am not sorry in the least."

(Note scrawled in the margin by NW)
Lies! Damned lies!

The condemned waved away the hood he was offered. And then, as befit a peer, he was hanged about the neck with a rope of silk.

As the guilty man kicked out his last breath on the gibbet, the proceedings were enlivened by the death of a mysterious Gypsy woman who heaped curses on the murdered man and the people in the crowd, vowing vengeance before throwing herself from a window.

(Only I was there to see. And I swear, I will live to prove the truth of your innocence and avenge you, Father. NW)

A NOTE ON HANGING

Hanging, as we might have seen it portrayed on television or in the movies, with a "long drop", a quick stop and a sudden death, is quite different from what was practised during the Regency. It was not until 1888 that the Home Office came up with the Official Table of Drops to document the length of drop by height and weight of the criminal in an attempt to come up with a more scientific and efficient method of execution.

Hanging in the days of this story was a grisly affair, definitely not for the squeamish. In the late 1700s, the drop was only a foot or two and death was the result of slow strangulation rather than a broken neck. If friends of the criminal were present, they might speed his or her end by pulling on the legs of the condemned. Although, as my son pointed out to me, perhaps a true friend would have cut poor William Wardale down.

After the execution, the family of the deceased would have to pay to claim his body. And it was wise to get the rope as well, for there was a brisk trade in the souvenir collecting of hangman's ropes.

Since William Wardale was a member of the peerage, he was hanged with a silk rope. Many people believe this is a myth, but research exists that a regular rope wrapped in silk might have been used.

Although we'd never think of it today, hangings were a popular form of entertainment with a seat in a window overlooking the gallows going for as much as ten pounds. Peddlers hawked broadsheets to the crowd, with woodcut drawings and grisly confessions, much as the one poor Nathan found. These were collected in a popular series of books called *The Newgate Calendar*, and kept in many homes to be read as cautionary tales for children.

GAMES OF CHANCE AND SKILL

Hazard: A dice game considered to be the ancestor of the modern game, craps.

Faro: A card game that involved betting on the identity of cards drawn by a dealer from a special faro box. An easy game for the house to rig.

E & O: For even and odd. A wheel that was similar to roulette, with Es and Os around the perimeter instead of numbered blacks and reds.

Piquet: A game for two players, using thirty-two cards. The piquet pack is made by discarding cards lower than seven from a normal deck. An excellent game for a serious player like Nathan Wardale, since it involves time, skill and concentration.

Vingt-et-un: The original version of twenty-one, or blackjack.

Macao: Similar to vingt-et-un. Another game that required minimal skill, but an ability to bluff.

Read all about it...

AUTHOR BIOGRAPHY

Christine Merrill is probably the only author of Regency-set historicals ever to fail a college English class covering Jane Austen. If pressed, she will insist that the F had more to do with her feelings on *Tristram Shandy* than *Northanger Abbey*. After she graduated with a degree in English and theatre education, and could go back to reading for fun, she discovered *Pride and Prejudice* and learned the error of her ways.

She has been by turns a theatrical costumer, a mum and a librarian. She is a terrible housekeeper, a mediocre cook, and she has a sense of direction so bad that she can get lost pulling out of her own driveway.

It is probably a good thing that she really likes to write, since it means she can stay at her desk. It keeps her out of trouble.

Chris lives in Wisconsin with her husband, two teenage sons, two cats, a pond full of goldfish and a labradoodle named Havoc.

Read all about it...

AUTHOR INTERVIEW

What do you most enjoy about writing as part of a continuity series; how does it differ from writing a single-title?

For this one, it would have to be the people involved. We had a pretty tight-knit group, by the end of it. Getting to create the universe and the characters and all the back story was a real joy. Also, watching the working process of the other writers was eye-opening.

What did you find most enjoyable about writing in an historical setting?

I think there are a lot of plots that can't be done now, that work much better in a historical. The diminished position of women a hundred or more years ago is an almost instant source of conflict in any story. It's a challenge to navigate in society, trying to give my heroines as much independence as I can without slipping too deeply into anachronism. And an alpha male hero is a given, to a certain extent. Even a timid man would, to a certain degree, have a sense of entitlement about marriage, money and property.

I can let my historical heroes do things that I would have absolutely no patience for in a contemporary. Much as I wish it to be other-wise, I don't think I'd last five minutes without picking a fight with Mr Darcy, if he wanted to talk to me at all.

But being able to imagine the meeting in candlelight and fancy dress does a lot to im-prove my opinion of it.

Would you have liked to have lived in London during 1814?

Definitely not! I am very fond of modern conveniences like running water and flush toilets. Also, I doubt I could live without television or the internet.

And there is the fact that my ancestors tended to be hearty peasant stock. If I were transported to 1814, odds are good that I would be the maid that had to heat the water and carry it up three flights of narrow stairs, so the heroine could have her bath.

It is much more fun to imagine the Regency the way I want it to be and play all the characters myself than to have to live with the truth.

Where do you get your inspiration for your characters?

From all sorts of weird places. It doesn't take much to get me daydreaming. I can get the start to a whole story from a facial expression in a picture or a line from a song. But it's generally the emotion of the music and not the words that set me off.

I watch a lot of old movies that actually have very little to do with the story I'm writing, but that give me an idea for a conflict between the main characters. I think I started out *Paying the Virgin's Price* by watching *Guys and Dolls*. And although my Nathan doesn't have much to do with Sky Masterson or Nathan Detroit, there is a lot of Sister Sarah in Diana Price.

What do you think makes a great hero and/ or heroine?

Is it unfair of me to say pain? I like to have characters who have been hurt badly in some way and I like finding a way to overcome that and move on. Although the love story and the happily-ever-after has to be a priority, I am always interested in how the two main characters got to where they are by the time the story starts and what it is about their pasts that make them perfect for each other.

Which character did you find the most interesting to write about and which one do you most associate with?

I loved them all. But if I had to pick a favourite, it would be Stephano Beshaley. I wanted to work on him almost from the moment we created him, even though I knew it had the p otential to be a really bad idea. If you've read any of the stories, you may have noticed that he has some serious character flaws. But after hearing of his childhood, I felt instant sympathy and wanted to forgive him anything.

Of course, it helped that he was tall, dark and mysterious. I find that a little hard to resist.

I think I most associated with Verity and her frustration at always being the nice girl and her chance to go wild with the Gypsies. At her age, I had a serious case of the goody-goodies. Looking back, I wish I'd cut myself some slack and misbehaved a bit more.

This Regency series is set against a backdrop of scandal, seduction and redemption; what do you think it is about these themes that continually appeals to readers?

I think some of these were around before we started writing down the stories. There is an element of gossip to a scandalous story, a chance to see what the neighbours are getting up to. And, of course, it is much more fun to see someone else's scandal than to be involved in one of your own.

If the good are rewarded and evil are punished? Good. But if the bad people see the error of their ways? Then I like it all the better. I want to believe that flawed people are worthy of a happy ending.

And as for seduction? Who doesn't like that? Reading romances is like a chance to fall in love, over and over again.

When you are writing, what is a typical day?

A typical day writing for me begins before eight, with breakfast at my desk, while I check the news, the e-mail and do an online jigsaw puzzle. By 8:30 or so, the puzzle is done and I have run out of reasons to dodge work. So I open up whatever manuscript I am working on and try to figure out where it was that I left off from yesterday.

Usually, about the time I am settling in to accomplish something, my labradoodle, Havoc, shows up with a tennis ball and a sad look. This means either I will have to take a break and play with him or my husband will take him out. Then I will have a few minutes of peace, until Havoc comes back and bounces the ball under my desk, loses it under the computer or filing cabinet and accidentally unplugs some cords. Lately, a lot of the morning is spent writing a few sentences and then crawling around under my desk while a wagging tail hits me in the ribs.

My usual goal is a thousand words a day, which amounts to four pages or so. Even with the dog interrupting me, I try to be done by lunch or early afternoon. Then I can keep writing or spend the rest of the day doing what I want (or what I have to do, should there be promotion to do, or editing, or working on other projects).

Tell us about the project you are working on at the moment.

Right now, I am working on a book which will be out sometime in 2011 (I think). The hero and heroine are Adrian and Emily and they have been married for several years, but have been estranged because he is trying to hide the fact that he has gone almost completely

Read all about it...

blind. She comes to London to retrieve him. And when he can't immediately recognise her because he can no longer see her, she decides to teach him a lesson.

There is a character who just recently appeared named Hendricks, who is a sort of secretary to Adrian and friend of Emily, who will be the hero of the book after that, which will have a runaway heiress for a heroine.

Regency Silk & Scandal
continues next month — when scandalous
Honoria encounters a wicked rogue in
The Smuggler and the Society Bride!

THE SMUGGLER AND THE SOCIETY BRIDE

While the first boat sailed out of sight, she saw the dark form of a man tumble over the side of the second skiff.

Curiosity changed to concern. Though the waters of the cove were shallow at low tide, the man would still need to swim some distance before he'd be able to touch bottom. Had he been injured by the fall – or did he not know how to swim? She hesitated an instant longer, watching as the man bobbed back to the surface and sank again, making no progress toward the shallows.

Murmuring one of Hal's favorite oaths, Honoria looked wildly about the beach. After spotting a driftwood plank, she swiftly stripped off bonnet, cloak, jacket, stockings, shoes and the heavy skirt of her habit, grabbed up the plank and charged into the water.

Still encumbered by chemise, blouse and stays, she couldn't swim as well as she had in those childhood breeches, probably not well enough to reach the man and bring him in. But she simply couldn't stand by and watch him drown without at least trying to wade out, hoping she could get near enough for him to grab hold of the plank and let her tow him in.

Shivering at the water's icy bite, Honoria pushed through the shallows as quickly as the sodden skirts of her chemise allowed, battling toward the struggling sailor.

She had about concluded in despair that she would never reach him in time when suddenly, from the rocks far above the water at the trail side of the cove, a man dove in. Honoria halted, gasping for breath as a rogue wave broke over her, and watched the newcomer swim with swift, practiced strokes toward the downed sailor. Moments later he grabbed the sinking man by one arm and began swimming him toward shore.

Relieved, she turned to struggle back to the beach. Only then did she notice the string of tubs bobbing near the cliff wall on the walk side of the cove. Suddenly the game of racing boats made sense.

Free-traders! Tethered in calm cove waters must be one of the contraband cargoes about which she'd heard so much. The first boat had apparently been trying to lead the second away from where the cargo had been stashed under cover of night, to be retrieved later.

Weighed down by her drenched clothing, Honoria stopped in the shallows to catch her breath and observe the rescuer swim in his human cargo.

Her admiration for his bravery turned to appreciation of a different sort as the man reached shallow water and stood. He, too, had stripped down for his rescue attempt. Water dripped off his bare torso, from his shoulders and strongly muscled chest down the flat of his abdomen. From there, it trickled into and over the waistband of his sodden trousers, which molded themselves over an impressive – oh, my!

Face flaming, Honoria jerked her eyes upward, noting the long white scar along his rib cage and another traversing his left shoulder, before her scrutiny reached his face – and her gaze collided with a piercing look from the most vivid deep blue eyes she had ever seen.

"Well, lass," he said as he approached, his amused voice carrying just a hint of a lilt. "Is it Aphrodite you are, rising out of the sea?"

© Janet Justiss 2010

REGENCY
Silk & Scandal

*A season of secrets, scandal and
seduction in high society!*

Volume 1 – 4th June 2010
The Lord and the Wayward Lady
by Louise Allen

Volume 2 – 2nd July 2010
Paying the Virgin's Price
by Christine Merrill

Volume 3 – 6th August 2010
The Smuggler and the Society Bride
by Julia Justiss

Volume 4 – 3rd September 2010
Claiming the Forbidden Bride
by Gayle Wilson

8 VOLUMES IN ALL TO COLLECT!

www.millsandboon.co.uk

M&B

REGENCY
Silk & Scandal

*A season of secrets, scandal and
seduction in high society!*

Volume 5 – 1st October 2010
The Viscount and the Virgin
by Annie Burrows

Volume 6 – 5th November 2010
Unlacing the Innocent Miss
by Margaret McPhee

Volume 7 – 3rd December 2010
The Officer and the Proper Lady
by Louise Allen

Volume 8 – 7th January 2011
Taken by the Wicked Rake
by Christine Merrill

8 VOLUMES IN ALL TO COLLECT!

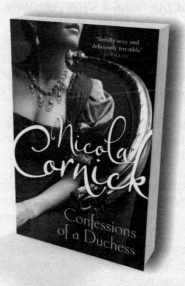